My Christmas Present... Has WHAT?

LK Kelley

DragonEye Publishing

My Christmas Present… Has WHAT?
Copyright © 2018. By LK Kelley

Publisher info. Contact
DragonEye Publishing
753A Linden Pl.
Elmira, New York, 14901

For Questions Phone: 1-(607)-333-5256

For information about our books, and for special discounts for single / bulk purchases, please contact DragonEye Publishing Ordering Dept. at:
Website: DragonEyePublishers.com
Email: Orders@DragonEyePublishers.com

To request one of our authors for speaking engagements or book signings, please contact DragonEye Publishing Publicity Dept. at: Directors@DragonEyePublishers.com

Published by, DragonEye Publishing

ISBN 13: 978-1-61500-222-1 (Paperback)
ISBN 13: 978-1-61500-223-8 (EBook)

Library of Congress Control Number: 2018963773

DragonEye Publishing First Edition: 2018
First Printing: December 10, 2018

10 9 8 7 6 5 4 3 2 1

Manufactured in the United States of America.

~ Dedication ~

This book is dedicated to my husband, who really puts up with a whole lot while I'm writing; my beautiful daughter, who is a true inspiration for my main characters with her indomitable zest for life; a brilliant young man who is a true inspiration for overcoming incredible odds; and my amazing Twitter followers who have been so patient and supportive in my writing efforts; and special thanks to Anita Meyers, Author, Georgia Trosper, and Patti Champion, who absolutely are the kindest and most supportive friends I've ever had.

Above all, I have to thank the Lord, Jesus for my true faith.

My Christmas Present... Has WHAT?

~ Prologue ~

"It's Christmas! It's the best time of the year! It's Christmas, and Santa Claus is coming to town! Rudolph's red nose is blinking red, and he's zipping Santa's sleigh through the night sky! So, kids, you'd better be good, 'cause he's a-watching! It's Christmas, and Jingle Bells are rockin' through the city!" declared the bouncy radio DJ, before he announced the next song. I was late in driving to Ronnie's home, because of a last minute "I have a Christmas decoration emergency" from one of my clients. Emergency, my eye! One of the garlands along her stair railing had come loose! The sky had let loose a torrent of rain and thunder, just as I left, and I was certain we were under a tornado watch, if not a warning. The radio was the *only* thing keeping me awake at the moment, despite the noise from the storm. Suddenly, I jumped for joy, when one of my favorite Christmas songs came over the air. I opened my mouth to sing right along. "I'll Be Home for Christmas" had always meant a lot to me, because I had not had a home since I was four years old, and it always made me cry for something that I had lost – family. Nope! No crying happening tonight for me, though, because despite all the corny things the DJ was saying, I have joy in my heart! All because of my very best-est friend and her "pull-off", as she called it, was why I was heading out so late at night!

My singing was abruptly, and rudely, interrupted when a huge burst of lightning, followed by thunder, scared the heck out of me, reminding me I was also driving in a horrible storm. I decided that I'd sure as hell had better start paying attention to my driving.

Beep, Beep, Beep, the automated radio warning came across in its usual staccato voice.

"The National Weather Center has issued a tornado watch at ten fifteen pm for the following counties in Arkansas…"

After what seemed to be about a thousand counties were named, the current song came back on, and actually started at the beginning. So, I opened my mouth to sing, again, while paying careful attention to my driving!

"I'll be home for Christmas....You can count on me." Rumble-rumble, ligtning, thunder. "Please have snow and mis-tle-toe and presents on thheee tr...!"

Rumble, ligtning, thunder resounded. I stopped singing, when I realized I had finally arrived at my destination. I turned into the drive that led to Ronnie's house. A massive gate loomed as the lightning lit up the sky, my foot hit the brake, and I began to hyperventilate.

"No Way! Uh-uh!" I denied to myself, shaking my head as if what I was seeing was real.

Holy monsters of all mansions, Batman! There just wasn't another way to describe it! While I sat, trapped in my car – by my own startled and frozen choice – I started thinking about how everything over the past three weeks had led up to this moment. In the middle of my musings, the only thing that made me mad was that Ronnie had not once told me how big her house was! I mean...look at this place! It's the size of Disney World – with all the parks put together! OK. So, maybe I am exaggerating, about it being that size, but it was at least as big as half of the Magic Kingdom! No! Really! It was that big!

I gaped at the monster mansion feeling as frozen as a statue that might very well be placed on its lawn.

Leaning forward as far as I could, before being stopped by the steering wheel, I peered through my rain coated windshield. Dang it! My wipers were not keeping up with the rain. Each time the lightning lit it up, I gasped. How was I ever going to decorate that place? It was going to cost them a fortune! Ronnie surely knew it! But, Ronnie is the one who set it all up for me! It was obvious, too, that the cost would not be an issue. I rubbed my head, feeling a headache coming to a brain near me!

OK. I can do this! I have to, if I wanted my Holiday decorating business to get off the ground in a huge way. I sighed, and felt myself begin to calm down, thank goodness, so I focused on just getting up to the door. I drove up to an intercom system that was underneath an awning. At least the owners were nice enough to consider the weather. I rolled down my window, and punched a button, waiting on someone to answer.

"What do you want!" a male voice demanded.

Wow! Rude! I stumbled with my words.

"I-I'm Ronnie's best friend? I am here to decorate the house for Christmas."

Silence followed. After what seemed like forever, the voice answered, as if angry, but resigned.

"Yes. She told me. You may as well come on up!"

I heard a clanking sound, and saw the gates open slowly. I put my car into gear, drove past the gates, and up the long drive to the monster mansion.

Very little kept me down long, and I had to admit that my favorite time of the year is Christmas! So much so, that I recently decided to open my very own Holiday Decorating Business called Noel's Holidays at the insistence of my bestie, Ronnie

Blood. Seriously, I still wanted to know where the heck they came up with that name? I remembered the movie "Captain Blood" with Errol Flynn, and wondered if someone adopted that name in Ronnie's family? What is it with last names these days? I mean, come on! Did I just have to be called *Noel Snow*? Combine that with my best friend's name? The first names are bad enough! But, Snow? Blood? Bloody Snow? Oh, for Santa's sake! If that wasn't enough to make you toss your cookies! And, you'd think it couldn't get worse, right? Were you never taught to never ask that question? It always – *always* – gets much worse! How? Well, I was born on December 25th twenty-nine years ago. I am rather short at five-feet tall, and not exactly skinny, but not fat either. I have an ample bust, small waist, and my hips were probably a bit larger than I wanted. My hair is a platinum blonde, thanks to a bottle, although it natural condition is dirty blonde, with some red highlights. My nose is small, and my eyes are brilliant green. Oh! And, I have no neck at all! Anyway, to continue, my Mom and Dad had a stroke of "genius", naming me Noel. Yes, I know. Stupid, but Snow really was my Mom and Dad's last name. I guess they thought it would be hilarious by giving me a first name from Christmas.

I know. I'm rambling, but the truth is? I absolutely love my name! Can all of this get more corny, you ask? The answer is a resounding why yes…yes it can! Just you wait till you hear my crazy, mixed up story! Even today, I don't even believe it really happened, and yet, here I am…smack dab in the middle of it all!

~ 1 ~

~ NOEL ~

Continuing on from the ridiculous to the absolute impossible, my life was always boring. And, when I say boring, I mean that with a capital "B". I'd been working as a data entry clerk, making only nine dollars an hour, which just wasn't enough to keep that wolf from the door. Originally, I opened my own decorating business in my tiny apartment, and while I'd had a few bites, and a few small jobs, it just wasn't going to hack it. I needed something else if I wanted to get out of the cubicle at my job. I needed something big to showcase my talent.

And, that's where Ronnie came into the picture about eight months ago. We had accidentally met, when she bumped into me with a hot latte mug, and dumped it all over me. As girls, we couldn't have been more far apart in looks. In contrast to my green eyes and blonde hair, Ronnie was a five-foot seven, raven haired, dark brown eyed beauty! She had a Baywatch Babe figure, and her perfect proportions would have made me jealous if I was petty. Her skin was rather pale, even compared to my fair skin with freckles, and she told me that her family had a alight allergy to the sun. Not overly strange. I'd heard of it. Yet, Ronnie had not a vain bone in her body, despite all the looks she always received when we were out in public. From that first meeting, we became almost inseparable as friends. It was her idea to suggest backing my Decorating business with her own money, as well as market it. She wasn't really working for me, because low and behold, I didn't have money to give her a paycheck. However, she didn't mind, since she doesn't worry about money. Her family, more specifically, her oldest brother, was as loaded as anyone could get. Oil, I think. But, Ronnie had a huge background in marketing and public relations. And, believe me! She stuck her neck out for me more than once.

Getting back to my money woes, which I know you all really, really wanted to know, right? I was about to lose my apartment, and be tossed to the streets, when Ronnie came up with a perfect idea to decorate their house for Christmas. She called some contacts she had to get my designs published in their magazines and websites after it was completed.

There was only one tiny small problem. Her brother just didn't like Christmas, for some odd reason or other, but Ronnie did. She would never have allowed me to go on the streets, anyway, so she had bugged her big brother, Damian Blood, to let her hire me to do a Christmas makeover for their house. Her brother fought her tooth and nail, even offering to put me up in one of their many classy apartment buildings just to keep me out of the house, but Ronnie is a real go-getter. What she goes after, she gets. And, she got her way in this, and now...wait! Did I happen to mention that she has an awesome website that features small businesses? I didn't? Well, you do now.

Now that you have my basic background – oh, except I forgot to tell you that I was orphaned at the age of four, because of a car accident, in which both my parents were killed. OK. Now, you know about my life before Ronnie.

Back to the here and now.

"I sure won't get to that monster mansion by sitting here...in this massive storm...at one o'clock in the morning. Ronnie, not once, told me how wealthy her bat shit crazy brother was! I drove my little burgundy, paint-pealing-off Taurus slowly through the deluge to the front door. I mentally slapped myself. What the hell was I doing here? I'd only decorated a few, small traditional houses, so far, but this place? Holy crap! It's so out of my league! I sighed and put the sputtering car into park, then turned the key. I just sat there, trying to come to a realization that I was here to do my first, big job. But, this was nuts! I stared at the curved, covered front porch. I was about to call the whole thing off, and reached for my phone to call Ronnie, when the huge, hand-carved, wooden double doors were thrown wide, and Ronnie ran down the steps.

"Crap! So much for running away," I muttered, as I reluctantly opened the door of my car.

"It's about time you got here, Noel! It's raining cats and dogs! For goodness sakes, what took you so long to get here? Where's your luggage? In the back? Pop the trunk, and I'll grab it. Did you bring all your stuff for measuring, drawing, and your computer? Hurry up! We have to get out of this rain! Come on! Well, why aren't you answering me?" Ronnie exclaimed. Without a pause, she continued to dig into the trunk grabbing at everything.

I had passed giggling way back, and proceeded to double over in laughter. Ronnie was my perfect friend. I was usually serious; she laughed and smiled all the time. Right now, though, I was howling. Ronnie could really get so excited, that she would not draw a breath, until she got everything out she wanted to say. But, while she was standing in the rain, I had an umbrella, not that it was doing me much good at the moment.

"Howze about we 'grabs' everything, and I'll answer your questions – after we get inside and out of the cats and dogs rain, OK?" I laughed, not even questioning her destruction of the English language.

"Whatever!" Ronnie answered, heading to the back of the car for the next load. She continued rambling. "OK, with your first million, I expect you to buy yourself a new car!"

"Riiiiight. My first million bucks. Just let me write that down in my 'to do' notebook," I laughed. "I'll get right on that one!"

Ronnie only rolled her eyes, while quickly gathering my supplies, grabbing my suitcase, and somehow, carrying everything else as well. Then, the two of us dashed up the steps. A man was standing just inside the door, waiting to take my ragged and worn little suitcase that was just an embarrassment after seeing this house. Seeing the scowl on the man's face as he reached for it, I knew it had seen better days. The orphanage gave it to me seven years ago when I left – correction; I was tossed out into the world. And, there went another memory about the accident that killed my parents. I had visions of it for years. It was so real, it was impossible for me to tell the difference between reality and false memories. I shook my head. I didn't have time for this.

Ronnie grabbed my hand and pulled me into the foyer, where I just came to a standstill in awe and shock. This was a decorator's dream! Crap! Was my tongue hanging out? Whew! That really would have been embarrassing, I thought after I checked! The floor was a slate gray stone, and when I say stone, I don't mean tiles. I mean stone...as in a solid piece! Where in the hell did they get this? Actually, *how* did they do it? Did they build a house on top a rock? My eyes left the stone, and traveled around the room. A Duncan Phyfe table stood between two curving staircases, which obviously lead to the second and third levels.

"Hmmpf! Did you guys just have to build in the Ozark Mountains, in the middle of nowhere, that took me at least an hour and half to get here? House, indeed," I muttered.

"What?" Ronnie asked.

I just shook my head. On the table was a huge, Waterford lead crystal vase filled with poinsettias, and apparently the only nod to Christmas in the whole place. The walls were solid mahogany! I'd bet my bottom dollar on it – if I had a bottom dollar, that is. The staircase was also made of mahogany and the stairs looked as if they were cut from that same gray, solid piece of stone in the foyer.

"Holy shit!" I said under my breath. Then, I turned to Ronnie. "You have to be kidding me!"

"Again, what?" Ronnie asked.

I stared at her in shock. She had to be kidding, right?

"Kidding you? Since when have you ever known me to kid you?" Ronnie quipped, and I rolled my eyes. "Come this way. You gotta see the living room! It's like something out of a medieval castle in the modern age!"

Ronnie dragged me along behind her, although truth was, I'd follow her like the good little obedient best friend that I was. And...I came to my second halt within minutes of the first shock, pulling on Ronnie's hand as she proceeded forward. I didn't budge. She dropped my hand, puzzled at my astonishment.

"Oh! My freakin' gosh!" I said aloud, slapping my cheeks in stunned wonder. I refuse to take my maker's name in vain – especially at Christmas. "This is...I...is that a Rem...holy shit!"

Ronnie turned to me with a grin.

"You like it?"

"Come on, Ronnie! Who wouldn't love just these two rooms! I can't imagine what the rest of the house looks like!"

"Yeah, yeah," she replied, grabbing my hand once more. "Come on. I'll take you upstairs to your room, and let you get settled. I know driving an hour and a half in the dark, in the storm, was stressful for you, since I know how storms whack you out."

Well, I couldn't argue with her, because that's exactly how I felt right now. Normally, the drive would have probably taken about thirty-five minutes to an hour, but the storm just made the drive much longer. I hate driving at night, and especially in the rain! Taking a deep breath, while trying to pay attention to where Ronnie was going, I silently followed her up the left side of the staircase. We turned left into a monster of a hallway! I really, really needed to stop using that word! But, truth was, the monster hallway seemed as if it went on forever. I had a sudden deja vu thing, remembering the movie series "Rose Red", where the unoccupied house just kept getting larger and larger, but no one knew why or how a house could procreate. That caused me to shiver a bit.

Several doors – fifteen to be exact – were lined up on either side of the hallway with the last door at the end. The floor was like the others – solid wood, and I bet it was not stained mahogany, but was mahogany. A runner in a crimson oriental design, stretched the length of the hallway, covered with many colors of flowers and leaves carved into it. And, talk about plush! I sank into the carpet with every step! Various paintings of people hung on the wall, and Ronnie began a running commentary on the characters imprinted on canvas for all time.

"...and that is Damian's Great Uncle Dominion. He was a real odd-ball, and never had a nice word to say about anyone."

I stared at him. He gave her the creeps! Dominion was obviously extremely tall, his eyes were black, his skin...really an odd pale color for such a bold painting.

"Wait! Did you just say Dominion? Why is he so pale?" I asked.

Either the odd glance at me from Ronnie was real, or I was imagining it was almost irritation. Not at me, though. More at this guy hanging from a nail on the wall.

"Huh? Oh, yeah. I guess he was a bit pale. Never really noticed that aspect of the painting. Maybe his parents must have had a morbid sense of humor. Or, they wanted him to rule the world. Really, don't know whether they wanted to do that, or they were just crazy. Either way would work. I vote for crazy as loons."

She turned with an evil grin, and that just made me grin right back at her. When she didn't elaborate, I just followed her to the door on the right at the end of the hallway. Ronnie grasped the door handle and turned it. She walked through the door, and motioned me inside. I did another shock moment of stopping dead in my tracks. I had no words. I had never seen a more beautiful room in my life! A hand-carved ceiling of mahogany (they really liked mahogany, I'd decided), looked down upon us. The walls were painted a hunter green, while the drapes and bedspread – uh...excuse me...that would be "duvet" – were crimson red, trimmed in gold, with golden tassels as tie backs on the windows. The bed looked like something out of a castle, and had a small canopy jutting out that covered the head of the person who was sleeping. It was also covered in red and trimmed in gold braid. The floor, strangely, was covered in green, wall-to-wall carpeting. I frowned at Ronnie, who understood.

"Yeah. A few years ago, an employee left the water on the tub above us run. By the time, we discovered it, it had crashed through the ceiling, and slammed into the floor below. Damian had two choices: either completely redo everything, or repair the ceiling, and the place where the tub landed. At that time he was, uh, preoccupied, and left things to Caleb, who didn't want to spend the money, so he just had the carpet put in here and in the room above as well. He's kind of a stingy bastard."

"The stories this house could tell!" I added.

"You have no idea!" a voice laughed.

~ 2 ~

~ NOEL ~

Both girls turned. Leaning against the doorjamb, stood the most lick-lippin', panty droppin' man I had ever seen in my life! But the truth was that he was a player, if I was a day! Besides, I knew he was full of it, and not my type, but he looked like he'd be fun to be around – and I was in no doubt that he loved to play around! His eyes were full on black, kind of like the painting of that Dominion relative, or was that a navy color? His skin pale as it could be (like everyone else around here), with his blonde hair cut short, he casually leaned against the doorjamb, laughing at us. His mouth was perfect, and naturally rose. His nose was rather patrician. He stood at least 6' 3", wore a turtleneck of charcoal gray, and a black blazer o over solid black pants. And, I would have given ten to one that he had six-pack abs, and what was below that...well, nope. Better not go there! In other words, ladies? He was yummy with a capital YUMMY! But, he wasn't my type, so I felt nothing at all for him other than eye candy.

"Hey, Caleb," Ronnie said, rolling her eyes.

"Hey, little sis! And, who might this gorgeous creature be?"

I caught the narrowing of Ronnie's eyes, but man! Was I melting under his gaze!

"Back it off and turn it off, Caleb. This is Noel – my best friend! Noel, this is my bastard of a brother and resident man whore, Caleb Blood."

He walked leisurely forward with his hand outstretched. His lips turned up into a gorgeous and sexy smile. As he came to a halt by Ronnie, it struck me that the two of them were not from the same parents. No way could they be. Ronnie's body was every bit as flawless as Caleb. Sigh. If only I could be as perfect as they were! But, right now, I ignored Ronnie, and took his hand. It was warm, but cool. Don't ask. I don't get it either.

"Nice to meet you, Caleb," I said.

"You, too, doll face. Nice to put a face to Ronnie's best friend. You know she talks about you all the time, right?"

My eyes darted to Ronnie in surprise, while her eyes rolled.

"Now, pray gorgeous, what is a beauty like you doing in a place like this?"

Oh, man! He was a hoot and a flirt! I just couldn't help myself but throw back my head and laugh. He was going to be hilariously fun! But, before he could talk, Ronnie grabbed his arm, pulling him to the door.

"Go play with one of your hundreds of girlfriends, Caleb. We have work to do!" Then, she pushed him out the door, and slammed it in his face.

"I won't forget that, Sis!" They heard him yell, as his laughter and footsteps disappeared down the hallway.

"He always like that?" I said, jerking my head in his direction.

"Pretty much. He's a real drama queen! Now, where were we?" Ronnie answered, rolling her eyes. "Oh, yes. That door on the right of the bed is a closet. The door on the left is the bathroom. So, right now, since it's so late, just get some sleep, and I'll see you in the morning. After all, you are going to be here for a whole week! We'll begin in the morning. That okay with you?"

"Sure," I said, turning to see Ronnie walk to the door. "Hey, Ronnie?"

She turned.

"Thank you so much for giving me this opportunity. I don't want to fail you, or disappoint you."

As if she could read my mind, she answered, "There is no way – ever – that you will do either of those, Noel! You and I are besties forever!"

I just grinned at her as she walked out the door. Before she closed it, she stuck her head back in around the door, and said, "Noel?"

"Yeah?"

"Don't go wandering around the house at night. You could fall down the – uh – stairs and hurt yourself. You aren't familiar with it, yet, and you might run into things, OK?"

Barely listening, I nodded my head, and Ronnie shut the door. First, I decided on a shower, then I'd get some shuteye. I opened the door to the bathroom, and sighed with awe and happiness at the room. It was truly like a dream come true. I started stripping, and walked into the huge shower. I'll tell you how it looks later, because right now, I just want to get clean, and go to sleep.

I looked at my iPhone. Geez! It was 2 AM! I usually sleep like a log anywhere...any time. But whatever was happening, I was lying on the bed wide-awake! OK. So. I could either lay here awake, and try to force myself to fall asleep, which would only succeed in keeping me wider awake, or I could go downstairs with my iPad, take pictures of at least the living room and the foyer, then plan out my decorating scheme. What had Ronnie said? Don't go wandering around in the dark. But, I knew my way back to the foyer and living room, so I didn't see how that could hurt. Making a split second decision, I sat up, swung my legs off the bed, and grabbed my phone for its camera. I had packed my other one, but I really didn't want to drag it out yet.

"Yeah. I'll just get a head start on decorating! It's better than lying here, and not sleeping!" I said aloud.

Completely ignoring Ronnie's warning about not wandering around the house at night, I grabbed my short robe, and threw it over my tank top and shorts in which I always slept. Then, I grabbed my iPad, and headed toward the door. Opening it, I peeked at the hallway, and man, did it ever give me the willies. It was so quiet. In order to stay as quiet as I could, I tippy-toed down the corridor in my stocking feet. As I reached the stairs, I remembered Ronnie's warning.

"Well, she said I wasn't familiar with the house, but like I said to myself. I have been in the foyer and the living room, so I at least know where they are," I muttered under my breath, and started down the stairs. "I mean, that's right, right?"

As I shuffled down the stairs, I immediately knew exactly what the Christmas theme for this house was going to be for the magazine and website. In my mind, I decided that I wanted it very old-fashioned with a touch of contemporary. This house was old, and extremely beautiful. Everything about it screamed Castle! A Royal Christmas would be perfect! I stopped to take an elevated photo of the two circular staircases from above and below, then decided that I would drape real blue spruce garlands, tied with small blue spruce wreaths in between the draped garlands, and alternating red and white poinsettias with red and white bows between them. I actually used a minor app to draw these things onto the photo, so I could save my ideas, and present a photo to the clients. I also decided that I would use the tiny lights, that are reserved for smallest of decorations, intertwined within the garland and the small wreaths. I know I had pre-made commercial light wreaths and garlands, but I didn't want to use them. I wanted real greenery. I wanted a very subtle approach. In those long ago days, they had only candles for lights, but those just were not used any more. Way too dangerous. Even in today's world, some idiots actually put candles on their real and artificial trees! Oooh! The largest tree for show needed to go right in the center between these two staircases! And, the tree needed to be huge. I mean, like 20' tall huge! I knew I'd have to call Jackie Mann for a tree that large, and made a note to call him the next day. He was the best tree farmer in Arkansas, if not the United States, and I'd used him since I started my business.

I reached the bottom, and marched to the front double doors, turned and took a photo of the foyer, then sat on a bench by the front door. I used my iPad to sketch what I had in mind for the stairs and entry. I tilted my head to study it, and changed my mind in an instant. Most decorators would consider the foyer the focal point as one entered the house, and probably put a ginormous Christmas tree where the table was. But, no one ever said that I was like most decorators. I wanted more than one tree. I would make both the foyer and the living focal points, but my plan was to have a "grove" of Christmas trees of various sizes adorning the entrance, while others would be scattered throughout the living room! Each would be draped with lights so dense, it would look as if fireflies inhabited the trees. And, then, decorated with red and white poinsettias to match the staircases. The Duncan Phyfe table would need to be moved from its usual place, and the bottom of the trees covered with a red silk cloth with potted poinsettias in the folds, and the same very small lights woven in and out of them. Keeping the foyer simple, yet beautiful, was my goal. There were five entrances to other rooms from where I stood – and there would be larger, blue spruce wreaths dangling over the doorways with tiny lights. I could picture each doorway draped with garlands and light to welcome the visitor into each room.

"White or multi?" I whispered to myself. Personally, I had always loved multi, but would it be right here? I tapped my finger against my chin.

"Ah, hang it! Multi it is!"

That decided, I had a great wreath maker, Beth Rose, and decided to ask her to make two, Christmas tree wreaths with the multi lights to hang on the outside of the front doors. I also wanted some white peace doves, red and white poinsettias with some gold and silver decorations on them as well. It would be different, and something that everyone would love. Well, everyone but Ronnie's brother, if she were to be believed what everyone said, and that he did turn out to be a stuck up and pompous prick.

I stood, and quietly slipped into the living room. I began to take photos from each corner of the room, and one from each quadrant of the room as well. I walked around the massive room, studying the lay of the land. Three walls of windows wrapped around the room, while a monster of a fireplace dominated the one wall in the center of the front windows of the mansion. Chocolate brown leather sofas were placed around the fireplace in a "U" shape, taking advantage of the warmth of the fire. Noel could see a large garland draping the mantel of the massive fireplace, but without lights. There was no need for them, because the firelight would be the ambiance. The windows would have garlands, but only stretched above them like a valance. Behind all three sofas were sofa tables topped with unique, antique porcelains and lamps. Each of these tables would be perfect for cream-colored Luminara candles set inside wreaths of holly and berries – perhaps in staggering sizes and heights. But, the porcelains and lamps would remain on the tables. No one could ever make me touch those things! Nope, I thought. Never gonna happen!

Scattered around the living room were wingback chairs sporting gradient upholstery in teals, creams, and chocolate. Most were in groupings for people to converse, while a couple of them were placed as single seating with tables and lamps. I noticed, at that point, that one could easily see the circle drive out front, and decided to place a blue spruce tree to the left side of the center, and maybe a life-size Santa to the right of the center. They would be surrounded by fake presents.

"Yes! Perfect!" I said to no one. I tapped my finger on my chin. Something was missing. I looked up to the ceiling, and brilliance hit me like a ton of bricks. I grinned as I made a quick note. "Snowflakes falling delicately, and intricately in different heights from the ceilings both in here and the entry way! And, even possibly in the dining room!"

~ 3 ~

~ NOEL ~

I yawned a couple of times, realizing that I was finally getting a bit sleepy. Maybe I could finish all of this before I went back to bed. I plopped down on one of the sofas, imagining in my mind's eye how the fireplace should look. It was the size of the Empire State Building! I know. I have this tendency to exaggerate, but it was still the largest fireplace that I had ever seen. Certainly big enough that someone could cook something the size of a large man, with all kinds of room left over! Well, that was a morbid thought, and I have no idea where it came from, so anyway, I decided that it might be prudent to use a fake blue spruce garland around the fireplace for safety. Covering that with scattered red and white poinsettias, and it would be gorgeous! I decided to change my mind, and use the tiny lights there as well. On the mantel, I think scattering some red and cream-colored luminara candles of different heights would look beautiful placed among a topper of holly and berries.

That reminded me. The chandelier in the foyer could be dripping with holly and berries. Since it was crystal, the lights would create a wonderful aura of the true spirit of the season! Now, if it were my home, I would have set up the small towns that had been so popular a few years ago, simply because they were just fun! From what Ronnie had said, I was almost certain that the "master" of the mansion wouldn't appreciate my levity! I also decided to scatter Luminara candles all over the house in various sizes, heights, and groupings for warmth. The windows came together in the corner of the room, and that was where I would place the main Christmas tree for the house, where all the wrapped, bright colored presents would sit for the family. Ronnie had also said something about a party, but nothing had yet to be decided. I'd work on a preliminary design for it, after I saw their dining room.

I yawned, and decided maybe a little nap right here would be a good idea. That was my first mistake. My second mistake? Well, that was having Ronnie as my best friend. I was really having a great dream, where I was the top Holiday Decorator in the world, and acclaimed by everyone. I woke with a start, when I felt a large hand slap over my mouth to keep me from screaming. My eyes met those of a man whose eyes were red. Not red from being drunk; crimson, like blood! I tried to struggle, but his hands were like a vise, holding me down easily. What the hell?

"Shhh, little pussy," his voice cooed.

I wanted to throw up at his sickeningly sweet and lust-filled voice. Did he really just call me a "little pussy"? Oh, shit! I couldn't talk; I couldn't move, and all I could do was listen. And, only hell knows I wish I could stop remembering that moment in time. But, even after all this time later, it still manages to make me sick!

"Now, now, little pussy. Let's be a quiet little human, Hmmmm? We don't want the others coming down here, and interrupting our little sex fest, now do we? Of course, if they wanted, they could join us, and we could have a whole lot of fun, don't you think? I'm not at all opposed to sharing, you know. Our kind love orgies!" His eyes closed as he sniffed deeply.

He opened them. They looked even more red! "You smell so delicious, little pussy! I wonder if your pussy tastes as wonderful as you smell?"

Without a pause, his hands turned into claws, and he ripped my robe and tank top off, exposing my breasts not only to the cold air in the room, which made my nipples pebble, but to his lust-filled, red eyes. What the hell was he? Holding both of my hands over my head, he quickly jabbed something nasty in my mouth. It tasted tangy and almost like iron. A bloody rag? Oh, God, NO! His other hand rubbed my breasts. He squeezed, pinched, groaned, and began lowering his head to suck them in his mouth. I couldn't move at all, and tears ran down my cheeks as I felt his teeth scrape my nipple. He then bit my nipple so hard, it bled. I saw his eyes grow even redder as he watched the blood run down my skin. My nipple was in horrible pain, and all he could do was grin like a lunatic. His tongue flipped out, and began to lick the blood that continued to flow.

"Mmop!" I tried to yell.

The next instant, I felt a sting as he slapped me, causing my head to bounce, and slam into the wood trim that surrounded the sofas, and hard enough for me to taste blood. I felt it trickling down my chin, from my lip. It literally almost knocked me out from the viciousness! I wouldn't be at all shocked to have a concussion. Then, he slapped me again and yet again, my head continuously slamming into the same wood. My head was pounding, and I was in the worst pain, ever! I could feel my face running with tears and blood all while feeling his tongue lapping my blood like a dog would lick its master! Then he bent his head to my other nipple, biting it as well, and drawing even more blood. This time, my swelling eyes met his, and I saw his fangs. FANGS? Oh, my God!

"Mmampire!" I screamed, but it was muffled.

"That's right, sweet, sweet little pussy. I am. I will only drain you dry, when I am finished biting you all over. Then, I'm going to drink you!"

He leaned down, sniffed my face, and then yanked my head to the right, causing severe pain to my neck. I felt his fangs scraping my carotid artery, just below my skin, and I knew I was dead. He was going to kill me! I gained enough strength to start to struggle. I kicked my legs, and pulled at my arms! He just laughed, and gripped my arms even tighter as he straddled my legs to keep me from kicking.

"Uh-uh. Not so fast, bitch! We are going to have fun in another way, first. I promise to be quick when I kill you, but you are too luscious for me not to fuck several times before I gulp down your blood!"

His free hand went down to his pants, and I heard him unzip his zipper. I panicked! He was going to rape me! And, I was powerless to stop him. I saw him free his cock, which was not all that impressive! Oh, crap! I didn't want that pissant thing in me! He put his hand on his tiny hard-on, stroking himself in front of me. I tried to close my eyes, but the swelling wouldn't allow me to do so voluntarily, but I was hoping that they would swell up, so I wouldn't be able to keep them open to watch. He grabbed my hand, and put it on his cock.

"Masturbate me!" he ordered.

I drew up my face in disgust, even though it hurt. It was already bad enough that he ordered me to – gross – masturbate him, but when I touched it, his cock was clammy and wet. I didn't want that nasty thing inside me, let alone touch it! Finally, anger filled me with hatred, and I began to twitch violently. Because my hand was free, I yanked it off him, fisted it, and hit his face. Oh! That wasn't smart! He was as hard as stone! But, still, he wasn't going to have me without a fight!

"Stop it!" he ordered, trying to gain control, until he finally penned me down, again, and I saw his fingers grow into claws.

He used them to rip my sleep shorts off along with my panties. He pushed my legs apart, and then just as I felt his cock head pushing through my opening, he was just – gone.

"Oh, My God!" a man's voice roared.

"Noel!" cried Ronnie. She quickly covered my nudity with her own robe, then helped me sit. I yanked the stinking, bloody cloth out of my mouth, spitting blood from the cuts that were inside my mouth, all over the floor. Ronnie's arms came around me to hold me steady.

"Who sent you!" a man's voice demanded.

I turned my head to see what was happening, and shock set into my bones. There stood the most handsome man I had ever seen in my life – and he gripped my rapist by the neck, holding him in the air as if he weighed nothing! I wrapped my arms around myself, holding Ronnie's robe in place, and despite the beating I'd received, I couldn't turn my head from the drama unfolding in front of me. I watched in stunned silence, as everything I had ever believed or known went up in smoke! The bastard just smirked at the beautiful man. And, the battle began. Between the gorgeous hunk and the rapist, I realized I wasn't watching just an ordinary battle, but I wasn't sure what I was seeing. I decided I'd file that all away to think about much later.

"That's for me to know, Damian." His voice turned deadly. "No matter what you do, you are going to lose. You know it, and so do they!"

"I will not ask again. Who. Sent. You?"

His staccato words only served to emphasize what Damian was asking. Wait! THAT gorgeous hunk of man was DAMIAN? That was Ronnie's *brother*??? The surprise almost made me totally forget what I was seeing. Unfortunately, though, that didn't last that long, and there was more happening.

A gasping laugh escaped that bastard's lips, but he still said nothing. Nor did he even attempt saying anything else. He just held the perpetual smirk, as if he knew something Damian did not know.

"I know you, Galel. You think I won't kill you," Damian warned.

The restrained rapist...uh...vampire, began to laugh almost maniacally.

"No, you won't. You lost your mojo long ago, and your courage right along with it! Everyone knows you haven't the balls to fight any more, and your days are numbered!"

Damian looked at him. I jerked backwards as I realized Damian had turned to look at me in disgust, and with another set of red eyes, complete with fangs!

"Oh, shit!" I mumbled to myself. I had walked into a nest of the impossible! Vampires! As a human, that's a bit disconcerting. Ah hell! It was a lot more than diconcerting! Suddenly, I had a terrible suspicion, albeit almost unbelievable. I had an insane idea to laugh at this point. Closing my eyes, I slowly turned to look at my best friend in the world, terrified at what I might see. When I opened them, and met her eyes, I gasped in shock, even though I already knew what I was going to see! Ronnie's face was full of

guilt, sadness, and remorse. No matter, though. The problem was that I was not prepared for the shock of seeing her red eyes.

"Noel, I…," she began, but I held up a hand to stop her excuses.

She snapped her lips together, and her eyes returned to their natural color of brown. Instead, I turned my head back to the two men. I really didn't want to watch, yet I was helpless not to do so.

Damian kept a tight grip on Galel's throat. My eyes met his as I realized he was still staring at me, and despite the shock I was experiencing, I felt a slow burn deep inside my womb – as if I craved his dick in me! I looked down, and saw that he was far more well-endowed than any man I had ever seen...big, hard, and I realized that this type of confrontation is what turned him on! My eyes fled upward in embarrassment, and I blushed like a tomato. His eyes met mine with an arrogant smirk, and I knew he caught staring at his package. The left side of his mouth turned upward into a huge grin, before it disappeared, and he looked back at his prey. Isn't that what they called humans? Prey? Obviously, it wasn't completely relegated to humans.

"Wrong answer," he said quietly and controlled.

In seconds, Damian held Galel with one hand, and with his right hand, correction, his right *claw*, he literally plunged his hand into Galel's chest. In the next second, just like sacrifices of old, where a beating heart was cut out of one's chest, Damian retracted his dripping and bloody hand. In it, he held a black mass of flesh – the heart of Galel, whose eyes looked completely shocked just before his head fell backward, and Damian released him. And, then, Galel disappeared in a puff of smoke, as his entire body disintegrated, leaving nothing behind except the heart dripping in blood that Damian still held in his hand. A vampire had saved me from another vampire, but I had no idea if he wouldn't actually kill me himself. He turned to me to watch my horrified eyes as he squeezed his hand together. Seconds later, nothing of the heart or blood remained, as it, too, disintegrated into ash. Then his face turned to anger, as he slowly approached the sofa. Had I just signed my death certificate?

~ 4 ~

~ NOEL ~

"Andrew?" he said to someone, who was behind me without looking at him.

His eyes held mine as he gave orders. I wondered, vaguely, how many people were actually in this mansion.

"Yeah, boss?" His voice sure sounded Australian.

"I need you to find out who sent Galel!"

"No worries, mate!" he said, turning to leave

"Oh, and Andrew?"

Andrew turned back to him.

"Find out how the fucking hell did he get into this house!" Damian asked, then, "And, Andrew? No survivors."

The dead calm in his voice, scared the fuck right out of me!

"Understood," Andrew nodded once, and left the room.

Now, Damian turned his blood red eyes to me. Uh-oh, I thought, watching him walk toward me. I couldn't move. His quiet, but lethal voice, had me shivering. His eyes raking over me were enough to make me sink even deeper into the cushions of the sofa. I had forgotten that I was nude under the thin robe Ronnie had given to me, and the last few minutes caught up with me. I began to shake, realizing that blood still covered my body. My damn head felt like a damn piece of bloody meat, and my damn eyes were swollen. I could barely see him. I might as well be dead and six-feet under I was so cold. After what seemed like forever, Damian stopped in front of me, and glared. I watched his eyes turn from crimson to ice blue in an instant, and gasped.

"And, just why is this one here?" he pointed to me.

"Damian, I told you all about her coming here, so don't pretend you didn't know. " She" is my best friend, and we are going to help her out with her new business! Noel is here to decorate our house for Christmas, so she can hopefully win a contest for best Christmas decorating. There's one-hundred thousand dollars on the line! She really wants her business to be full time."

"That is not a good enough explanation, Ronnie! This will not be tolerated! My laws are quite clear!"

"Damian, cut the crap! You've known all along about her being my friend. The only reason that you are bringing up those laws, now, is that this is the first time that anyone in this house has ever broken them! And, that was you! Besides! You made them, you can change them, so don't give me all that bullshit!"

I knew Ronnie wasn't wasn't telling the exact truth, but who was I to bust that bubble? It was quite apparent that he had broken whatever laws there were. Damian knew it, and smirked at her. I looked at him, then Ronnie, then back to Damian, I couldn't stop the words, that came out of my mouth.

"You know something?" I said to him, standing, almost falling over. I reached out to grab the hand Ronnie extended to me, until I was steadier on my feet. Then, I poked him in the chest with my index finger. "You are a real, fucking douchebag!"

I slapped my hand over my mouth in shock, Ronnie gasped, then threw her head back and roared with laughter. I had never, *ever* said that to any guy in my entire life! Looking at Damian's stunned face was almost worth it! He looked as if he had never had anyone talk back to him before! It was one of the MasterCard moments – you know, hire a Christmas decorator – $40 per hour; gas money to get there – $30 a tank; shock a vampire by calling him a douchebag – priceless! And, if I hadn't made such an outrageous remark, I just made everything worse. So why not make his "I'm going to kill the bitch" look worse.

"You bastard! Right! Let the human female get mauled, beaten, and almost raped, but hey! No worries! I know what you're thinking! 'She's nothing but food anyway'!"

Again, Ronnie doubled over in laughter, and my hand covered my mouth, again! Shit! He was going to kill me!

"I just killed a vampire because of you! I do not want to hear it!" Damian's anger was roiling from him.

You'd think I would shut up, right? Are you kidding me? Of course not!

"Oh! So, vampires great; humans, prey!" I threw up my hands. "That's it! I'm out of here!" I whirled on Ronnie. "And, by the way...thanks, girlfriend, for letting me in on your "little secret"! I don't need you, or anyone else! I can't believe I fell for all of this shit! I can't even believe this period!"

Forgetting how hurt I was, I stumbled trying to make my exit from the room dignified, fell on my face, then picked myself up off the floor to storm up the stairs, and into my room leaving a trail of blood behind me. I collapsed against the door after slamming it shut. A vampire! They were all vampires! This just can't be real! I shook my head of the memory of Damian tearing that vamp's heart out of his chest. I mean, I wasn't angry about it, but I was damn sure he'd raped and beaten women before, maybe even killing them. I couldn't get that picture out of my mind! And, Damian, just proved that Galel was more important than she was. I frantically looked everywhere around me. I must resemble a trapped animal, as I looked for an escape route, but the only way out was back the way I had come! I couldn't function right now. I needed to regain my composure, and try to clean my bloody self up, before I left! So, I did the most logical, most mature thing any adult female in the mess she found herself would do. Grabbing a blanket off the bed, I ran straight into the huge walk-in closet, and yanked a fluffy robe off the door. I removed Ronnie's slick and slinky silk robe, put the fluffy one on, and shuffled into the back corner in the dark, under the clothes where I was effectively hidden. Even though I was covered in blood, I sunk to the floor, and started to cry.

Now, I didn't just cry! Oh, no! I sobbed so loud, I was sure that I could be heard across the country! After what seemed like a very long time, I finally started to gulp and sniff. I was beaten and completely worn out. I leaned my head against the wall, and drew my knees to my chest, linking my hands around them. What the hell had happened? My best friend was a vampire, and so was her family! At least, I thought it was her family. I shook my head. Of course it was her family! But, the worst part of this whole thing, I'm ashamed to admit, was when Damian looked into my eyes, I almost melted like Frosty the Snowman! My knees wobbled, my stomach turned inside out, and I felt dizzy and faint. I sniffed again, and was overwhelmed by a metallic odor.

"Shit!" I said aloud. "I stink!"

I put my hand on the floor to rise to my feet, intending to head to the bathroom for a shower, when a voice interrupted.

"The only reason you smell is because Galel Harkness stunk to high heaven. He always did! I can smell him on you!"

My head jerked upward to stare into the iciest blue eyes I had ever seen, and they belonged to the very man – uh, vampire – who so obviously hated my guts. And...his chest was bare. (No pun intended). Oh, who am I kidding? Of course, pun intended!

"What?" Well, that was a really, great nothing I had to say!

"Galel Harkness, vampire, extraordinaire. Or, at least he was in his own mind. I never liked the bastard. So, I came up here to thank you."

He reached out his hand to help me up, but I froze at his words.

"H-huh?" I stammered. "W-wait a minute. You were angry that I had 'made' you kill a vampire. So, why would you thank me?"

He obviously decided to ignore me.

"Thank you. I have tried to find an excuse to kill that jackass forever. Well, maybe the last four hundred years or so, but still, thanks to you, I finally found a reason."

"I have no idea what you are talking about," I answered with a frown, wincing from the pain in my face.

"Harkness is an ancient vampire – one from the old school."

"Huh? Old school? Like I said. I have no idea what your are talking about!"

"There are a group of vampires that hate the laws that I implemented about seven hundred and fifty years ago, which ended randomly turning humans at a whim. I...."

"Put your foot on the brake, and back the hell up! Did you just say four hundred years? Seven hundred and fifty years?" My head was having a difficult time wrapping around the fact that the old tales of vampires living for hundreds, and even thousands of years were true. And, now, I was being thanked for my help in the demise of one of them? He continued as if I had never said a thing.

"...deliberately placed restrictions on the vampire world for several reasons, but the first one was that humans could no longer be turned without petitioning the Vampire Court. And, then, only in extreme cases. Rape is strictly forbidden, and punishable by death, Noel."

When he said my name, everything else he was saying flew out the window! Gosh! He was gorgeous! I checked quickly to make sure I wasn't drooling. He was at least six-feet four inches tall, his skin was not as pale as ge others, but hovering between pale and light honey. Dark, chestnut brown hair, he was the epitome of a businessman who took charge in everything he did. And right at the moment his chest was completely bare, covered with dried blood as were his six-pack abs! I tried hard not to stare, but what else could I do? I was, after all, a red-blooded American woman sitting in the floor of a closet with a half-naked man, who was looking down at me, while I was naked even if I did have a robe covering me, because I had just lost my mind by crying like a maniac. If I allowed it, my tongue would be hanging out of my mouth, dripping with drool. How I ever kept it in my mouth has always been, even today, a complete mystery to me!

He reached out his hand once more, and this time I took it. I was on my feet, before I even realized it, and splattered flush with the bare-chested god standing in the closet! Anywhere else, it might have been sexy or romantic, but a closet? Not feeling it, and one look at his face said he was still mad – at me.

"Well, you're welcome! I'm so happy I could make it easy for you to kill a vampire. I get it. You're angry with me because you think I made you kill him. You even just thanked me for giving you an excuse for killing him!"

I was angry, now. I wiggled out of his arms, but he didn't try to stop me. I walked around him, stomped into the bedroom to rustle around in my suitcase, and grabbed a pair of panties, a bra, and a shirt. Then, I turned, and rushed into the bathroom – running into a hard body. I blinked in surprise as I looked up at him. They really did move that fast!

"Look, If you don't mind, I'm going to wash off this blood, get dressed, and then, I'm leaving! I can't believe that I have actually stumbled into a mythological situation that turned out to be real! I…me...even if I said something to someone, I'd be put in the looney bin for the rest of my life! So, believe me! I would never say a word about this insanity!"

My chest was heaving up and down, and I stood aside with my finger pointing at the door, indicating that I wanted him to leave! When he just stood there, I started tapping my foot.

"Well? What part of get the hell out of here do you not understand?" I asked him.

"Are you seriously asking me to get out of a room in my own house?" Damian said in surprise.

"No! Of course not! I want to shower in front of a vampire, so he can sink his fangs in my neck, and drain me dry!" Sarcasm be damned! "Are you crazy? No, I don't want you in here! I'm going to take a shower, and get this fucking blood off me, so I can return to the world of real, and get away from you!"

Damian took a step forward, his face so angry, his mouth drew back to show me his fangs. Oh, fuck!

"Never...NEVER dare to speak to me in that way again! I am a Vampire, not a fucking human! And...."

Did I even learn? Of course not! I got right into his face, and poked his chest – that gorgeous naked chest – with my finger. His eyes quickly turned to red, and I just didn't give a shit any more!

"OK. That's it! Now, you listen to me, *Vampire*! I don't give a fuck who you are or what you are! I am in no mood for your shitty bravado and bragging! I've had enough of all this shit! I am going to shower, then I'm going home! And, I'll be damned if I will ever darken your 'bat cave' ever again, let alone talk to Ronnie!" I pushed him toward the door – or at least I tried. He didn't budge. I lost my anger as exhaustion took over, and I hated it, but I was reduced to begging. "Please, Damian. Please...just l-leave!"

Damian's eyes returned to their blue, and without another word, he stepped through the door. I slammed it, and leaned against it sobbing. Oh, I knew he could hear me, but I didn't care. I couldn't believe all that I had been through over less than twelve hours! I came here with excitement to design, and decorate a monster of a house, and I landed splat in the midst of a den of vampires! I gulped as my laugh became miserable. Was that even what it was called? A den? Vampires? Was all this real? I heard a door slam with a bang, and knew Damian had left. I stepped into the shower of dreams, and scrubbed my skin raw. Honestly, even though I scrubbed and scrubbed, I still felt the bastard's skin on my skin. I wondered if I would ever not feel it. I finally gave up, realizing I wasn't going to get rid of it. It was there; I couldn't see it, but it was there. I felt like Pilate who tried to wash Jesus' blood off his hands, but couldn't, no matter how much he washed them.

I quickly dressed, throwing all my stuff in my case, and even though it was heavy, I hoisted it as if it had no weight at all, because of my pure, unadulterated adrenaline rush, because I was in a hurry to get the hell out of this house! I carried it down the curved stairs to the front door. No one lingered to stop me, so I paused long enough to look back at what I had wanted so badly to make my dreams a reality – my real break. With tears flowing down my face, I walked out the door, shut it softly, got into my broken down car, and drove out of sight of the house without a backward glance.

~ 5 ~

~ NOEL ~

"Hey, Noel! Mrs. McDougal is on the phone – again. Did you order those garlands and the two door wreaths her?" Sally called from reception. Actually, it sounded more like whining. Mrs. McDougal could be such a pain in the ass!

"Yeah, I called yesterday, Sally! Tell her that they should be in by five pm on Friday, and we'll call when they are here!"

It wasn't as if both of them had told her the same thing, when she came in yesterday to order them. Both of us told her that they would be ordered and should be here on Friday. There was nothing worse than a client who believed that they were the only clients that I had! And, that described Mrs. McDougal perfectly! In fact, the whole group of them were pains! Oh, crap. No they weren't. Well, except for Mrs. McDougal, that is. I was still angry about how I'd been played by Ronnie. I shook my head, then looked at the clock. It was past time to send Sally off for the Holidays! I fished around in my purse, and pulled out the tickets for her and her boyfriend that I had bought her for Christmas. Sally had it tough. For years, she had taken care of her invalid Mother, sacrificing her own life to do so. When her Mom had passed four months ago, Sally had been at a loss of what to do, so her boyfriend of five years had asked her to move I with him. She had been so happy since then, and I felt she should have a real reward.   I admired her so much, and wondered if I could have done the same. I had a couple more surprises, too.

Standing, I turned off my computer, and traipsed into the reception area.

"Well, Sally, I think we can safely say that we have everything done. The McDougal's decorations are ready for James and Terry to deliver when they come in, and…yep! That's finally everyone! So, you can go," I told her.

Sally looked up at her, and grinned. Two whole weeks of paid vacation! She and Sam were going to enjoy just being together!

"I can't wait! Sam and I are going to have so much fun. Thank you so much, Noel! You are the awesomest boss ever! How can I ever thank you?"

She gave Noel a hug, picked up her purse, then started toward the back entrance.

"Oh! I almost forgot, Sally! Here's your Christmas present!"

Sally turned in surprise.

"But, the 2 weeks paid vacation is it – isn't it? I couldn't ask for a better gift!"

"Well, here. I wanted to thank you for everything you do during the year, and putting up with my jack-assiness!"

Sally laughed, and took the envelope, opening it. She pulled out two airline and hotel tickets to.....

"Hawaii? Hawaii? Y-you bought u-us tickets to Hawaii for Christmas! Oh. My. God!" She looked at Noel in stunned surprise. "Ten days – in Hawaii? Are you serious?"

"Yep. Sure am! Seriously, Sally. You deserve far more than that and a paid vacation. I couldn't run this place without you!"

Sally threw her arms around Noel, tears rolling down her face. She and Sam had never had a real vacation in their relationship, and now this!

"Now, now!" I said with a huge smile. Then, I added to her excitement. "Oh! And a raise of four grand a year when you return, too!" Sally froze, gaping at me with a flood of tears streaming down her face.

"Get out of here. You leave in two days!"

"Thank you, Noel! I can't wait to tell Sam!" she said, sniffing, and turning to run out the back door.

I honestly was so happy that I could give that small gift to Sally and Sam. I had saved all year just so I could give her those tickets. She put up with a lot from me, took care of her Mother, and he put up with a lot from her, because of me. Sighing, I turned to walk to the front door to lock it, only to feel a light gust of wind, and two people appeared before me out of nowhere. I frowned, and anger started to spread across my face when I recognized who it was. It had been three weeks since I had gone through my vamp ordeal. I was still angry a Ronnie over it!

"What the fuck are you doing here, Ronnie? Caleb?" I demanded, fiddling with my keys to open the door. "The exit door is right behind you. Get out!"

"You have to come with us, Noel," Ronnie said without emotion.

I looked at her in disbelief, the keys suspended in my hands.

"You're joking, right? Why would I come with you? Haven't you done enough to me? I've kept your secret, so why are you here?"

"You don't get it," Caleb said. "You are in serious danger."

"I've already been there, done that! Get the hell out of my store!" I ordered a second time.

"Sorry. No can do," Ronnie told me, and grabbed my arm.

Before I knew what was happening, I was being put down in front of the mansion where they lived, and promptly puked my guts up, because of the speed we had traveled. I was inside the grounds of their mansion, and wiped my mouth off after I emptied my entire lunch onto the front porch. Yuck! My mouth tasted horrible! When I looked up, Damian, Ronnie, and Caleb stood next to me, and at least three other vamps stood outside the gates. Ronnie was positioned on my left, while Caleb was on my right, acting as if they were guards. Damian was actually standing in front of me, almost blocking my view.

"Damian! What the hell?" I exclaimed. He didn't answer me. "Dammit, Damian! Move!"

No one paid one bit of attention to anything I said, but they continued to talk to each other.

"You know the rules, Damian. She does not bear your bite of bonding, and without it, she is fair game. She's never been yours. We've had our eyes on her for a really long time!" One of the men said, who was standing outside the gates.

He wasn't my type at all, but he was really good looking with his almost sun-bleached hair and dark streaks running through it. His hazel eyes were piercing, and his six-foot two frame was pulled up to its full height. I was also certain he, too, had those damn six-pack abs that the male vampires seemed to have in droves! His words finally penetrated my brain, and I wondered what he meant, when he said I didn't "bear his bite". Ronnie shifted uncomfortably, and that made me look at her. She looked very worried. Not scared, exactly. Just worried. I turned my head when I heard the other vamp talking, again.

"Stand aside, Damian! We are claiming her, and you have no right to harbor her!"

"Landon, do not push me," Damian warned him. "I have already killed one vampire, lately. Don't make me kill you!"

I cocked my head to the right. Hmmmm. If I had to bet on one of them, my money would be on Damian. The other guy was blustering. Right now that guy was laughing as if Damian's words were hilarious. But, I was curious why they did not come through the gate. If they wanted me so much, I was standing right here.

"The rules are set forth, specifically, because of just this type of situation. And, might I remind you it was *your* law! Now, again, Damian, I will say this only one more time. Stand aside! We do not have to have permission to come onto your property for an unclaimed and unbonded human!"

Unclaimed? Unbonded human? I looked at Ronnie. I was still angry with them, but I had to ask.

"Unclaimed? Unbonded? What is he talking about?" I asked her.

Ronnie scooted closer to me, then whispered.

"Any human who is with a vampire, or who knows about vampires, must claimed and bonded to one of them. That means bitten. If the human is not bitten, then he or she is not claimed nor bonded, and can be claimed and bonded by another clan of vampires."

Horrified, I asked, "You mean turned into one of you?"

She giggled, and looked at me.

"No. A human can be bitten, but not turned. A claimed human is one who has been bitten, and bonded. He, or she, becomes the 'property', as it were, of the vampire who bites him or her. The vampire is then responsible for the welfare of the bonded human for life. He or she will either be allowed to do whatever they wish, or they can come to work for him or her."

My mouth just dropped open. Was she kidding? A bitten human was a slave.

"Slave? Are you serious?"

"No. Not a slave. More like a butler or lady in waiting, as it were, to the vampire who bites them."

"So. Like I said. A slave!" I repeated sarcastically.

"There is a real difference between an unclaimed human and a claimed human. By our rules, a bonded human can become a mate to a vampire, but a claimed human cannot become a vampire mate."

I darted my head around, desperately looking for a way out of this nightmare. Claimed? Unclaimed? Bonded? Mate? Did Ronnie mean that if she didn't claim me, or any of the others, I could be claimed by that horrible vamp, who was forcing his way through the gates right now? And because I wasn't claimed that meant he was welcome to take me?

"Oh, hell, no!" I screamed, and turned to run toward the house. Futile, I know, but I had to try.

In seconds, I felt hands grab my shoulders, and turn me around to face the other vamps, who had come to an absolute standstill, staring in shocked disbelief. I felt a hand in my hair, yanking my head to the left – hard. Then, I felt something that had my stomach plummeting down into my feet. Fangs lodged deep inside my neck over my carotid artery, and then, a sucking sound as my blood was sucked from my body. The sudden pain of the bite almost made me scream. But, then after a moment, I began to feel lightheaded and almost euphoric. Suddenly, the fangs and the sucking motion sent pleasure straight to my core, making me very wet. The sexual pleasure was unbelievable! I wanted to strip right there, and let whoever was suckling on me take my body, and do whatever he wanted! I knew it wasn't a woman, because Ronnie was standing over me, eyes bugged out and wide. But, frankly, I wouldn't have cared one bit if he took me in front of everyone right here, right now! I groaned in pleasure, and I could swear I heard an answering groan, coming from whoever was biting me. Still, the suckling continued, and as I lost consciousness, I heard Ronnie cry out, "Damian! That's enough! You're killing her!"

I was still partially conscious, so when he withdrew his fangs from my neck, I felt a lick before his mouth left me. Then, there was something very warm pushing against my mouth, and I heard, "Drink. Dammit, Noel! *Drink*!" So, I opened my mouth, and drank the sweetest liquid I had ever tasted. The flavor was a cross between cinnamon and chocolate! And, because it was my favorite combination of food, I drank greedily. When the drink was taken from me, I felt tears of frustration run down my cheeks. I wanted more of it, but I passed out cold.

~ 6 ~

~ DAMIAN ~

Shit! I couldn't let Landon take Noel! She was completely innocent in all of this, but even so, I couldn't let them take her. Just because she happened to be a good friend of Ronnie's, she had been placed in this situation. The surprise I had felt when Landon had said they'd been watching her for a long time, I wondered how Ronnie had been able to hide her all this time. Why did they want her? What was their game?

While I was pondering this, Landon and his goons were advancing. There was no doubt in my mind that she had been staked out a while back – more than likely before she even met Ronnie. I couldn't stop him from taking her unless.... In an instant, I made up my mind. I quickly whirled around, grabbed Noel, pulled her in front of me, and fisted her hair. Yanking her head to the left, I lowered my fangs and bit into her tender, white, delicious tasting flesh! I saw the shocked look Landon and his goons had on their faces, and felt a sense of victory. Oh, God! Noel tasted so heavenly! Her blood was cherries and blueberries! I had forgotten how those tasted! I closed my eyes, and drank deeply. And, that wasn't enough. I wanted it all! Draining her dry was the only way I knew that I would be satisfied. Until a voice broke through with hands pulling on my arms.

"Damian! That's enough! You're killing her!" Caleb yelled.

"Please, Damian! Stop! Please, don't kill her!" Ronnie cried.

And, that is what got through to me. Ronnie. What was she saying? Stop? I'm killing her? Suddenly, my brain broke through my blood lust haze, and I retracted my fangs. I looked down at the beauty in my arms.

"Shit!"

I'd taken far too much blood from her, and could barely hear her heart. It wasn't too late, thank God, so I tore a gash into my wrist causing blood to gush. I raised it quickly to Noel's mouth, and pushed it onto her mouth.

"Drink. Dammit, Noel! *Drink*!" I ordered, using a bit of mind control on her.

In a moment, and thank God, she began to drink from me. I couldn't believe the ecstasy that hit my groin as she drank. I grew hard and my sacs filled full. What the hell was going on? I had never felt this way in my entire life! I fought against looking down at Noel drinking from my wrist, and my eyes met those of Landon's. The surprise on his face was priceless. I smirked, and his anger was palpable as he was forced to retreat off of my land.

"She's under my protection, now, Landon. She is now my bonded human. Tell that to you 'boss', and do not return! Do I make myself clear?" I warned him with a sneer.

Caleb snickered as he watched the other vampires leave.

"Wonder what part of she's your bonded human, now, that he didn't get?"

As Landon exited through the gate, he turned.

"You will not get away with this, Damian. She will be ours!"

The three of them turned and were gone. I sighed in relief. Noel would be safe, unless I removed my protection, which I had no intention of ever doing. I looked at Ronnie.

"Thank you for stopping me."

"You're welcome, Damian. But, what was that?" she asked him.

"Honestly? I don't know. I was not going to let them take her, though. It's obvious that they have been watching her for quite some time – even before you brought her here. I wonder why they would want Noel in the first place."

Ronnie shrugged. "I have no friggin' idea, Damian."

I felt Noel's sucking still, and removed my wrist from her mouth. She was asleep.

"OK. Let's get her inside to her bedroom to rest, then we'll try to figure this out," Caleb suggested.

I picked her up in my arms. She was light as a feather, and so tiny! Her petite structure only served to let me know just how humanly fragile she was...and, that I had almost ended her existence when I drank her blood. Thank God that Ronnie had stopped me. I couldn't let her die. Not now. Not when her blood had a hold over me. I was almost eight-hundred years old, and no woman had ever held my attention, my heart, or called to my soul. But, Noel's blood called to mine. I desperately desired her mind, love, and body! With her blood inside of me and my blood inside of her, I could always find her wherever she was, but I didn't want it to be as my blood-bonded human, Dammit! A vampire my age should have known better! It should have been easy to stop myself! But, I knew it wouldn't happen! Her blood tasted like the finest nectar of the gods!

When Ronnie started to open the bedroom door where Noel had stayed weeks earlier, I shook my head. I had changed my mind. She was mine. She belonged to me, and I to her. I bowed my head, hearing Ronnie's deep sigh of resignation.

"She stays with me, Ronnie." I turned to look at her as I began to climb the stairs to my room. "She is mine."

I had no answer for the startled look she had just given to me, even though she quickly hid it. Wise of her. I had made my declaration to another vampire, and as such, had just signed not only my name to my eventual death by the council, but Noel's as well. For if I died, she would die. Such was the strength of bonding. Silently, Ronnie followed me to my room, and she opened the door, following me into my room. I strode purposely, and gently, placed Noel onto my bed covered with royal blue sheets. Her blonde hair spread over one of my own pillows, where I spent my solitary nights. It was the first time in my life that a woman would share my bed, and I was quite sure that she would be furious with me when she did wake. That was arousing, and frankly, I looked forward to her anger.

"Damian...you...you are going to be a gentleman, right?" Ronnie said in a small voice, grabbing my arm.

Without taking my eyes from Noel, I said, "Yes", while at the same time crossing my imaginary fingers. The truth was, I had no idea whether or not I could keep my hands off her. They itched to touch her, to caress her body, to make her mine forever. What the fuck was wrong with me?

"Yes," I repeated, then turned. "I promise, I won't touch her unless she asks me to."

I watched Ronnie's mouth drop.

"You can't seriously expect her to ask you to seduce her?" she gasped.

"I don't know, Ronnie. Drinking her blood, and giving her mine was the most erotic thing that I have ever done in my life! And, no matter what anyone says, I know she feels the same. I'm not sure that I can keep my hands from her indefinitely, but I promise I will try."

"Do you think that she is your mate?" Ronnie said, as she had an epiphany. "You? With a mate? And, my very best friend?"

"Mate? No! Of course not! Why would you say that? She is my bonded human. The idea she is my mate is not possible."

If I could win a medal for the biggest liar with the biggest lie I had just told, I would have earned an Oscar. The truth was that I already knew the answer. I just had a hard time believing it after all of this time. But, whether or not I believed it was irrelevant. Even though the laws were concise, I could not say that I would never claim her as my mate. However, even if I did not, she would forever have my protection. "Let's get out of here. We need to make plans. Landon will waste no time going to his boss, and we need to be prepared."

As they left, and closed the door, Ronnie asked, "Why? Why do they want her so much?

"I don't know. What do you know about her past?" I asked, and shut the door.

~ NOEL ~

Holy friggin' crap! Where the hell am I? I had awakened a few minutes ago, and I certainly didn't recognize this room. Everything I saw was actually rather enjoyable, because it was decorated in different shades and tints of blues. It was beautiful and very relaxing! But, still...where was I? As my head cleared, I realized that I was right back at the Blood mansion with Damian, Caleb, and Ronnie. I rubbed my head, because it was pounding. Sliding off the bed, I almost fell flat on my face. And, why the hell was my core wet and throbbing! Terror hit me. Was I raped? I calmed down almost as fast as the feeling of terror. No, of course, I wasn't. But, I sure felt as if I had sex! OK. So, I didn't know what it would be like, but if I had, I would think I'd feel like this! My legs wobbled, and I wanted to get clean. I managed to stumble into the bathroom, making sure I grabbed whatever was in my path on my way to keep from collapsing. I turned on the faucet, and began to splash my face with icy water that poured from it. When I remembered what had happened out in the front of the house, and almost being kidnapped by one of them, I finally lost my balance, holding to the sink as I sank to the floor. I guess Ronnie and Caleb were right. I really was in danger, and it was very obviously they protected me. And, Damian, too. He'd held me tightly, goading the three vamps into trying to take me. I lowered my hand to my aching neck. I had the granddaddy of all cricks in the neck!

"OUCH!" I whined, grabbing the sore spot. Why the hell was it hurting so badly? I grabbed hold of the sink to pull my body to a standing position, and leaned forward to look at myself in the mirror. "Shit!" I looked like a ghost, I was so pale! My eyes were sunken in just a little, and honestly, I felt as if I was low on iron. I had no idea why. What I really wanted, and needed, was to get clean, and no matter what, I was determined to do that right now.

"Oh, wow!" I muttered in surprise, seeing the tub and shower. It was the most luxurious thing I had ever seen, and I was comparing it to my own room when I had stayed here! That bathroom would have fit into this bath ten times over! The shower was attached to a sunken tub! Well, maybe I should call it a pool, because it was large enough to be one! Why would a vampire have such a large tub? Just as fast, my face heated up as I blushed, thinking about how many women would fit in it! It was so fancy, I knew, without a doubt, that this was Damian's room. Damn! There went that weird feeling, again! My core became wet and began to throb. With all the women he's had in his life, why would I feel this way about him. Why was I in his room? The only time I had really spoken to him was when I stayed here, and he was a perfect jackass to me! Oh! The throb became stronger just thinking about him! Even though, I'd never had sex before, I had fooled around with a couple of boyfriends in my past. However, when they discovered I wouldn't put out, they put it in drive, and ran out on me. Not that it really mattered, but it had been a bit of a letdown for me. You'd think some guy would want to take me to bed, right? But, no. They didn't even really try! I am sure of one thing! If Damian tried to take me, I'd let him without blinking an eye! What the hell was wrong with me?

In the meantime, I decided to take a shower or a bath. Which one? Maybe both! I just had to try them out! I quickly locked the door, and stripped to my birthday suit. Once I washed out my underwear in one of the two large sinks, I hung them on the heated bar to dry. I figured as warm as it was, my bra and panties would be dry before I finished. I turned on the "pool" faucet, standing in surprised as I watched a real waterfall run down the rocks on the opposite wall. I walked down the four steps into the sunken tub. There were seats and lounge seating, so I chose one of the loungers, and waited for the pool to fill. As the water crept up over my very sore and turned-on body, I turned on the jet dial, noticing that there were numbers of ten, fifteen, and twenty. I figured out that those were timers, so I turned it to twenty and closed my eyes, groaning as I relaxed. The warmth cradled my body, and I let it do its work. I was really lucky that those programs were on there, because I must have fallen asleep immediately.

When I did wake up, I did so, because something was bothering me. The water was still warm, but that wasn't it. I heard a slight shuffle behind me, and turned my head. Oh, my freakin' Aunt Fannie! Damian stood behind me, holding a huge, white fluffy towel! Was he expecting me to step out of the tub? OK. So. The water wasn't exactly hiding anything, but at least the water was still gently bubbling from the jets, so that helped a bit to hid my body from his gaze. My eyes widened. Did he expect me to step out of it? Naked? Over my dead body!

"What?" I asked him in a sarcastic manner. "You did notice I'm in the bathtub, right?"

Damian gave the very definition of a smirk. "I did."

"And? You are standing there hovering over me why?"

"Because you've been in my bathtub for a bit too long. Don't you feel a bit pickled by now?" he snickered, waving the towel just a bit. "Get out."

I shook my head.

"No way, buster! Leave the towel, and *you* get out. You didn't buy movie tickets to this show, so you are not going to get to be a voyeur any more than you already are!"

Shit! If he didn't get out soon, he would get a great show! It irked me to know that he was right. My skin was starting to resemble a raisin.

The two stared at each other. It was just a matter of time, before one of us broke. There was no way that I was going to be the one! It became a battle of wills, until I felt a tug, and without being under my own power, I literally stood, and walked up the stairs into the waiting towel, being held by Damian. Gently, he wrapped it around my body. The "tug" left me, and my face instantly was red from embarrassment! Damian just looked into my eyes. Damn! Did he just have to be such a studly stud? Because he was. He truly was the most amazing looking man – vampire or no – in my entire life! And, he'd just watch me walk out of the bath naked, and that...was totally unacceptable! Or...did he compel me to get out just so he could see my nudity?

~ 7 ~

~ NOEL ~

My only offense was a defense.

"You! *You* made me get out! How? With what? Using thrall? Isn't that what they call a vampire's influence?"

Damian's mouth dropped. She was kidding, right? OK. So, maybe he did use a tiny bit of influence on her mind, because she had stayed in the tub too long, but he didn't use his whole power. If he had used his full influence, she'd be nothing but an automaton! A lot of vamps loved using it to get whatever they wanted from their bound humans, because they considered them slaves, but he would never have done that to her. He much preferred willing women, and one in particular. It made a much better and rewarding experience.

"No, I didn't. Where did you get that word?" he asked with a hesitant grin.

I held the towel tightly with one hand, while I marched to the bathroom door. Instead of answering, I lifted my arm, and pointed my finger. It was clear what I was telling him. Get the hell out of here!

"Huh?" he asked with a puzzled look. Then, after I growled at him, he understood. "Ah! You want me to leave?"

I nodded. My face was still red, and I almost felt humiliated in a way, but...a bit excited in another one. Why would I even feel excited around Damian anyway? Why wasn't anything making sense?

Finally, he nodded, and turned toward his bedroom. I slammed the door on his amazing, and very sexy, backside. I needed to get dressed. I was just too vulnerable, naked with only a towel around me. And, I really, really, *really* didn't need this man in close proximity to me right now, either. What was wrong with me? Just looking at him made me wet! This was ridiculous! I grabbed my dry panties and bra, which I knew that he had seen, and looked into the mirror. My red face stared back at me. I turned my head to the right, and yelped. I grabbed the left side of my neck, again. I still had that damn crick in it! I turned on the bright lights above the elaborately, gold gilded framed mirror over the two bowl sinks, and pulled aside my shoulder length hair. I leaned forward to see if there was something there. Nope. Nothing there! Wait a sec...! What is tha....

My eyes widened as I remembered something. A sting on my neck – as if I had been stung by something. I squinted my eyes, until I could barely see two, almost healed small holes, straddling my carotid artery. I stood up fast as I realized what they were. Oh, my God!

"No!" I gasped.

I was bitten? By a vampire? But which one? I tried to remember more, and while I could remember seeing Ronnie and Caleb at my side, while the bad vamps were closing in on us, there was one, missing vampire.

"Damian!" I exclaimed in anger.

I pulled open the door, and stormed out into the bedroom in my bra and thong panties, which literally covered almost nothing. I was so angry, it's very obvious that I wasn't thinking with a full deck.

Damian stood at the window, and turned when he heard the door bang against the tile. I heard something break and almost cringed. I knew the tile had been broken. But, that was very tame considering the fact that the vampire looking straight at me at the moment had bitten me! My hands on my naked hips, I glared daggers at him.

"You! Bit! Me!"

~ DAMIAN ~

I knew that Noel would not remember everything immediately, but I had heard my bathtub waterfall filling, and knew she was in the tub. Right now, the bite would seem like nothing more than a crick. If I were lucky, she wouldn't remember me biting her. That was basically a hopeful thought, but I knew that eventually, she would. And, with this woman, it would be sooner rather than later. After a couple of hours, Ronnie stuck her head into my room to ask me if I knew where Noel was.

"She's in my bathroom, taking a long soak, I think," I told her.

"She's where? In your bathtub!" Ronnie asked me, opening the door wider, pinning her with my red eyes.

"Back off, Ronnie. She's mine, now," I reminded her. "I claimed her, and bonded her to me."

"Yeah, yeah. I know. Blah, blah, blah. I am grateful that you saved her, but did you just have to bring her to your room?"

"She is tied to me forever, Ronnie," I reminded her.

"I know that! What the hell were you thinking? You have never had a bonded human before! Why would you claim her? Why her? She was under my protection, not yours! I mean...you didn't even like her! Why would you bond her to you forever?"

I just looked at Ronnie without answering her, because I didn't know why I had done it, either. That woman made me madder than I had ever been, especially when I was forced to dislodge the heart from Galel Harkness who broke into my home for God knew what. I knew it might have been a case of opportunity. Ronnie, I knew, had befriended Noel a long time ago, but I was angry at Noel and Ronnie for keeping Noel's arrival from me. So, why had it been kept it from me? Noel's fury had her leaving the mansion, and I didn't want to stop her. I wanted her out of it! The next thing I knew, rumors were flying around about an unbonded human who knew who, and what we were, and that put her in total danger from any vampire out there. Stranger, however, was that we heard there was a race to get to this, specific human. The question was who wanted her, and why? What was so special about Noel? I had sent Ronnie and Caleb to get her, even while I wondered why I even cared in any way. When they had returned, and I saw the three vamps behind her, my mind went the way of insanity. Because of her unclaimed status, she was fair game, which allowed them to enter my home to get her without my permission. I didn't think. I acted. I whipped her to me, bit her, and bonded her to me forever. Her blood held me in its grip as I tasted Noel's blood, and felt it run down my throat. Closing my eyes, I remembered how sweet it had been. I moaned as I remembered her tasting of cherries and blueberries! Two flavors of my past that were my favorite! I sank into blood lust, pulling at her vein to hard, and I had taken just a little too much of her blood, forcing me to give her mine. Because of that, she had become my first, bonded human. Truthfully? That act could easily have changed her real connection to me, and it was a connection I didn't want to think about, because it would mean something far more than I was willing to admit. Many vampires kept more than one human, but I had always deemed it as barbaric. To force a human to bond to me was a horrible thought! It gave the humans special privileges and rights that others did not get. Yet, now, my very own, my very first, blood-bonded human was in my bathtub, as was her right. Just as it was her right to be in my room, and it was my right to take her to my bed, if I so wished. To take her body, and do with it as I wanted. And, I wanted Noel. There was no doubt about that, because right now, my pants were far too tight to be comfortable. For a vampire to be uncomfortable was not at all normal! I reached down to my crotch, and repositioned my hard-on. Ronnie noticed my action, and her eyebrows drew into a frown. Of course she would. Nudity and sex was common with our species. Hell! Orgies and sex were used all the time with blood-bonded humans, but for some reason, I didn't want that for Noel. I could easily smell her arousal through the door, and it was that of an innocent. Surprising me that she was a virgin, that just made this all more complicated, because it would require gentle handling! I desired to take her hard and fast to make her mine immediately, but I knew that would not be wise. Just the memory of tasting her blood sent me into waves of desire for Noel. Great! Not only did I desire this beautiful woman, but she was a virgin! How was I supposed to deal with that? I was used to very experienced women whether human or vampire. I never boned a human virgin in my life! But, right now, it was all I could think about, knowing her naked body lounged in my own bathtub right behind that door! The idea of that sent my dick straight up and even more rigid. I reached down to readjust it, and answered Ronnie.

"I don't know, Ronnie, but that is neither here nor there. She is mine. I will protect her, this I promise you."

"I know you will, Damian. But, can you protect Noel from you?" she asked him.

"No," I answered, after a moment's hesitation.

"Well, at least you're honest!" Ronnie snorted.

"Yeah, well, get with Caleb, and see if you two can find out why they wanted her so much. It's obvious that she is very important to several vamps."

"OK," Ronnie said, turning and walking toward the entry. Before she disappeared, she added, "Damian...just don't hurt her, OK? I know you are responsible for her, now, but so am I. I brought her into our world, but I never had any intention that she know about it."

I nodded once. How could I promise Ronnie I wouldn't hurt Noel, when even I didn't know if I could hold back? Ronnie shut the door quietly as I opened the door to my bathroom. I hadn't heard anything for a few minutes, and I knew she was fine, but I still needed to check on her. I walked into the bathroom, and saw Noel's blonde hair sprawling across my tub, slightly damp from being wet. Closing my eyes and sniffing, her blood was intoxicating, and so was her skin. My first instinct was to strip off my clothing, and take her in the tub. I managed to stop myself when I felt my arms automatically pull my t-shirt over my head. I stared at her. She would never be able to leave him like she had done before for it would cause her a type of physical pain that would only get worse the longer they were apart. And, she could never resist him, if he decided to make her his completely and physically. Being inside of her would be the most incredible form of pleasing torture!

Right now, though, her skin was looking a bit wrinkled, so I grabbed a towel off of one of the warming racks, noticing her bra and those thong panties, hanging on one of them. I almost hyperventilated – or would have if I could breathe, but the bra was pink and her panties were a red thong making her the picture of a Christmas gift. For me, it would be a present for me to see her in them, just so I could remove them. Her anger at me standing over her almost had me laughing. But, then, she refused to get out, so I used a tiny bit of persuasion on her. Noel stood without question, stepped out of my tub, and into the fluffy towel, where he dropped the influence, and she yanked the towel from me.

"You are a real piece of work, did you know that?" she yelled at me. "You made me get out! What? Using thrall? Isn't that what they call a vampire's influence?"

I did a double take, and my mouth almost dropped open. Was she serious?

"No, I didn't. Where did you get that word?" I asked her, not wanting her to know that I had used just a little bit on her.

Naturally, Noel didn't answer. No. Instead, she pointed at the door to get out! So, I decided to let her think she kicked me out, when in reality, I left the bathroom, because the vision of her naked almost caused me to take her!

A few minutes later, though, she bounded out of the bathroom – dressed in that bra and those almost non-existent red thong. I thought I'd seen everything, but Noel standing there presenting herself to me in her underwear? Nothing was as gorgeous as she was at that moment! My present awaited! Until, she said something I wasn't expecting her.

"You! Bit! Me!" she accused.

"Noel...," I started, only to have her interrupt me with a wave of her hand.

Noel stood in front of me, hair wet, dressed as my ideal of the dream of a naked woman. I wanted her desperately. She stared up at me, and because she was so petite, it was almost comical, seeing her stand up to me. Her finger started to poke me – yet, again. That was really going to have to stop. Before she said a word, however, I grabbed hold of her finger.

"Noel, listen to me. Either I claimed you, or those three vamps would have tried to claim you just as Harkness almost did when I killed him. They are not part of my clan, so I had no control over them at all. If they had grabbed you, there would have be nothing I could do to stop them, because without my bite on your neck, you were fair game, and I guarantee you that they would not treat you with respect at all. They would have raped and taken you without your consent or will!"

~ 8 ~

~ NOEL ~

I struggled to get my finger back, but he just wouldn't let it go! Damn him! Those last words, however, did sort of cause me to freeze for a minute. Considering Harkness was some nasty bad-ass vamp, and this man in front of me...OK...vampire – just said that he would have had no control over those guys at the gate if they had wanted to take me and rape me, was enough to make me ask the obvious question.

"Why?" I demanded.

"Please, Noel, sit." Damian indicated the bed.

I glared at him. But, being me, of course, I was obviously not going to obey him. My stubbornness was really going to get me into real trouble one of these days. Instead, I turned and stomped toward the chairs at the window. Holding my towel tightly, because I didn't really trust the knot at the top from coming loose, I plopped down, crossed my arms over my chest, and looked at him. He rolled his eyes, then came to sit in the other chair.

"Any unclaimed human – one who has never been bitten – who discovered us, becomes a free for all immediately...fair game to any vampire at all. Without protocol, we can take that human, and use them for anything we wish. If you are a bonded human, it is forever, and you can be used, abused, raped, and anything else at a vampire's will. Or, depending upon the vampire, you could be treated like a queen. Some vampires see themselves as superior to humans, and believe that they are here to be used at their will. There is danger everywhere within our world."

"Huh?" I asked, my eyes wide. I had understood what Damian was saying, but it just wouldn't register. So, I stammered, "Anything?"

Damian leaned forward, his fingers tented as he spoke, eyes slightly red, and staring into mine.

"Noel...think about this. You know about vampires, now. Harkness sealed your fate when he revealed himself to you...."

"And, tried to rape me!" I broke into his sentence.

"...but," he continued, as if I hadn't said anything. "what we don't know is why even more vampires are so eager to nab you. Another vampire is out to get you. You saw them. Landon had no problem whatsoever to coming onto my property to take you and to claim you. They were willing to risk everything to grab you. And, I'm very certain that they would not have claimed you, but they would have taken you back to their sire, so another could bite and bond you. Once you were his, I could have done nothing."

My eyebrows rose in horror, as I realized what he was trying to tell me.

"Are you telling me, that this vampire, whoever he is, has sent out a basic 'hit' on me to have me kidnapped. And, in addition, he could have claimed and bonded me as you did, and there would have been *nothing* you could have done? Not even Ronnie? I mean...*I'd have been lost*?"

"In a word, yes. You would have belonged to him. A vampire this eager to claim you cannot have your best interests at heart!"

My eyes widened in shock, as I realized what he was saying, but before I could ask, he nodded, with a smirk the moment I realized the truth.

"Yes. You, now, belong to me."

"No! No! No! That can't be! It just can't be!" I said to myself.

"B-b-but, you tore out that vamps heart! You killed Harkness!"

"Yes, I did. I officially broke our laws, when I did that. We are never allowed to kill another vampire without a very good reason. Being a human female does not enter into something considered a 'good reason'. However, the only reason I will be allowed to get away with it, is because of who I am, and he had broken into my house. The grounds are fair game, but not within the house."

Well, that was just great! I was a bonded human, now, to a vampire who claimed me and was his, now. Now I had others after me.

"So, are they still after me? But, if I'm your bonded human, why?"

When Damian just looked at me, he shrugged, but didn't answer. I leaned back in my chair with a thump.

"Terrific!"

~ DAMIAN ~

Noel started to talk, but what I had just said finally got through to her. She stood, walked in a daze toward my bed, and sat down. Oh, hell! Did she just have to sit on my bed? Why couldn't she have just stayed in the chair? She was mouth watering. Her fair skin was in stark contrast against my royal blue duvet. And, that towel was driving me crazy! She was definitely a candidate for high blood pressure, because she was so obviously prone to overreacting. Her pressure had been sky high, since she walked into this whole world. I wanted to stay away from her, but I was helpless. I stood and walked over to the bed to sit next to her.

"Do you really understand anything I have told you?" I asked.

She nodded, then looked at him.

"I – I think so. You are saying that what they meant was that I did not have a bite by any other vampire, and I was up for grabs."

I nodded.

"Essentially, that is correct, Noel. If I, or Ronnie or Caleb, had not bitten you in front of them, and claimed you as a bonded human, I would have had to let you go with them."

She looked at me with the most innocent of eyes, and my gut turned.

"Look. I know you didn't like me. So, why didn't you just give me to them? You'd have gotten rid of me and been happy again. Why tie me to you?"

"I don't know, but I just couldn't do it," he admitted.

"Oh, I get it!" she said in a soft voice. "You saved my life."

I could have heard her no matter how softly she spoke. My body coursed with her blood flowing through me, and I honestly wanted more. Well, I would get more, eventually. Neither of us could go long without tasting each other. As time went on, our desire for each other's blood would become less, but we would always crave it. I wondered why I had no problem with that, now. A bonded human had to have the blood of their vampire. Initially, it would be almost weekly, but after about a year, that was a reduced to about once a year. It was a type of symbiosis, and we would depend upon each other, but still it was not quite a mating bond.

"Are there any blood-bonded humans in the house – I mean, besides me?" she asked.

"Well, yes. Ronnie has three. They are Ronnie's boyfriend, Sam Nichols, whom you have already met. He is our butler. Then, there are Tina and Larry who are our chefs. They were married when she took them as her bonded humans. Caleb has four, all married to each other, who are our grounds keepers, Ferdinand and Margita, and our housekeepers, Ronald and Lydia."

"And, you? How many do you have?"

"Me? I have never had a blood-bonded human, Noel…until now."

She gasped in surprise. I stood, and darted to the fireplace. Staying seated next to her was really trying my patience. It was way too tempting to sit with her, while she was on my bed. I shook my head. I shouldn't have these feelings for my bonded human, yet I did. They should be more like a deep friendship, but that is not what I felt for her. After Rebecca, I never wanted to get involved with anyone, again – ever. She had been a human who had come into my life, but refused to become my bonded human, and above all, didn't want to join me in my life. She had passed when she was barely thirty-seven, which was quite old in those days. After almost 800 years without anyone, I did not want to get involved with Noel. Unfortunately, it was already done, and there was no way out of this.

"Well, it's neither here nor there. But, we have to figure out why you are a target, and why they are desperate enough to come after a bonded human. Whatever it is, they know something that we do not. They were sent to get you. This is more than just a simple claim. You've had not just one, but four vampires coming for you. What worries me is why they are not stopping."

"None at all?"

"I do not know," I told her, looking into the fireplace.

That's when Noel asked me something I would never have expected.

"Damian?" He gave me a questioning look. "Who's Rebecca?"

My eyebrows shot up at the name.

"How…?" I began, then stuttered, because it was unbelievable. "H-how did you know about her?

She looked at me, and cocked her head to the right, then shrugged.

"You just said her name," she deflected.

Seeing the surprise on her face, I knew something was odd in the state of Arkansas.

"No. I didn't," I disagreed.

"Sure, you did! I just heard y-you!" she insisted, stuttering on the last word. The change on her face turned from surprise to wary.

"I did not, Noel."

I was in her face in an instant, my hands on her arms, lifting her into the air. I was getting very angry with her, knowing she was flat out lying to me. My fangs lengthened, feeling my eyes burning bright red. It was a threatening device used by vampires on their prey to get information – just before we killed them.

"Noel…how did you know about Rebecca? Did Ronnie say something to you?" Ronnie had promised to never, ever mention her to anyone. She never had, well that I knew of anyway, but I needed to know why she had mentioned her to Noel.

"N-no! She didn't say anything, Damian! Really! I'm not ly-lying. But, I *h-heard* you say her name! It's the first time I ever heard it! I promise! Please, Damian! You're hurting me!"

Tears ran down her cheeks from the force I had used on her arms. And, that was all it took to knock me out of my red haze. I gently let my fingers stop digging into her arms. When I saw blood run down both arms, I realized that my nails had grown into dangerous claws. I was horrified! It was beyond any vampire to hurt their blood-bonded humans, and I had just hurt Noel! The shame was overwhelming! I let quickly let her go, and I watched as she tried to grip the wounds to staunch the blood. Obviously, it didn't work, because blood was still oozing from between her fingers, and now, dripping onto my floor. I had never, never felt as low as I did right that moment! I'd hurt my blood-bond human!

"Noel, I'm really very sorry. I have no excuse, but if you will let me, I can heal those wounds."

She looked at me with tears, fear, and wariness, then she bit the right side of her lip as she considered my offer.

"H-how can you do that?" I asked.

"My saliva or my blood can heal a wound on a human."

"You want to lick me? Or do you want to feed me your blood?" she squealed.

Oh, shit! The idea of Noel letting me do either, or even both only caused me to harden instantly! I immediately pictured laying her on my bed, stripping her nude, and licking her skin free of blood, and it just caused my desire for this woman to skyrocket! But, the idea of her drinking from me? Damn! That only told me that I would love for her to drink from my neck! I gulped.

"Y-yes," I stammered. I never stammer! I quickly dampened my need, and continued, unhindered by my momentary lapse. "Trust me, Noel. I didn't mean to hurt you! Truly, I didn't. But, I can heal you."

She thought for a moment, then looked into my eyes, before she nodded, and held out her arm. I gently took her left arm, and brought it to my lips, letting my tongue rake the wounds all the way around her upper arms. I saw Noel watch in shock, as she watched my lick – Oh, fuck! I licked her! – heal her wounds right before her eyes. She held out her other arm, and I licked those wounds as well, while I fought to pretend that her taste was not affecting me!

"Wow! That's nifty!" she grinned, using an old slang term.

"Yes. It is...uh...nifty!" I answered.

Crap, crap, crap! Her smile undid me, and I grew impossibly harder. My fangs did not disappear, nor did my red eyes, but I did manage to withdraw my nails. I wasn't going to hurt her, again!

"Now. Back to my question, Noel. How did you know about Rebecca?"

She narrowed her eyes at me. Had he said her name aloud, or not?

~ 9 ~

~ NOEL ~

Oh, shit! Damian hadn't said Rebecca's name out loud, had he? What did that mean? When Damian had grabbed my upper arms, I had felt several sharp things dig hard enough into my skin to cause blood to flood down my arm! He begged my forgiveness, so I just had to forgive him, didn't I? His sad and horror struck face was enough to make me want to forgive him. But, when he asked me if I wanted him to lick my wounds to heal them with his blood or saliva? I guess some of the stereotypes were real. Wait! He just said he wanted to *lick me*? Oh, damn! There went my pussy, throbbing and flooding with desire! I noticed his nose twitch slightly. Oh, fuck! Smell was an enhancement in vampires, according to all the books I had read. They also said that vampires could smell arousals. Can he smell mine? Shit! And, what if I told him the truth about me? Would he be disgusted? Why in the world would I even care? This vampire bit me, and turned me into something other than human!

I was also feeling terribly guilty. I had never even told Ronnie about my gift! I thought back on my life and the fact that I had always believed I was insane. But, when my foster family took me before a judge on a complaint from my foster family that I was filled with the Devil, he refused to put me in an insane asylum! After that day, I am still thankful to God, because He let me get the opportunity to run from my foster family's home, and never went back. I had been seventeen at the time, and I just disappeared in the middle of the night, after I packed what little things I had. I would turn eighteen in three and a half months, anyway, and neither they, nor the government ever found me. I managed to stay out of the way. Strangely enough, my social security card, which I had lost the year before, had the wrong name on it. It had been listed as "Show," but their computers had it correct as Snow. I was issued a new one, and I never looked backward. My first job was as a waitress in a fine restaurant in Fort Smith, AR, and I became one of the best servers. The tips I earned actually paid my way through college. My gift, or curse, if you ask me, reared its ugly head one day when Ronnie had to cut our only day off short. She told me that she was going to the library, but, I knew she was lying. I could feel very strong emotions, but I couldn't read someone's mind. I had simply told her to have fun with her boyfriend. The surprise on her face, caused me to back off, and never say anything to her again. Luckily, she forgot about it.

Now, it just had to come up, again, but it was different this time. I know I heard him actually say the name, Rebecca, inside my mind, but I thought he had said it aloud. She had been his, but she hadn't been a blood-bonded human nor had he turned her to a vampire. Shit! I had been caught! I needed to leave – fast! I turned to run, forgetting I only had a towel around me. He reached out and grabbed my arm.

"No. You are going to tell me how you knew about Rebecca!"

Damn! I looked at his eyes, and knew I was caught, but good! I just had no other option. Not this time. I was going to have to tell him. And, my sarcastic side flew from my mouth as easily as duck a takes to water.

"OK, vampire!" I whirled on him. "Listen up and listen good, because I am never saying this, again. When I was a little girl, I started exhibiting odd behavior," I began.

His eyes widened.

"What kind of odd behavior?"

Geez, he sounded puzzled. *"I can't imagine why,"* I thought sarcastically. So, with trepidation and a lot of pacing, I told him my story.

"You are the first person – uh – being I ever told this to, Damian. So help me! If you ever betray my trust I'll…" What? Kill him? He's already dead! I mean undead.

"Whatever you tell me will never go beyond these walls, Noel."

I stared at him, trying to get a read in his eyes, but all I saw was kindness.

"OK. The first time I knew I had some sort of special gift was when I was a junior in high school. One of the teachers was talking to a boy I only knew as David, and I overheard her ask him if he was fine. He said yes. I made the mistake of asking David about his Dad in front of the teacher. I will never forget the shock in his eyes, nor the sound of hatred in his voice, telling me that his Dad was just fine. But, David wasn't. His Dad was an abuser. I could feel David's pain, and I just knew things like why. He had never told me, nor the teachers. I always went home from the rear of school, and that day, he was waiting on me. He grabbed my arm, told me never to say another word about his Father, and asked me how I knew. I was too frightened to answer, and he slugged me in the mouth. I decided, then and there, I was never going to open my mouth again, and say a thing. Two months went by. The teachers gathered us all together in the gym to tell us that David was dead. They didn't tell us how it happened, but I knew his Dad had beaten him to death. Sometimes, hindsight is better than foresight. Should I have told? I will never know, but our teacher remembered what I had said in class, and grabbed me after the assembly. She towed me in front of the police and the principal for questioning. They wanted to know why I had mentioned his Dad to her two months earlier. For the first time in my life, I lied through my teeth, and stuck to my story that I had never said what she said that I had said. That teacher kept calling me a liar in front of everyone, but I wouldn't deviate. That caused the police to rethink that she was the one who imagined everything. She was disgraced, and she quit, leaving the state. I never knew where she went, but I had been far too terrified to tell the truth. I kept it to myself. Short story is that I went home to my foster family, who really hated me, packed what little I had, and left. I came to Arkansas. After I met Ronnie at UAFS, she said that she was going to the library, but I just told her to have fun with her boyfriend. She looked at me in surprise, then frowned and left the room. I never said anything again."

Damian's eyes turned back to their normal bright blue. I could see a strange awareness in his eyes, but what I didn't think about was why.

"Holy shit! You're an empath!" Damian gasped.

"I'm a what?" I squeaked. "What is that?"

"A person who can feel others' feelings, Noel."

I just stared at him.

"I don't understand?"

"Do you feel someone when they are angry? Mad? Happy? Excited? More?"

Well, I couldn't doubt that was true, so I nodded.

"Do you have electrical impulses that make you unable to wear anything touching your skin, because it will drain a battery?"

OK. Now, he was starting to scare me, because that described me in full detail. It was so true. I couldn't wear a watch. I was lucky to be able to carry a cell phone. They had some kind of internal protection that kept me from draining the battery. When I got around computers, though, certain ones didn't always have that, and I could zap them dead. I did that, once, at an airport. When I joked about it, the girl just glared at me. She took me seriously, too. I had grinned at her and left quickly.

"Can you influence other objects that have electricity running through it? Like a stop light? Do you have a lot of electrical impulses in your body? Do you know something about that person that can come true?"

I nodded, again.

"Sometimes, I can do the trick with the objects, but it's random at best. How do you know all that?" I asked, my hands and legs shaking.

"All of that is the description of a highly developed empath! It usually doesn't exhibit so strongly in most. It usually takes years, but most never proceed beyond the beginning stages. It's obvious your gift has been with you all your life. You were born as a strong empath. But, you can also read minds, and that is just something that is impossible!"

"Read minds?" I questioned.

"Rebecca. I didn't say that aloud, Noel. The fact you could hear me, only reinforces that you do read minds – or at least hear thoughts. Who knows? Eventually, you could read minds! Damn! No wonder they want you! But, how would they have known about you, I wonder?" Damian puzzled to himself.

"I-I don't know. Damian, if what you say is true, now I really am terrified! I don't want this!"

Damian turned to me, and pulled me to him, cradling me in his arms.

"I know, Noel. The truth is that none of us wants any of these things, but we each must deal with what we are dealt with in life. I had to deal with becoming a vampire; you will have to deal with being an empath."

He rocked me gently back and forth, and for the first time in my entire life, I felt secure. Suddenly, I had a desire to drink his blood! Why? That was just gross! So, if that really were so gross, then why would I lick my lips as if I wanted to do it? And, da-amn! He was now staring at me as if I was the last girl on the face of this planet – and I swear, desire was in his eyes. His eyes took on that red color, once more. I gasped in surprise, when he grabbed me by my waist, and pulled me back into his arms. I sighed with relief, as his lips met mine in a frenzied lip coupling! At first, I was completely shocked, but as he teased and licked my lips, I happily opened my mouth, and let him inside. He devoured me with his tongue and his lips.

Oh, dear God! This man could kiss! I briefly wondered if he was so experienced at kissing, would he be that experienced if she let him inside her body to give it what I wanted. Well, of course, he would! He was almost eight-hundred years old! To think of that long without having sex was just stupid. In moments, I was wetter than I had ever been. The towel dropped from the friction between us, and my thong was not holding the liquid flooding my legs. My bra was just way too tight, because my breasts were swollen and heavy with desire. In seconds, I had his shirt unbuttoned and he yanked it off, tossing it onto the floor. Then, he had my bra off just as fast, he drew me back to his chest, and our flesh met. Moans dominated the room, as we kissed. He finally lifted his head, and stared into my eyes. I needed him to seduce me! I needed to drink his blood! I needed so much right now!

"Please?" I asked, begging for him to help himself to my body.

In answer, Damian flipped onto the bed with me on top of him. That's when he spoke, and everything I had ever believed, and accepted, was dashed in that split second.

"We need to talk. I think I know why the other vamps are after you."

Wait! I'm straddling him on a bed, naked, and this is what he wants to talk about? I would have been, should have been, insulted, but, I was too curious as to what he meant.

"You do? Why?"

"Somehow, some way, someone knows the truth about your gift."

I looked at him in horror.

"How would they know that? I've been so careful all my life to keep it under wraps! How could anyone have known?"

"I have no idea, but we need to find out. Whoever knows about you, has told some of the worst vamps in the world. Why, though, is the other question. But, if they, now, find out that you can hear minds...."

"Do you think it's because of our blood-bond?" I asked.

"I don't know, but it does sound like a logical conclusion. Imagine if a supernatural being had you as their property! Your value as a commodity would be through the roof! You would not only be taken and used – against your will – you could be used for horrible things. This gift, as you call it, would be priceless to the highest bidder. To have someone who could read minds, would put most everything in that vampire's power. That is how you knew about Rebecca, isn't it? I kind of put it together from what you told me. Noel, you are in real danger. I don't know why they want you, but I'm sure your gift is involved."

"I guess so. It was easy to hear you. But, again, how would someone know?"

"No idea, but we need to find that answer."

I was way too upset over this. I had been so careful, so quiet about it. Who could have told someone about my gift? And, why tell vampires?

"Wait! I'm your blood-bonded human. I belong to you, right? Then, no one could take me from you."

"Well, if they kill me, they could take you."

"I knew it would get me in trouble, some day! I'm so fucked!" I almost yelled.

"Fucked is right."

Damian reached up, and flipped me over, landing me underneath him, his body holding me down. Truth be known, that just excited me even more than I already was despite the revelation of my gift, and others somehow finding out about it.

"We will find it, Noel. Now, it's time to talk."

~ 10 ~

~ NOEL ~

"More talk? About what, this time? Really? Right now?" I huffed, crossing my arms over my chest.

I was getting frustrated. Here we were. Nude. I was wet and ready, and his arousal was positioned at my core. And, he wanted to talk? What guy does that?

"We have to discuss this, before anything else happens between us, Noel. You need to know everything, first."

His eyes were turning even more crimson, if that were possible. I felt his hardness flinch against me. How was I supposed to take his "we have to talk" business with it doing its jerking thing? I needed him off me, before I went insane. Just because I was a virgin didn't mean that I didn't have the same urges as a woman who wasn't. Sighing, I gave him a small push, and he rolled off of me. I pulled the duvet cover over me.

"OK. Talk," I told him.

Quickly, he pulled the sheet over his lower half. I was really glad about that one. No. No, I wasn't.

"You need to know what it means to be a blood-bonded human, before we go forward."

I stared at him with a "get to the point" look.

"The first thing you need to know is that once we were bonded, no matter the reason, we will need to take each other's blood frequently for a while. It's a type of survival mechanism, I guess you'd call it." When I would have protested in disgust, he held his hand up to silence me. My mouth pressed together in irritation, but I nodded. "Usually, and unlike you, the human has not ingested the vampire's blood. The only time that usually happens is to heal, or to take a mate. After completed, it requires both vampire and human to drink from each other. When, I bit you, I took far too much blood from you, and it was almost too late. If Ronnie, had not gotten through to me, I would have killed you. I am truly sorry for that. I haven't lost control in blood lust since I was first turned."

My mouth was hanging open at his declaration. Not since he was first turned had he suffered blood lust? He could have killed me! Holy crap

"Without taking each other's blood, the bond will weaken."

"So, if it weakens, what's the big deal?" I asked him.

"Because if it does, and we go too long without, we will both die."

"What!" I squeaked.

"I told you. Once bonded, Noel, it is forever."

Forever.

"H-How often?" I asked. "What do you mean by forever, Damian?"

I shouldn't ask, but I couldn't keep my big mouth shut! I wasn't really all that keen to drink the forbidden drink of blood, but damn! I so wanted his. Wanted him.

"At first? Daily. Within three years, it will be needed once a month. As time progresses, say in a hundred years or so, it will become less and less, until we will only need to feed on each other on occasion, but the bond will be older and secure, so the frequency will eventually stretch to once every ten years, give or take a year,"

Part of his words didn't make it to my conscience immediately, so my mind blocked it out and ignored it for a moment.

"How does this work, then? I-I mean...I'm willing, if it will keep us alive. I mean, I don't have fangs, so how can I bite you? And, how do I know that you won't drain me dry like you almost did earlier?"

"I will never wish to drain you – unless you decide to join my world. That, though, is your decision, and I will never push it on you. For me, my fangs will do the work on your neck. For you, this will have to suffice," he grinned, sticking his finger in the air.

The surprise on my face when I saw his fingernail lengthen, must have been priceless, according to the huge smirk he sported. That's when my brain fart woke, and I realized what he had said earlier. He did not just say....

"Wait, wait, wait, wait, wait! Tell me – please, please, please tell me, that you did not say a hundred years?" I paused to put my hand on his chest. "You didn't, did you?"

Hopeful thinking was good, and worked, right? Of course it didn't.

"I did. When I bonded you to me, Noel, it means that my blood – immortal blood – is running through your veins. While a blood-bonded human may not live as long as an immortal, they have been known to live up to about two-hundred and fifty to three-hundred and fifty years."

Suddenly, I started to shake hard above him, and I was cold. Very, very cold. Rubbing my arms to try and get warm, the question was how could that be true? I wasn't good but for maybe 75 to 90 years, right? But, the thought of being around as long as he had just told me was terrifying. I mean, I'd outlive everyone I knew. I'd see the future, and all its changes. What if those changes were horrible? What if I couldn't hack it? No. No. I shook my head.

"No! No! I-I can't do that long! Damian! I just c-can't!" I cried, looking into his red eyes.

"Yes, you can. I will be here, and so will Ronnie and Caleb. So, will their blood-bonded humans."

"No!"

I kept repeating, then felt a sharp pain in my left shoulder, followed by what I could only describe as an orgasm of monstrous proportions! I groaned heavily, when I realized that Damian had sunk his fangs into my neck, and I could feel him pull on my blood as he drank from me. "Oh!"

Next, I felt him withdraw his fangs, and the next thing I knew, he had sliced his own neck, and placed my lips over the cut. I automatically opened my mouth and tasted the delicious, warm red liquid that touched my tongue. I drank deeply, feeling it warm my esophagus as it slid downward into my stomach. In moments, his immortal blood flooded my entire body with its warmth, and I almost felt drunk on it. I let go of his neck, and watched his wound heal almost instantly.

I didn't understand any of it, but the truth was, I hadn't realized how badly I was feeling until now. Weaker, I meant. But, now? I felt strong and...oh, crap! I felt horny! So horny, I realized I was grinding my core against his leg. I wanted him to pound into me. I could feel my womb throbbing in harmony with my

upward movements as I humped it. My head was thrown back in obvious ecstasy.

"Noel? Stop, please! Noel," he muttered.

I stopped humping and looked into his red eyes, which were boring into mine.

"Huh?"

"Stop humping my leg, please!" Desperation was in his voice. "If you don't, I'm going to ravish you!"

Well, I guess he thought that it would stop me, but I wanted him to ravish me. I wanted him to remove the duvet and thrust into me!

"Noel! It's not you! It's our blood! It's similar to an aphrodisiac! Please, stop!" he begged.

I stopped my grinding, and looked at him. Oh, my God! I felt the red rise in my face, and I have never been so humiliated in my life! He was wrong. It had all been me...ALL me! Not him! I had literally tried to seduce him! I pushed off him, and he flipped off the bed in a backward flip. If I had been in my right mind, I would have noticed, but I wasn't! The heat burning through me was not normal! I was in lust. And, one look at his tortured face told me he was every bit as affected by this as was I. I reached, again, for the duvet that had slipped, and yanked it back over my nakedness, my face redder than it had ever been.

"Is this even normal?" I asked, panting with need.

"While it is always a possibility, I've never heard of this kind of desire happening! Never!"

"Are you trying to convince me, or yourself?" I asked.

Damian just stared at me. His eyes narrowed dangerously. His eyes traveled from my face, to my seated position on the bed, which even I had to admit, was probably very suggestive and sexy.

I was leaning back on my arms, one leg flung out on the bed. Under the duvet, my other foot was against my crotch. I just couldn't breathe, and my pussy was soaking wet. Thank goodness he couldn't see that, too! Quickly, I pulled in my leg, and made sure the duvet covered me as much as possible. I looked up under my lashes to see if he was still looking at me. He had closed his eyes, but I could tell he was sniffing me. There was something just so creepy about it! My eyes widened when I realized he was smelling my desire. Oh, shit! That just sent more of my juices flowing!

"How long will this last?" I gasped, holding the duvet as tightly as possible.

"I have no idea. I-I have to get out of here, Noel!"

Damian turned, and was gone. I mean one second he was there, the next he wasn't. I nibbled on my nails a bit. I was so turned on, I had to do something! Quickly, I threw off the cover, and ran into the bathroom. Turning on his shower, I slid under the water. Darn! I had my little toy with me, but it wasn't in his room! And, this was not a case of "getting off with my fingers"! I needed something hard enough to take care of this desperation. I left the shower, and donned the robe that I had seen hanging behind the door. It was long, and drug the floor. I had to get to the room I had used earlier. I had left my sex toy in my rush to leave the house days ago. Holding the robe together, I peeked out the door. I didn't see anyone walking down the hallway, so I started to run. I tripped a couple of times, and almost fell down, but I reached my room, slammed the door, and ran to one of the drawers in the dresser where I had left it. Rustling around in it, I pulled out my vibrating toy, threw off my robe, and ran into the shower. In moments, the warmth of the water allowed me to sit on the ledge that was built into the wall. I guess it was for someone to shave their legs, or just to sit. For me, the warmth and my vibrator would save my sanity. Turning my vibrator on, I spread my legs wide, and while I usually needed to work it into my pussy slowly in the past, this time, I shoved it up into it in one, fast thrust, moving it in and out of me as fast and as hard as I could. The vibration worked on my clit and sweet spot, while the movement was bringing me to an orgasm. I came harder than I ever had in my life. So hard, I actually peed myself. It was rare that it happened, but in this case, I didn't even care! I needed to come! I continued to moved it slower inside me, and leaned my head back on the tile as I brought myself down to Earth. Then, just the thought of Damian's naked chest, sent me over the edge again! I slammed the toy inside of me even harder, this time, until I came, once again. If I was feeling this way, then what was Damian feeling?

~ DAMIAN ~

The second I saw Noel grab the duvet to cover her nude body, and her desirable, very wet pussy, I knew I had to get out of my room! Her desire hit my nose hard. This was not acceptable behavior for a vampire and bonded human union. I knew that Ronnie and her blood-bonded Sam had a sexual relationship for over a hundred years. Even so, the two of them were inseparable. In fact, every time she was home, it was rare to see her, since the two of them spent the majority of their time in her room. Was this what it was like for them? Had something gone wrong with me?   I'd seen many, many other blood-bonded humans, and I could not think of anything like this. I needed to talk to Ronnie. Well, I needed to jack off first…and perhaps even several times. I had heard Noel leave my room and then, slam her own bedroom door. The thought of her naked in bed almost consumed me with lust. It was not like bloodlust or physical lust. Those I'm familiar with, but it was an all-consuming lust. I craved her blood, her body, and above all, craved putting my seed into her body. Filling her fully with my semen was all I could think of at the moment.

I sighed when I heard her shower start, but when I heard her grunt and groan several times, my dick shot up harder and even larger. I started up to my bedroom, when I heard her grunting again. Her moans of pleasure were coming from her room. I stopped to listen at her door, imagining my cock slamming into her! What was wrong with me? I was just causing myself more pain! My balls were locked and loaded, and as hard as mahogany. I knew when I did jack off, there would be a lot of seed shooting from my slit! And, my cock was harder than I ever could remember. Still, I allowed myself to be tortured as I listened at her door. Without thinking, I found myself reaching down to grasp my own dick! I pumped it, desperately wishing it were her hands – or her gorgeous mouth. I heard her panting hard, until finally I heard her sigh. The picture of her masturbating herself with her own hands was too much. In half a second, I was in my own shower, pumping my dick faster and harder. I felt as if I would explode. And, I did! I pointed my dick at the tile, threw back my head, and cried out, feeling my desire move into my shaft. But, what amazed me the most was to see the white semen,

explode with an unusually thick stream onto the green marble tile without stopping! I imagined it shooting into Noel's body, and it was all that could think about at the moment. I wanted to feel it flood into her body, knowing it was filling up her womb. After depositing my seed inside of her, I wanted to watch as my seed flowed from her. I wanted to spread our juices all over her, and lick it off, sharing it with her through a passionate kiss.

And, that had me seeing her suck on me, again! Damn! My dick hardened. I pumped it harder than before, and to my surprise, my dick threw my seed even harder, and higher onto the tile. I sank to my knees afterward, watching my semen slowly slide down the wall. There was so much, and it was so very thick! Irritated, I realized I was angry that it was not inside Noel! That it was not inside of her – my mate!

When I said the word "mate", I collapsed onto the floor, lying under the water in complete and total shock. Mate? Noel was my mate?

"Not possible! She can't be my mate!" I practically whined – and I never whine! I rose on my knees, and began to relieve myself, once again. As I shot my seed on the tile, I thought of the impossibility of it. "I've lived almost eight hundred years, so why would I find my mate now?" I muttered.

~ 11 ~

~ NOEL ~

I sat in the shower for a while, after I was empty. Being a vampire, I was never exhausted, but at this moment, my mind was tired, and my movements slow. The emotional toll was nothing like I ever experienced. I got up, dressed, and sought out Ronnie. She was the closest I had to a sister, and I needed to know if Noel was really my mate. I needed to talk to someone, and she was the most logical. After all, Ronnie was a girl, and if Noel was my mate, then there was another ritual that had to be performed. If I had found my mate at the same time I blood-bonded with her, none of our rules could apply, because as far as I knew, no documentation existed, because it had never happened. The rules could be broken, but only under true, mitigating circumstances like Ronnie and Sam. It was rare to find a mate among blood-bonded humans, but it did happen on occasion. Luckily, I wouldn't need to turn her, but the ritual was private and quite bloody to make her my mate forever – unless I had already completed the mating bond.

I wandered throughout the house, and finally found Ronnie with Sam in his room. I waited until their cries of pleasure finished, before I knocked on the door. Sam opened it, and was naked.

"Damian? What is wrong? Did you need something?" he asked me.

"Is that Damian?" I heard Ronnie ask from the bedroom. She was still breathless from their humping activity. Oh, hell! What I really needed was to fuck Noel!

"Yes."

Ronnie came out of the bedroom, dressed only in a thin, silk robe. Sex among many vampires was not necessarily a private act. It just depended on what their mood was. However, I had always maintained Sam and Ronnie's relationship was a private one, and accorded them as such, until I realized that they were mates, and I intervened for them. Ronnie took one look at my face, and turned to Sam.

"Can you give us a minute, love? It looks like Damian has some questions. And, I'm pretty sure that it's all about his mate."

Sam looked up at me in shock.

"You are mated? To Noel?"

"I don't know, Sam."

Sam slapped him on the shoulder. No. Sam was not a normal butler, but he was as much a part of my family as were Ronnie and Caleb - and now, Noel.

"So, you've made it into the mated ranks, huh?" he laughed at me, grabbing my hand, and slapping my shoulder.

I just glared at him. Until I realized exactly what he had said. I looked at Sam to Ronnie, and back again.

"So, it worked?" I asked in surprise.

Ronnie leaned her head against Sam, and nodded.

"Since when?" I asked them.

"Since last night," Sam answered. "We are finally mates, Damian, thanks to you. I don't know why it took us so long to figure it out."

"Congratulations! It's about damn time! You must allow me to throw a mating party for you both!" I said in an excited voice.

"Of course, you can," Ronnie answered. "But first things first, Damian. I know you have some questions."

"You have no idea."

When Sam started to go into his bedroom, I stopped him. I couldn't deny it. I was a wreck after everything. "Please, Sam. I need you as well."

Ronnie and Sam indicated the sofa, and after Sam had put on a pair of pants, I put my head in my hands. Ronnie brought me a glass of O- blood, which was one of my favorites.

"OK, Damian. Give."

~ NOEL ~

My legs felt like spaghetti! I limped along the bathroom, and out into the bedroom, dressing in a pair of panties, no bra, because my breasts had swollen with my desire, and had yet to return to their normal size. I completed it with leggings, and a long, dark blue sweater that hung almost to my knees. And, then, I fell into the bed. It felt weird not having Damian in it with me. Why? I'd come several times, yet still, I wanted him inside me. I wanted him. What the hell was wrong with me? He was a vampire! Something wasn't right, and I didn't know what it was. I had to get my mind off him, now, or I'd go crackers! So, focus, Noel! You were hired to make this house a Christmas wonderland. I turned my head, and noticed that my iPad was on the table next to the French doors. I briefly wondered where it had come from, because it wasn't with me when I was brought back to the house. Maybe I just needed some fresh air.

I got off the bed – a huge problem, because I was so tired – and picked up the iPad. I slithered through the French doors. One thing about an iPad. Even on the darkest night, you can use it. I saw some chairs on the balcony attached to my bedroom, with a wrought iron railing surrounding it. Standing at that railing, looking up at the starlit sky, I felt as if I was in a dream! Winter was my favorite time of the year! I mean....

"Look at those stars!" I whispered in awe. "So bright! I wonder who, or what is on the planets around some of them?"

Suddenly, I got an idea. It was rather ambitious, but I was sure it could be done! I sat down in the chair, and began to sketch out my idea on the iPad. I honestly don't know how long I sat outside, but I began to notice how stiff my fingers were, and began to flex them. That's when I realized I had been out here for – I looked at the clock on the iPad.

"Four hours? I've been out here for four hours. How is that even possible?" I stood to go into the bedroom, and that's when I noticed that I wasn't really all that cold. My feet were warm, my body was warm in what I was wearing. So, why wasn't I cold?

"Why am I not cold?"

"Because my blood runs through your veins, Noel," came the one voice that stirred her body with just the sound of it. I looked at Damian who was leaning against the doorjamb, and knew, in that instant, he was mine, and I was his. I stood and stepped past him into the room. He backed up, and shut the doors behind us. Placing the iPad on the table, I didn't hesitate, but walked right into his arms. Damian held me tightly, resting his head on top of mine. It felt right, perfect.

"This bonding stuff is heavy," I said, trying to make the moment light.

"It is, yes, but that is not what this is," Damian answered.

I looked up at his gorgeous face, and frowned.

"What do you mean?"

"The reason the bond is so strong, Noel, is because...because...."

"Wow! It must be pretty bad, the way you are hesitating!" I joked half-heartedly.

"It depends on what your definition of 'bad' is."

That's when I remembered my new design.

"Hold that thought!" I grabbed my iPad, and turned it so that he could see it. "I had an idea while I was outside."

Damian put his arms around my waist, pulling me back toward him. I relished his body next to mine, but I wanted to tell him my ideas, before anything else happened – or at least what I hoped and wanted to happen.

"Damian, look. I just realized that Christmas is all about lights. Oh, we could go the old fashioned route, too, but I was thinking...how about a combination of both?"

"Both? Everyone does both."

"Yeah, but my idea is a bit off the wall. Look!"

I showed him my ideas, and when I was done, looked up at him. His eyes were turning red – slowly, but they were still turning red.

"I would never have thought of that!" he said to me. As if he was excited about it, he took the iPad from me.

"You know, when I heard about Jesus' birth, I...."

"Wait! Hold the mayo and the mustard! Did you just say when you heard of His birth?" I squeaked, or rather my voice did.

He nodded. "Of course, it was a couple of hundred years later, but I remember thinking that He must have been an amazing person. I mean...all his miracles and talks with the people! Even today, I find Him fascinating!"

He looked down at me.

"What?"

"That's just creepy! You are almost as old as Jesus?" I shook my head in awe. "Wait! You are a vampire! Why would you even want to talk about Him? Isn't He taboo with your kind? How about the whole supernatural world?"

He looked at me with a shocked look on his face.

"Well, technically, he has a thousand years on me. But, why would you think that He was taboo?"

"Oh...well...doesn't that go with the whole package of undead and what not?" I muttered.

He threw his head back and laughed, while I narrowed my eyes, and crossed my arms over my chest, pushing my breasts upward. I started to tap my foot.

"Well?" I demanded. "Just what's so funny?"

"What makes you think that we don't accept Him – or at least some of us do, like humans? I mean, look at all the things He did that you would, or should, consider supernatural. A name is still just a name, Noel. Speaking either His name or the name of God isn't going to change what we are, and nothing is going to happen.

"Oh!" I thought about that for a minute. "I never thought of it that way, and no."

"I never even thought about the miracles that He did as being supernatural. It was just a given."

I stopped, and he let me think about what he said at that point.

"Another question, though, is why do vampires drink blood? I mean, what's the real reason? Is there even a reason?"

He huffed.

"OK. You are a part of our world, now, so I will try and explain it. You have that right as my…."

He broke off whatever he was going to say, walked over to the bed, and patted it. She didn't hesitate, but plopped her butt right next to his. His arm went around her.

"There is a good reason why we do drink blood. Vampires – the first vampires – were not from Earth."

~ 12 ~

~ NOEL ~

My eyes got wide at his admission. Not from Earth? Of all the things I expected to hear, it certainly was not those words.

"What? Seriously? Then, where are you from?"

"The original vampires came from another planet, and their planet was dying. There were other species on the planet as well...," he began, and Noel interrupted him.

"What species?"

He didn't answer, but gave me the "be quiet, and you'll find out" look. I smacked my lips together, and just waited.

"Until the planet began to die, the creatures of that world lived in harmony with each other. But, like all politics, they began to argue. No one knew exactly what they should do, except that they knew they had to leave the planet or die."

I leaned back on the bed, placing my hand on the side of my head, holding it up so I could see him. Holy crap! He followed, and mimicked me.

"Well, they almost argued their way into destruction and almost waited just too long. At that time, their world was allied with several other worlds, and two of them came to their rescue, offering ships to ferry them to one of the worlds that was sparsely populated, but still had the atmosphere conducive to the different species. The trip helped for a while, and essentially, they were cooperative. The ship that brought them to Earth left as soon as they deposited their cargo, because tarrying would have meant danger to them. They couldn't breathe Earthly atmosphere."

"Wow, Damian! That's sad and happy…and sad," I told him.

He nodded in agreement.

"But, what they didn't know, and they were never told, was that theirs was the only ship to make it to Earth."

He paused to look at me. Was he gauging my response? I wanted to ask the obvious question, but decided not to do it. So, I waited for him to continue.

"No one knew what happened to the others, but the small contingent who did make it were left to fend for themselves. To this day, no one really knows what happened. Their population was very small compared to humans on Earth, which was good in one way…."

"Food," I guessed.

"Yes. Food. They had a few choices."

"Which ones made it past the initial landing?" I asked, very, very interested in this story.

"The way I understand it, on the ship, there were both vampires and werewolves. Of course, we discovered, to our detriment, that the werewolves could pro-create on Earth, but the vampires could not."

"Werewolves?" I sat up and sneered. "Really?"

"You want to hear it or not?" he snickered.

"OK. OK. But, why could werewolves pro-create and vampires could not?"

He shrugged.

"I don't really think we will ever be able to figure that out. Whereas both species could procreate on the original planet, vampires, for some reason, were unable to do so here on Earth. Yet, the werewolves had a huge uptake in children and were highly fertile – far more than on the original planet. Someone finally theorized that the Earth's atmosphere had something to do with it. There was something else on this planet that kept us from procreating, while giving the weres the ultimate fertility."

"As if it took the ability from the vampires, and gave the werewolves double fertility?"

"That's interesting. Perhaps you are right, as of right now, they are still actually trying to figure out why, but the bottom line is that vampires have never been able to have children. Anyway, nature made up for this oversight, because we discovered that humans were perfect for both species. Both of us had fangs, and where werewolves could mate with humans, or turn them with a bite, vampires became the perfect killing machines. They could mate with humans and turn them as well, adding to their numbers, but only if they drained them dry, then fed them their blood. Unfortunately, there are always bad eggs in all groups, and some used it to rule over humans. In some cases, they were used for nothing but food. And, some of the weres were just as bad."

"Dracula?" I said, enlightened. Come on! You were all thinking it.

"Yes. He was the worst vampire ever created. His extraordinary hatred of both vampires and humans allowed him to do horrible things. But, you already know the things he did. He was selfish, and his hatred turned him into the most evil vampire who ever lived. Today, we know he was a turned vampire, but something went wrong. Sometimes, it happens. No one knows what, but some believe that he was already crazy, and the vampire who turned him was just as insane. Whatever happened, he killed his sire, and then he went on a killing and impaling spree. Impaling is not a lot different from the cross, of course. It took a long time for the council to gather enough proof against him to put him to death. From what I know, they impaled him alive, stripped his skin from his body, and broke every bone in his body, before they dismembered and burned him."

"That makes my sick just hearing about it!" I gagged and ran to the bathroom, where I promptly threw up anything I had eaten that day. Damian was right behind me, holding my hair out of my face, and bathing my forehead with a cool cloth. After I was finished, I stayed to brush my teeth, before he carried me back to the bed, laid me down, turned off the light, then climbed onto the bed to lie down beside me. I knew my heart was beating like crazy, and I was sure he could hear it. But, as much as I wanted the night to evolve with us, I was just too curious.

"OK. I'm ready. What happened?"

"You sure?" he asked, watching me nod. "OK. Where was I? Oh, right. After Vlad, the council began to make rules – many developed by me. One of these was that no vampire or werewolf could change anyone at their own whim any more. If it continued, we would have no food, left. One of the main procedure of the law was that any vampire and werewolf were forced to petition the court to be able to change a human. They didn't think it was a smart idea to just turn someone at will."

"Blood-bonded humans!" I said, understanding where he was going with all of it.

He nodded, and grinned, turning his head to look at me.

"Yes. Only certain humans would be granted blood-bonded status, but they could not be a mate of a vampire. For werewolves, they were only allowed to turn their mates, if the mate wanted to do it."

"That doesn't sound fair," I said.

"That's what the vampire world said. But, because of Vlad, we were forced with even more rules and regulations, and as I said, I was one of the sponsors of those laws. However, as time evolved, the more we understood why they made that decision. A werewolf's mate would still be alive with a beating heart, but vampires had to drain their mates dry, and give them their blood to turn them. Essentially, we would have to kill them in order for our mates to live."

That made some kind of weird sense, but I still didn't think it was fair.

"Still not fair," I said, crossing my arms in solidarity. "What if the mate decides she or he wanted to become like their vampire mates?"

"Doesn't really matter. The law stands – even based on the vampire mates desires. They are not allowed to be considered. The rules evolved as time went on, and the Vampires were allowed to have a blood-bonded mate if needed, but without turning them. However, if a mate was found among the blood-bonded mates, that mate could decide for themselves whether or not they wanted to be turned. As you know, it's not necessary."

"No, but the blood-bonded human would have to realize that he or she would not live as long as their vampire mate, right?"

He nodded.

"I was turned at a time, before the time of the blood-bonding."

"Oh. I'm so sorry," I said, staring into his red eyes. I watched him shrug.

"It's not a big deal. The deed was done, and it was done during the time of war. I was born in the year 173 AD in Caledonia. The Dark times followed."

I recognized that name, but the war? No. If I learned about Caledonia in school and, like most of us, it went in one ear and right out the other, I didn't really….

"Caledonia?" I petted my chin. "Wait! I do know that name! Wasn't that in Scotland?"

Damian grinned very big.

"Very good, Noel! Yes. Anyway, when Septimius Severus invaded, we fought, but I was killed in battle."

Even though I knew he had been turned, it still surprised me, so I gasped.

"A vampire named Curttis, turned me. He made it his duty to make sure he made vampires to keep Rome from conquering the people. And, it worked. When Severus fell ill around 210, and died 211, the war was called off, and they returned to Rome."

"He fell ill?" I questioned. Then, realizing what he meant. "You mean someone bit him."

"Perhaps. We were never able to confirm it one way or the other, but we like to think one of us killed Curttis. The truth was, though, for whatever reason, he became about as evil, if not more so, than Vladimir Dracula. Strangely, he disappeared, and no one was ever able to find him."

I narrowed my gaze. Did he really mean that or did he mean he'd taken care of him?

"Who are you really trying to convince here? Me or you?" I asked.

"Maybe both?"

"So...you think he's still alive?" I asked, but received no answer, and any time someone has a vague, or no answer, it means that is a bad thing.

I narrowed my eyes at him, and noticed an almost imperceptible smirk on his lips. I took that as to mean that he had something to do with the whole thing. I started to ask, but he darted his head at me. I saw his eyes brighten with humor, and it kind of shook me up at that moment. But, not for long. If he had something to do with it, I knew that it was his secret, and his alone. I decided that perhaps I really didn't want to know the whole story, so I pushed it to the back of my mind to lock it away somewhere.

"And, Jesus?" I asked.

"Oh, yes. When I first heard of him, I became a convert. He is the reason that I have tried to be a better vampire since that day. I am not perfect, and I have slipped a few times, but I have never questioned my belief. He does forgive, and it is because of Him that I have the family I have today."

I thought about him. His belief was very inspiring. I really wanted to have the same confidence, and belief, but my life had been full of hatred and hurt. Losing my parents, and being plunged into the governmental system of foster families, had sort of soured me on anything such as faith in something bigger and better. But, then, I thought that if Damian – after everything he had been through could believe, then why should it be that hard for me?

"Oh! I just found out that Sam and Ronnie mated last night!" Damian told me.

I suspected, from his huge grin, and blue eyes, that this was a great thing. So, I smiled, too. I was happy for Ronnie. She deserved to be happy.

"So, what does that mean? You said that you can take a mate from the blood-bonded humans, right?"

He nodded.

"Oooh! Does that mean a party?" I asked, clapping my hands.

"I thought you might want to throw it for her! I did tell them I'd give them a mating party."

"Christmas! We can have a Christmas Mating Party!" I squealed, bouncing all over the bed. I flipped up on the bed, and settled on my knees. I grabbed his hands. "Can we, Damian? Can we have a Christmas Mating Party for Ronnie and Sam?"

Damian laughed at my exuberance! He pulled me to him, and I fell on his lap, laying my head against his chest. It felt so right! I felt content, happy..., and pretty damn horny, too! It was just like I was a young teenager who was having my first date! And, maybe I was. He kissed my hair, and I watched him tip my happy face up to him. For a moment, we looked at each other, then Damian lowered his lips to mine.

~ 13 ~

~ DAMIAN ~

I went straight to find Ronnie after we shared blood. Both of them had already concurred that there was no doubt that Noel was my mate. Oh, hell! I knew it. I wanted to confirm it, or not to confirm it, for myself. I was confused by my feelings – especially after what had happened earlier. So, here I was, showing up at their door. Sam and Ronnie gestured for me to sit.

"What happened?" Sam asked.

"I'm not really sure. We shared blood, again. I just need to know if she is my mate."

Both nodded. That was a given, or they both would die.

"It was afterward that was very strange. I've never heard of it before," I told them.

They didn't say anything, and I was grateful, while I gathered my thoughts.

"The desire...," I started. "It was.... I mean, it was so damn strong. Hell! I had to jack off in my shower, and what came out of me was unbelievable!" Two sets of eyebrows rose. They looked at each other, and nodded.

"What about Noel?" Ronnie asked.

"I know she felt something, too, but if I hadn't gotten out of there, I would not only have taken her, but I know I would have drained her, and made her like us. It was so strong, Ronnie, I have no idea how I stopped myself!" I hung my head in my hands. It was shame I was feeling.

Sam stood, and walked back and forth across the room. I watched him, until he stopped.

"You didn't blood-bond her at the same time you mated her did you?"

"No," I protested. I hesitated. "At least, I don't think I did?"

Ronnie put her two cents into the mix.

"You know, Sam, you may be right. But, what if...," she paused. "...Damian, what if you did bond her at the same time you made her your mate?

"Never heard of such a thing!"

"I know. Neither have I. Is it possible? I mean...is it possible that when you shared your blood the second time, that your body was demanding that you claim her? You know that you almost took too much blood. I'm wondering if it could have happened without your knowledge. You think that hers was just as strong?"

I thought back after the sharing a few minutes ago. There was no denying it.

"Yes."

I watched Ronnie text on her phone, and seconds later, Caleb was at the room.

"What's up? For goodness sakes, guys! I was getting some tail!" he whined, trying to buckle his belt in his haste to get dressed, and get to their room.

"Grow up, Caleb!" Ronnie said, only to get a sneer from him. "We may have a problem."

"OK. So, what's the problem?" he asked.

"We think that Noel and Damian are mates."

Caleb's eyes darted to Damian.

"Mates? Wait, but she is you blood-bonded human! She can't be both! Not unless the ritual was done."

"Yeah, yeah. Settle down, Caleb," Sam said. "We think Damian did not realize this until the blood-bond took place. Do you know anything about it?"

Caleb looked at the three of them. This could be very bad, especially if the council found out about it, and he had made her his mate without her knowledge.

"No. As far as I know, blood-bond and mating has never happened at the same time. Damian, did you just have to become the first – again?"

"I thought it would spice things up to defy the council!" My answer was dripping with sarcasm.

"Ha, ha. I'm not sure the council knows that it could happen. That's why they put the laws into place. Why?"

"His reaction to the second sharing of blood," Ronnie said.

"What reaction?"

"Desire like I've never felt before."

"Jack off?" He watched me nod. "What was different?"

"The amount and how thick it was. And, it happened more than once. I was hard for well over three hours, and I spent the entire time constantly jacking off on the wall of my shower."

"Shit! I've never heard of anything like that!"

Ronnie sat down, and closed her eyes. She always did this when she was thinking hard. She had this uncanny way about her, as if she could see patterns in things. Funny thing about it? She was always right. The three of us kept very quiet, while we waited for Ronnie to think. Sometimes, she could see the patterns easily; other times she had to wait for it to come.

"How about a drink?" Sam asked me.

"Whiskey?" At his nod, "That would be good."

"Caleb?"

"Yeah."

"Be right back."

Sam left the room to go to the kitchen. The minute he left, Ronnie opened her blood red eyes to stare up at me in awe and wonder.

"What?" I asked.

"I have to talk to Noel, first."

"Why?"

"I need her version, because if what I think has happened, it could be one of the most momentous, and monumental events in the entire world of the vampires! It's something that I heard long ago, but it's been just a myth."

I barely said "huh" to her, before she was gone. I plopped down in one of the chairs just as Sam entered. He had brought all three of us glasses. Staring at each other, we guzzled the dark amber liquid.

"Ronnie?" Sam asked.

"Noel," I answered.

"Ahhh," he responded in understanding.

~ NOEL ~

A knock on the door had me jumping off the bed, pulling open the door to find Ronnie standing in front of her. I grinned.

"I'm so happy for you! I can't wait to get ready for your mating party!" I gushed, as I hugged her, and she hugged me back. "So, Ronnie? Watcha needing, chicka?"

"I need to ask you a very intimate question," she said, almost a bit embarrassed.

That was weird. Since when are vampires embarrassed?

"Whoa! OK????" I said in the form of a question, and motioned for her to come into the room. Ronnie made her way to one of the chairs in front of the window by the table.

I sat down opposite with a wary look in my eye.

"What did you want to ask me?"

"Noel, Damian came to Sam and me. He believes you are his mate."

My hand went to my throat in surprise. OK, maybe not completely, but to hear it voiced aloud? That had my stomach gripping.

"Mate?"

"Yeah. Has he told you about being a blood-bonded human and mates?"

I shrugged. "Only that it shouldn't happen, because of the laws, unless we are truly mates."

"Yes. So, I have to ask you. When you shared blood with him, what happened to you?"

My face turned tomato red, I was so embarrassed. It really was an intimate question.

"Oh, well, uh, I, uh, you see, I brought my, uh, device with me, when I was here, last, and I had left it here. So...." I kind of left the thought hanging.

She laughed aloud.

"So, you were horny?" she giggled.

"Uh, yeah."

"How horny?"

"Why are you asking?"

"Noel, I believe that the two of you are, indeed, mates. And, I also believe that you were mated when he made you his bonded human, too. To our knowledge, to do so at the same time has never happened."

I had tried to interrupt, but her hand waved me to be quiet, so I didn't say anything.

"Let me finish. How many times did you use your toy?"

"I don't know. I kind of lost count."

"Intense? I mean your desire?"

"Ronnie, I have never, in my life, been that horny. I really, really thought something was wrong with me. Damian seemed to be suffering from it as well, until he ran out of the room."

"OK. Normally I wouldn't say this, but you need to know. It took him three hours, and jacking off multiple times, before he was able to relax."

My mouth formed into a surprised "O". The thought of him jacking off was a huge turn on, and my pussy was wet again. Damn! I'd just felt dry!

"He said that his erection was hard for those three hours - very, very hard. He, too, lost count as to how many times."

"I don't understand."

"I'm going to tell you what I think about it. Then, I'm going to tell Sam, so he can tell Damian." I just nodded, as I waited for her to explain. "I think the laws that were made against having a blood-bonded human, who was also a mate, was for a nefarious purpose. The fact that so few every found a mate in the bonded humans has to mean something. I think that we have been lied to all this time. I also think that the ritual that is performed between a bonded human and vampire, is a total lie."

"I don't get it? You and Sam did it, and are mates. What makes Damian and me any different?"

"I don't think there is a difference."

"Do you mean you two had the same feelings?" I asked, surprised.

"Yeah. This family has a tendency to do something, then think about it afterward. What I think," and her hand went to her abdomen. "is that it is nature's way of letting us procreate. But, certain things must happen in a specific way to do so. Whatever their reasoning, someone didn't want vampires to ever have children. I've always believed there was more to the story, but I could never prove it. There is a myth about vampires conceiving, but we have been taught to ignore it."

"So, what you are saying is that someone conspired to stop vampires from having children. That would mean that someone, way back when, discovered early on that vampires could procreate!" I said is surprise.

"Yeah. And, that also means that in order to prevent the pregnancies, they had to be on…"

"The Council," we finished together.

~ 14 ~

~ NOEL ~

"Who would have done that?" I squeaked.

Ronnie shook her head.

"I can't be totally sure, unless it happens, but it actually would make sense. The myth goes that when our people came to Earth, there was a strange consequence, and vampires could not procreate."

"Damian told me about that. But, he said he was a sponsor of the bill for certain laws like that of a blood-bonded human versus mate."

"Exactly. There is a ritual. Did he tell you about it?" I shook my head. "There is a specific ritual for making a blood-bonded human a mate, Noel. It's rather bloody as well."

I was wary, but I nodded for her to continue.

"The way it works is that a vampire and blood-bonded human cannot have intercourse, until after the ritual has been completed. The vampire must bite the blood-bonded human, and drink only a couple of sips. Then, there is a knife, and the vampire must use this to slit three arteries of the human – the neck, one wrist, and finally, the artery in the left leg. Bleeding must occur for a period of not less than ten minutes. Once that is completed, the vampire must take blood from each of the arteries, and they must be sealed immediately after each sip."

"That would be bloody," I said.

"Yes, it would. Arteries of a human allow bleeding out to occur very quickly."

"But why no sex before it, and why does the human need to bleed out for ten minutes?"

"That's the whole question. That myth I was talking about? According to it, a vampire and human are completely compatible for a child as long as the female or male mate is human. The way this happens is when mates have sex, and vampire bites the human while the human sucks the blood from a vampire through a knife cut in the neck's carotid artery. The odd thing? The bite and cut must occur at the same time as the male ejaculates into the female – and they both must drink from each other for a full, ten minutes after orgasm. I believe that this was deliberate on the part of the werewolves and the vampires on the council. The werewolves have always had this insane desire to stop the spread of vampirism, thus the dislike between species since arriving on Earth. And, during this ritual, which they deliberately stopped, the intense, almost insane desire, to have sex is something like I had never experienced. Sam and I broke the law, Noel. We decided to test my theory, and we had sex for four hours straight, which ended in an intense orgasm, followed by ten minutes of drinking each other's blood. Our desire was so strong, I couldn't bear to have him out of me at any point! And, Sam filled me full of hot, thick semen, Noel. When I mean full? I mean I was full to overflowing for hours, even after the desire had lessened. I think that the reason the vampire male has so much and it is so thick, it will coat the inside of the human female's womb so the eggs can be fertilized. To put it bluntly, the eggs are so strong, it would take something hard and massive in order to break through the membrane in order to impregnate them. When a blood-bonded female mate is made, there is a physical change in their womb, ovaries, and eggs, making them just as hard as those of a vampire female. This has already been documented medically. Damian said he shot his seed constantly onto his tile in the shower. He also said that it was unusually thick, and slid down the tile extremely slowly. A female vampire or human has a relatively slick womb, and that's a lot of the reason we have been unable to become pregnant. It has always slid out of them. But, I think that is because of the laws of making a blood-bonded human a vampire's mate. It was deliberate. I'm thinking that because the law states the human must bleed out for ten minutes, it makes the womb weak, so that the vampire's seed would still be thick, but the sides of the womb slick so it would not be possible for implantation to take place. I also believe that to be true for a human male and vampire female. The human male's semen is so thin, it cannot stay inside the female for any length of time. Therefore, the human male cannot procreate with a vampire female."

I just gaped at her. Did she really believe that?

"Ronnie...what are you on? Or has mating Sam sent you into weirdsville? And, since when do you lie to yourself?"

She hauled off, and slapped me – hard. It didn't hurt, of course, but it sure was humiliating.

"How dare you say that to me! When have you known me to lie? I can't believe you said that to me!" Ronnie cried.

Ronnie grabbed me by the throat, and lifted me into the air. I knew I'd stepped over the line, and I knew I deserved it, but damn! I couldn't breathe!

"Ca...bre-athe," I gasped, clawing at her hands. "Pl- pl-ease, Ronnie!"

I looked into her red eyes, and knew if I couldn't get through to her, I was a dead duck. Tears began to flow down my cheeks. I noticed her eyes began to turn back to her normal chocolate, and horror struck her as she realized what she was doing. She lowered me down, quickly, and let me go. I started coughing, and couldn't stop. How did I ever get into this situation? My hand went to my throat, as I continued to cough.

"Oh, my God, Noel! I-I'm so very sorry! I don't know what happened! Oh, God!" she cried out into the room. Her eyes were huge. They were chocolate, again, but huge. She reached out to me, and I flinched. The pain in her eyes as she saw me, caused her to lean back.

I shook my head, and tried to talk, but my throat felt bruised. I walked to the mirror, afraid to remove my hand, but I did. Yep. I had a bruise...a bad one stretching across my throat in the form of a hand. I opened my mouth to try and speak, but found I couldn't. Crap. My vocal cords must be bruised, too! It had happened once when I was twelve due to Red Rover and a rope that accidentally got wrapped around my throat. I couldn't talk for a couple of weeks. I had more than a bruise. I had a horrible rope burn. And, it hurt. A bruise was preferable, but still, had the same effect. I'd been through so many emotions over the last few days, it was a miracle that I had not passed out yet. And, that's when I fell to the floor unconscious.

Coming out of the fog, I heard screaming around me.

"What the fuck were you thinking, Ronnie?" Damian yelled.

"I'm sorry, Damian! Do you think I could feel any worse than I already do? For God's sake! She's my best friend!"

"Damian, she's sorry!" Sam yelled.

"I don't care! You hurt my mate, Ronnie! How could you do that?"

"I-I don't know! I've never had that happen before! I've never fallen over the edge like that!"

"Damian, don't hurt her. I don't want to have to hurt you!"

Sam's voice was deadly quiet, and I knew he would do exactly what he said, and that was something I couldn't let happen. Damian? Damian was mine!

My eyes opened slowly. I was in Damian's room, and three very, very angry vampires were standing in the middle of the room, glaring at each other, their fangs long and deadly. I tried to call out, but I couldn't say anything, so I pulled myself to a sitting position, and waved my hand, trying to get their attention. Of course, they were too busy getting ready to beat each other up – royally. That's when Sam and Damian became a blur. They flew around the room so fast, I couldn't even see them. I had to stop this insanity! I stood up, and started to move toward Ronnie, and I guess I should have zagged when they zigged, because I was hit. More like grazed, and I was thrown back into the chest and flat out against the wall. I hit, and slid to the floor. Ronnie was at my side instantly.

"Noel. Are you hurt?" she asked.

All I could do was shake my head, and hope I looked honest, because in truth? I was aching in every muscle, and felt as if my back had a slight, warm trickle of blood. I looked up and saw Damian and Sam staring at me in shock. Everything was hurting right now. My neck, my head was pounding, my chest was hurting, and I peed myself. But despite everything, I stared at Ronnie in total surprise and delight! I frantically pointed at Ronnie's belly. No one was paying attention to me. But, I kept on doing it. Ronnie frowned at me, and suddenly, she knew what I was trying to say! She was pregnant! Her hormones were completely off the wall! I just knew it. Her mouth dropped open in shock and the sudden realization had her mouth turning up into the biggest smile I had ever seen on her face.

"You think?" she asked in awe.

I tried to say I did, but instead, I just nodded, because I couldn't talk.

"Sam! Damian! Noel believes I'm pregnant!"

Both men looked at her in stunned silence. Sam turned to Ronnie in a silent question. She nodded. He scooped her up, but she stopped him.

"I'm so sorry, Noel. Now, I understand. My hormones are off the rail because I'm pregnant! I'm really, really pregnant!" she gushed.

"Sam…," Damian begged.

He nodded, and ran with Ronnie in his arms. Next thing I knew, Damian scooped me up in his arms, and was laying me on his bed, before I could catch my breath. He lay beside me, then removed his shirt in one movement. Damian allowed his nail to slice his throat. I almost forgot all about how I was hurting, while staring at his ripped abs, watching his delicious blood run down his strong chest. There was a trail of dark hair just enough to be sexy, and it spread into a "V" at his waistline, and I wanted what was beyond that. I felt him lift my neck towards his throat, and my mouth attached to it. That's when I remembered what happened earlier, and shook my head. I loved his blood, but I didn't really think I was that hurt.

"Noel. You are hurt very badly. You have several broken ribs, a huge gash on the back of your head, a cut on your back, and your arm was sliced open. You must take my blood to heal you."

OK...apparently I was hurt worse than I thought. I looked into his eyes in fear. He knew what I was thinking.

"We won't share blood this time. But, mine will heal you quickly. It shouldn't effect either of us since it's one sided."

I thought for a moment, and it actually made sense. I nodded, and he lifted my head to his neck. But, I stopped him. I opened my mouth, lowered my head to his chest, and licked the blood from his chest all the way to his shoulder to the gash. My mouth closed over it, devouring his delicious blood. I groaned at the taste, but more importantly, I felt something begin to knit together inside of me. My throat, first, felt much better, followed by my headache as it disappeared, then I felt my ribs healing rapidly. My cuts were healed almost instantly.

"OK, that's enough, baby."

Damian slowly drew me away from his neck.

My eyes were still closed, enjoying the favor of his blood. Finally, I looked up at him. But, did he really just call me "Baby"? Oh, man! Did that ever make me wet!

"Damian? I feel normal!" I paused. "Well, actually I feel better than normal!"

"Our blood has healing qualities," he said. "But, we must offer it to a human. A human cannot take the healing power from our blood."

"Please...don't hurt Ronnie? It wasn't her fault. It was mine. She was really angry. I called her a liar, Damian!"

"I don't care. She is leaving as of tonight! No one hurts what is mine without repercussions!"

I placed my hand on his chest, feeling it ripple in anger. I looked into his red eyes, and shook my head.

"No, Damian, she isn't leaving. Her hormones are off the wall. She's pregnant! And, that means that vampires can procreate! I was wrong, and so was she. You can't punish her without doing the same to me."

I watched his blue eyes return, and his lips met mine. I groaned, and opened my mouth. His tongue dove into mine, and they tangled together. OMG! He tasted so good! When he finally let go, I moaned at the absence of his lips.

"Understand this, Noel. You are mine. You are my mate." He stared into my eyes, and I felt him branding me with his. "And, baby, I am yours."

His mouth crashed into mine, and we kissed for...oh...who cares how long! I wanted him. Desperately! My hands raked across his strong chest, and I slid one down just past his waist, but kept it over his pants. I wanted to feel it. When he made no move to stop me, I finally reached what I was after, and ran my hand over it. It was hard for me. I was wet for him. Why are we not doing the "deed"? If we were truly mates, like he said, and I actually believed it, why weren't we making love? I heard him moan my name into my mouth as I stroked him gently. Finally, Damian cupped my left breast, and he squeezed gently, rubbing his thumb over my nipple. Without a bra, it pebbled immediately. That caused me to echo his moan. I wanted to feel flesh on flesh. To hell with the clothing!

"Flesh," I demanded in between his kissing my mouth and my neck.

He stopped to look at me, and saw the answer in my eyes. I had no bra on under my top, and I wanted to feel my breasts against his chest – his flesh. He took his claw, and sliced my top down the middle, baring my breasts to his hungry gaze. I wanted to rake my nipples across his chest, and feel his mouth on them! Just as I thought it, his mouth was suckling on my right breast. I arched upward, and yelled out his name.

"Damian!" I yelled. "Harder!"

I felt his teeth nip my nipple, and I writhed in ecstasy. He let go, and nabbed my other nipple, suckling, and nipping that one as well. My pussy was wet with desire, my juices flowing heavily. My pants were soaked, and I wanted him! Oh, I wanted him inside of me!

"Please, Damian?" I begged. "I'm so wet!"

His hands went to my button, and unzipped my pants. Without hesitation, I lifted my hips, and he slid both my pants and my panties off in one motion. Where they went, I didn't know, and I didn't care. I wanted his cock in me. I was lifted toward the head of the bed, and looked at him. He stared into my eyes as he slowly – too slowly – unbuttoned his jeans, unzipped them, and yanked them down over his hips along with his black briefs, stepping out of them. My eyes grew big as I beheld the most beautiful cock in the world. Standing tall, hard, and proud, his rod pointing at me as if it was claiming me! And, I wanted to be claimed! The bed dipped as he climbed back onto it, and his glorious, naked body covered my body, pushing apart my legs, and settling his cock at my pussy.

"Virgin?" he asked, as if he didn't already know.

I nibbled on my lips, thinking to tell him no, but I didn't. I just nodded. To my surprise, he grinned.

"Good. I am going to make you mine. Once I do, you are mine forever, Noel. Understand this. Vampire mate is forever. You will live as long as I, and we will never part. I will not let you go."

I lifted my knees, and spread them wider.

"I am yours, Damian. Forever," I murmured.

Finally, his cock entered into my core, and I screamed out his name.

"DAMIAN!"

~ 15 ~

~ NOEL ~

He was absolutely huge inside of me! Could I take all of him, and at the same time, I thought that yes, I could take every single inch of him!

"Don't go slow, Damian!"

"What?"

"Give it to me hard and fast!"

"But, it will hurt."

"Only for a moment. Don't you get it, Damian? I want you to take me hard and fast. I need it!"

Without questioning me further, Damian thrust himself into me fully, seating himself inside me all the way to my womb! My hips met his in an upward thrust. We were so desperately frantic with each other, the fleeting pain I had was nothing compared to the ecstasy I was feeling! We settled into a fast rhythm as we took each other as fast and hard as we could. I arched back, and screamed his name as my pussy clenched around his hard rod. Squeezing him with everything I had, I milked his seed from his body with each and every thrust! When he was done, he collapsed sideways, but still inside of me. He had filled me full!

"Baby! You are so wet and tight!" Damian was gasping for air that he didn't need.

I grinned up at him, his cock still hard and buried inside me.

"I thought that was what I was supposed to be?" I kissed his gorgeous lips. "Very, very wet, and extremely tight, in order to take your wonderfully hard cock and its white fluid."

His eyes grinned in laughter.

"Did you just say 'white fluid'?" I nodded, and gave him a "come hither" smile. "You know what it's called, I hope?" He teased.

I laughed aloud, and to get him back, squeezed his hard shaft with my internal muscles, his groan making me want him so much more. I wrapped my arms around his neck, and he pulled me on top of him, gently moving inside me, again. I lifted my hips up and down, taking him into my body slowly, taking the time to feel his cock inside. I leaned down, and kissed him in a slow, methodical kiss. Teasing him, I also brushed my nipple across his mouth, letting him catch it.

"You mean your semen? Your seed?" I whispered.

"Yes! You are my mate, Noel," he murmured softly in between licks.

"I know. And, you are mine, Damian!"

Our lovemaking was much slower and languid, this time. I don't know how long he was inside of me, or even how often we made love that night, but really, it didn't matter. By morning, he dragged me into his shower, and pushed me against the wall as he took me once again.

"So, are we mated, yet?" I finally had the nerve to ask.

"Our situation is a bit…unusual," he said kissing my nose, "but…."

I slapped his arm.

"Funny, are we? So? Give!"

While he soaped me down, he explained.

"Mating between a blood-bonded human and vampire is technically forbidden without the knowledge of the human. If I am right, I broke that law when I almost drained you, and I'm truly sorry."

I was a bit surprised.

"Wait! We are already mated? But, how is that possible?"

"Mating usually takes place with sex and taking each other's blood at the same time. However, when I bit you, I unconsciously, sent out the mating hormones into you. I really, really didn't realize I was doing it, so instead of making you my blood-bonded human and mating you as is the right way, I combined them, and that's the reason for all of our desire. It is our law that we ask the human to mate with us, before it happens."

"You mean what happened to us the other night was caused by this hormone?" my voice had risen in its pitch.

"Yes. But, it's never supposed to be that intense except with mates. However, after talking to Ronnie and Sam yesterday, I began to realize what I had done to you."

I waved my hand.

"I don't care if you mated me that way or the normal way, Damian. Between us, you asked me, and I said yes without hesitation."

"But, it's against our laws," he protested.

"And, who is going to know? Who is going to not believe me if I said I gave my permission? Ronnie? Sam? Caleb? They aren't going to betray us, so there is no one who will know. And, I certainly will not let anyone try to use it against us."

"Landon and his minions may not agree with you."

"So? We tell them that my yes was a whisper."

"We can hear those, Noel."

"Are you telling me that everything we whisper to each other, even in the form of a sighed 'yes', can be heard every single time by vampires?"

He yanked me to him, and crashed our lips together. In seconds, we were in the shower, and he pulled me to him in another mind-blowing, but romantic kiss.

"I guess we can convince them that you told me yes, but in a sigh. I mean. You sighed and moaned.

"So, we can convince them that I did say yes to you in a so soft sigh, that they could not understand it, right?"

"Yes. I love you, Noel," he murmured against my lips.

"I love you, Damian," I answered, kissing him tenderly. "Now that that is settled, Ronnie told me her theory about all the desire that hit us, and why I felt I had to run out on you."

"Really? What is it?"

"Wait! She didn't say anything to you?"

"What did she say?" he asked, while shaking his head no. I continued.

"Her theory is that the desire that we experienced, and that she and Sam did as well, would not be common between a blood-bonded human and vampire. That sexual desire had nothing to do with that type of bond. She told me what you had said, and done."

"You mean when I jacked off in the shower?"

I nodded.

"She said you said that it was very thick, and stuck to the tile."

"Yes. I thought it was very strange."

"Well, her theory is that you have all been lied to about procreation by this Council of yours. She believes that it is thick only during the time when the female – vampire or human – can become pregnant, but I'm not sure whether she knows when those times will be. Ronnie also thinks that's the reason vampires have been required to slit three arteries within your blood-bonded mating, and forced to let them bleed for ten minutes, before you drink from each other. And to top all that off, you cannot have sex, at the same time. She says she thinks it does something to the DNA of the human mate to keep them from getting pregnant. However, if it is done during the mating process, and skipping the arteries, it will remain permanent, and vampires can have children."

"I don't think...."

"No, Damian. Think about it. Your kind...."

"MY kind?" Damian asked with a smirk.

"Shut up! Yes. Your kind cannot procreate, but the wolves can. Why? Did you all ever really ask? And, also you said that the bloody ritual between was absolutely required between blood-bonded humans and vampire to mate, right?"

Damian nodded hesitantly.

"Well, like I said...do you know why all that bleeding was necessary? I mean...think about it. Who would stand to gain the most by lying to all of you. That's my contribution to all of this. Who set those laws, or whose idea was it? Was it yours? If Ronnie is right, then why did no one ever tell vampires the truth. Or, did *someone* know, and didn't tell you? Did the council tell you the truth?" I asked him. "Or was it someone else who put the bug in the council's ear to manipulate your population to be less? Again, *who would gain the most from lying to you?*"

~ DAMIAN ~

Was Ronnie right?   Was Noel's additional question also a possibility? Had they been lied to all this time? A better question was, *"Why have I never questioned it?"*

Noel's face had taken on a "I see you are finally making the connection" look. What would it mean to them if vamps could have children? For him, it would represent freedom from the darkness of having to live on blood, because he wouldn't care any more that he did need it. Drinking blood would be nothing but an annoying habit he needed, qne it would no longer dominate his world.

"Well, like I said...do you know who it might have been?" Noel asked.

"I never even thought about questioning our rules and laws. We were all told the same thing from the Council. I mean, why would we even think about doing it?"

"Well, I have another theory. A vampire and their bonded human might be able to procreate after they mate. I think Ronnie and Sam wanted to prove it. And, I think they have. I'm positive she is pregnant. She would never have acted that way toward me. So, it has to be something else. Hormones would be the most logical idea, only vamps would have a little bit more of a stronger reaction with them. Human females get a little cranky, but for a vamp, it would be magnified thousands of time."

I thought about that for a moment. There was no doubt about human women's hormones when pregnant. Rebecca proved that to me. Maybe Ronnie was on to something.

"So, you think that is why the thickness of the semen comes deliberately after mating?"

"Well, Ronnie thinks it is. Yes. And, I think the woman's womb is changed during the correct way of mating to take the thick liquid. It would stick to the womb and the ovaries, allowing the vampire's seed to enter the female's egg, because if it were that thick, a released egg would stick in the semen, allowing pregnancy to take place. She said that mating the required way. as the Council willed it, causes the female's womb to become slick through the loss of blood, and that it is just as permanent as when a vampire mating takes place without their requirements of law. And, it will only happen after we take blood from each other. I just can't believe the great man upstairs would have left you guys out of the procreation game! It would make no sense!"

I had never thought of it in that way before. We stayed quiet for a while, as we bathed each other, preferring to ignore Ronnie's idea. Still, it was in the back of both of our minds. The thought that Noel could swell with my child gave me a whole new feeling of want. I wanted her to carry and have my son or daughter. She would have to be a strong woman to do it, and she was the strongest human female he had ever met.

After a good shower and breakfast, Noel announced she had to get back to her store, and we decided to file the other away for considering later. The Christmas decorations were arriving today, and there would be no one there to accept the order. Against everyone's better judgment, and mine, I decided to let her go.

Because, as Noel said, "I'm not allowed to be taken or touched, because I'm yours, right?"

And, none of them could deny it. So, I drove Noel to her store, and parked my SUV in front of the shopping center, where Noel's business was located. She opened the door, but I put my hand on her arm.

"Sure you don't want me to come in?"

"Damian. This is for your home. We have the magazine photographers coming in a month! I have to do this!" she said, trying to placate him.

"Well...," I began.

"I'll be just fine. You can't keep me in a bubble, my love. You have to let me spread my wings, and I need to do something other than be in your bed." She grinned at me as I shook my head. I'd rather her be in my bed forever. "I have a lot to do, putting things together, closing out the year, and more. Pick me up at six, and make sure you have a van or something! I ordered a lot of stuff!"

All I could do was nod. Even though, in theory, no one ever took an already blood-bonded human from another vampire, let alone a mate. I just couldn't shake the idea there was more to all of this than I knew, especially with Landon involved. I watched her unlock the door, wave, and walk into the building. I made her promise that she would lock her back door, and I heard her do so. For the moment, there was nothing I could do, so I decided to drive back home, and get back to work myself. And, it was one of the longest days I have ever spent in my life.

My day was interminable! First, the computer for the shipping company went down, and I had to scramble to find someone to repair it. Then, there was some minor crisis between two of my employees that I had to referee. I had to talk to my online President for my store, because he couldn't find his own ass if it stared at him in the face! I had Caleb fire him, and to replace him immediately.   Caleb had a candidate already waiting, and did both in the same breath.

Finally, after one hell of a day, I was finally driving back to get Noel! Just before I left to get her, I had to contend with someone who was demanding that I drop everything, and immediately come to Italy to discuss the deal I was putting together in person. Not without picking up Noel first! I argued, but he was another vampire, and he was one of my best customers, so I finally acquiesced. I knew Noel wouldn't want to go, because she had the photo shoot coming up with the magazine. I called my customer back, and asked if he would mind if I had Ronnie and Sam come instead of me, and he was more than willing to do it. He really admired both of them, and he felt he could trust them implicitly. That having been done, I pulled into the back parking lot, and waited for Noel.

Noel never came out of her shop.

~ 16 ~

~ NOEL ~

"Owwwww!" I moaned, slapping my hand on my forehead. Man, my head was hurting! I opened my eyes, only to close them quickly against the bright light. After a few minutes, I opened them slowly, and pushed myself up only to fall back down. Where was I? Looking around, I noticed I was on the concrete sidewalk just outside the back door of my shop.

"Dammit!" I said aloud. But, I certainly was not expecting an answer.

"Language, Noel," a strange voice said, and my eyes flew open as I sat up in an instant.

The voice startled me, and I whipped around to find my eyes meeting those of yet another vampire! He was in shadow, so I couldn't see him very well. And, my sarcastic voice decided to pop out at just that moment.

"You're brave enough to say that to me, but too much of a coward to come out of the shadows? Sorry. Nope. Why should I listen to a disembodied voice?"

I slowly stood, realizing I had been laying on the concrete in the back of my store. Bracing my hand on the wall, I rose to my knees, reaching out to put my hand against it to help me stand the rest of the way. I could tell there was no way at all that I was going to be able to stand without assistance, so I leaned against the wall. I watched as a slightly slithery figure emerged out of the dark parking lot and into the light. He looked familiar, and like all other vampires I'd met, he was gorgeous. Truthfully, I had noticed the same guy the night that Damian bit me, but it didn't register. Then, it hit me.

"You're Landon, right?"

I made the statement, sure I remembered his name.

"You remember."

"Oh, yeah. I remember," I answered, my voice dripping with sarcasm.

"Good. There is someone who wants to talk to you."

"First, did you just have to whack me on the head? Second, nope. Uh-uh. Not going to happen. I'm claimed, now. You can't touch me," I warned.

"True, but I am not here to take you for claiming, so that negates the law, so that I can take you," he told me.

"Well, it figures."

"What?"

"There's always a way around the rules," I replied.

He grinned.

"Smart as you are, I'm not here to break rules. As I said…someone wishes to speak to you, and he will gladly answer any questions you may have. But, you must agree to stay overnight."

"Why?"

Landon shrugged.

"I do not know what he wishes to say to you, but he will have my head if I do not return with you."

"So? Why should I care whether or not you keep your head?" I sneered.

"Because, what he has to tell you will answer questions that you have not had answered in your life. Somethings that even Damian and Ronnie do not know."

I stared at him, my mouth in a tight line. My life. Answers. Well, I did want things answered, but was it wise of me to go with Landon? Probably not, but you know what they say? Curiosity killed the cat, and I was far too curious about what an unknown vampire knew about my life and why. I knew that Damian and Ronnie would absolutely be furious with me, but I had to go. Some things will always override your own good sense, and this was mine. So, I nodded to him.

"OK. I'll come. I will stay one night, and one only. If your – uh – leader doesn't tell me something that I don't know, then I'm out of there."

Landon nodded once, then motioned to a limousine, that I had not even noticed.

"Fair enough. He said to make sure you came, whatever I had to do to get you there. It's good you decided to do this the easy way."

I stumbled to the car, and Landon caught me before I fell. A tall vampire held open the door, and Landon helped me slide into the rear-facing seat, so I could keep an eye on him. Landon entered behind me, and the limo took off for parts unknown.

After a few minutes of utter silence, I was brave enough to look around my surroundings. Black leather seats adorned the inside of the limo. To my right was a bar that overshadowed any I had ever seen in any James Bond movies.

"Drink?" Landon asked.

I nodded. After asking my preference, he quickly made it, and handed me a Mimosa. I took a sip, still wary.

"Wow! This is really good!" I said to him surprised.

Landon only nodded his head again. As I sipped my drink, the luxury limo I was sitting in was way out of my league! How is it that these vamps were rich beyond human standards? Even though my rent had been paid by Damian for the next six months, it would stand to reason that their long lives would probably allow them to accumulate great wealth. Common sense told me that, and he'd paid for other things as well, I was sure. He used the excuse, originally, that it was part of being a blood-bonded human. I was determined to pay him back, one day, and I had told him so. He'd merely rolled his eyes, and walked away. But, Damian was rich; this guy was rich. Were there even any middle class or poor vampires? I had no idea, but the facts were stacking up in the "no" column of the list of pros and cons I had made. OK. I hadn't really made a list, but it was in my mind.

I continued to sip the most delicious Mimosa I had ever set lips on and settled back into the luxury leather seats of the limousine to join with Landon in a staring contest. Neither of us spoke for the thirty-minute ride to another mansion that wasn't quite as grand as Damian's, but it was pretty damn near it. As we drove through the privacy gates and up the long driveway to the house, I noticed it was lined with statues. On second look, I realized what I was seeing, and I knew my face turned beet red. One look at Landon's smirk told me he knew why I was blushing. The statues were all involved in some sort of sexual act. That very thing told me what I needed to know about him. He was a fucking pervert!

"So, what? Is your 'boss' a vampire pimp, because he is certainly a pervert!" I asked sarcastically.

Landon said nothing, but shook his head slightly to the left.

"And, you couldn't have at least warned me of these statues?" I asked. Landon still didn't answer. "So, I guess that's a no?"

This time he just nodded once. Damn vampire! Finally, we reached the front doors to the mansion. The driver stepped out and around to open the door for me. He reached his hand to help me out of the car. I put mine into his cold, dead one, and allowed him to pull me onto the stone pavement. The double, ornately carved doors opened, just as I began my walk up the steps, and against my better judgment, I stepped inside the door, whirling around when I heard the door shut behind me.

I was trapped like a turtle in a tank – with no way out of this fucking mess. Looking around, this mansion also had some similarities to Damian's home. I tried to put my finger on what was different, though, and finally realized I'd already said it. This was a mansion; a house. Damian's mansion was a home. My home, now. There it felt wonderful. You were cared for as if you were precious gems. From the treatment that Landon was giving the servant in front of him, that was a no go here. The floor was sleek, brown slate. Two large tables were parked on either side of the entryway, and a single staircase led upward, splitting, and continuing on either side. Kind of like the Von Trapp home in "Sound of Music". Two balconies were perched on either side, and another set of staircases rose on either side of them. At the top of the single staircase was a portrait of a very distinguished, middle-aged man. I couldn't see his eyes from here, but he appeared to be an aristocrat. How would I know what one of those looked like?

"Oh! Right! Now I get it!" I said aloud. "Politicians!"

Yep. That's exactly what he looked like! A politician!

"I have no idea what you are talking about," Landon growled from the entryway. "If you're finished ogling everything, follow me!"

He led the way down the right hallway that was at the side of the main staircase, while there was also one on the left. Neither joined up behind it, apparently. As we walked down the hallway, I realized how stark this place was. There was nothing really permanent here, and the statues that I saw on the way up the drive certainly were not echoed inside this house. But, that even made me more suspicious, not less. A man who had those kinds of statues out in the front of the mansion was no saint. On the contrary…it was more troubling than ever. Just what was he into?

Landon stopped, and I almost face planted into his back, only catching myself just a second before I did.

"In here, Noel," he said, and opened the door. "After you."

"Yeah, said the spider to the fly," I muttered under my breath, but I knew he could hear me.

I stepped into what appeared to be either a library or a study. It was almost too big to be the latter. I looked around. Wow! Books adorned the walls on all sides, with comfortable library tables, and leather wingback chairs of brown and black leather. Tiffany lamps were scattered around for good lighting, and a large desk sat opposite where I stood…with a very large man, resembling the man in the portrait, sitting in an equally large chair, staring at me from behind it. I wasn't really sure who he was, but he was older than other vamps I had met. He was very distinguished. His hair was cut very short, and graying at his temples. His face was stoic, I guess. As if he had been through hell and back. His nose was patrician, while his lips were full. His eyes were…amazingly green! That was really weird. I had green eyes, and mine were the most brilliant I had ever seen. But, his were almost a teal green, reminding me of the Caribbean Sea – as if I had ever seen it. His shoulders were broad, his chest quite large. And, now, he was standing – and standing and standing. How tall was he anyway? Finally, he stood to his full height of at least six-foot six! His waist was firm, and tight. Probably had six packs under all that muscle. Not that I wanted to know or see, but that was neither here nor there. His legs were strong and large. His skin was pale, golden tan, and he moved with exquisite grace. Not as attractive as Damian, of course, but he was very attractive for a man his age. Strangely, though, he seemed a bit familiar, but I couldn't figure out why.

"It's about time you brought her, Landon. Get the hell out!" he ordered, and I watched Landon leave, shutting the door behind him.

I slowly turned back to him.

"OK. I'm here. What the hell do you want?" I demanded with my fists on my hips.

"Ah, Noel. Don't be that way! We have much to discuss, and only a small bit of time to do so. I'm sure Damian will try to 'rescue' you and to assert his rights as regards his blood-bonded human," he sneered.

Well, that was interesting. Apparently, he didn't know that Damian had mated me. Geez! That word "mated" made me horny! Anyway, it was probably best I didn't mention that bit of information.

"I can't imagine what you and I have to talk about…uh…who are you anyway?"

"Oh. My apologies. My name is Richard. Richard South."

"South? Richard South. Really?" I gave him a sarcastic look, showing I didn't believe what he was saying.

"Yes. That is truly my name."

"Uh-huh. Well, alright if you say so," I said.

He walked toward one of the two wingback chairs facing his desk.

"I do. Please, Noel. Sit down." He waved his hand toward them.

No please; no thank you. Just an order. I not only defied him, I just continued to stand and to stare into his eyes. His eyebrows went up, so, naturally, I shrugged. I finally relented, because I didn't think that I was in trouble with this guy anyway, so I waltzed to the chair, and sat down, watching South move back around to his chair behind the desk. He sat down, leaned on his desk, and templed his fingers. He was staring at her, and that made her uncomfortable. Finally, he spoke.

"I can't believe how lovely you turned out to be, Noel. You are beautiful," he said.

I sat up straight, and scooted toward the edge. That was just too weird, and I was going to bolt if he kept it up. I didn't know him, yet he acted as if he knew me.

"Can you just get to the point?"

"No, really. You are more beautiful than anyone I have ever seen…except for…."

OK. That was it. I started to stand, grabbing the arms to push up off the chair.

"Yeah. Well, look. If that is all you have to say to me, then if it's alright with you, I will return to my own vamp."

"Please, Noel. I know I sound a bit…."

"Insane?" I finished.

"Well, I don't think that is the word I would exactly use. More…fatherly, I would say."

That did it. I stood, and faced him. He had said the one thing that really ticked me the hell off, because no one could take my Dad's place – even if I couldn't really remember him!

"You are not my father, so don't even say that! I don't know why you had your lackey bring me here, but I suggest you get on with it or let me go home to Damian! But, don't you *dare* put yourself in the same category as my father!"

He stood to face me, anger showing in his features.

"Do not dare to yell at me!" he ordered in a booming voice.

"Ah, hell! I'll yell if I want to, you pervert! Why not? You bring me here against my will! And, then you try to compare yourself to my father! How dare you! Just who the hell do you think you are, South? God?"

His eyes narrowed, and he lost his temper.

"Who am I? Who am I?"

He stomped around, and grabbed my arms tightly. Oh, damn! I knew I would be bruised.

"Who am I? Do you really want to know?"

I just shook my head. He was hurting me, but I wouldn't let him see it!

"Well, I will tell you who I am!"

I stared at him like I didn't give a rat's ass. And, I really didn't.

"It doesn't matter, because you are as beautiful as your Mother!"

I stared at him in stunned disbelief. I tried several times to talk, but I couldn't get anything to come out of my mouth. Finally, I managed to stammer.

"W-what did you just say? H-how could you possibly know who I look like?"

I saw his face contort. Oh, hell. I should have known never to ask a question like that, because just as sure as shootin', I was going to hear an answer I didn't like! He didn't disappoint.

"Because…I…I am your Father!" he yelled, and let me go with a push.

I fell into the chair as he let me go, staring up at him in shock. Had he just…just…just said he was…

"What?" I squeaked.

"I am your Father, Noel!"

I shook my head over and over and kept saying "no".

"Yes!"

He paused, when he noticed my arms turning red from his grip. He reached out his hands to touch the bruises, and I flinched away from him.

"I'm very sorry I hurt you, Noel. I knew better. But, you just made me so angry!"

"Anger is not an excuse to hurt anyone! You can't be my Father! That's not possible!" I whined. "My parents died in a car crash!"

He leaned against his desk, rubbing his face as if he was really tired, but I knew that wasn't the case. Vamps didn't get tired. Then, he started to talk. My stomach sank into the floor, my head shook back and forth in a perpetual "no", as I listened to him.

"That night of the accident, we were going home from church." He didn't look at me, but continued. "I remember how happy the three of us were, and your Mother looked so beautiful that night." His eyes shot to the ceiling as if remembering. "She wore the gorgeous red sweater that was her favorite."

Even I remembered that sweater, even though I was only two. It was her favorite. My bottom lip began to tremble. I wouldn't cry! I wouldn't give him the satisfaction!

"It was Christmas Eve, and we had been to the church play. All the kids in it looked so pretty, and they were so adorable. You were so excited to see everything. You loved Christmas every bit as much as your Mother and I did. We were headed down Free Ferry road, laughing and singing carols. And, then...."

He broke off his words. I saw him gulp, as he looked to me, his eyes so sad, it broke something inside of me.

"Then, I stopped at a light, and it turned green. I started to drive through it."

Again, he paused, pain crossing his features once more. I thought he was finished, and I really, really didn't want to hear it! Naturally, the Fates weren't on my side!

"We were hit broadside by a school bus that was returning from a play in another city. It slammed into your Mother's side of the car, and the car was pushed over fifty feet into a culvert with the car landing upside down. I heard later that the man who was driving the bus was drunk. Anyway, you were safe, because you were in the backseat, buckled into your car seat behind me. But, your Mother? She was gone. I won't tell you how I knew it. Just know I did. And, I was dying. My neck was broken. I couldn't feel anything below my waist at all, and very little above it. Blood ran down into my face, but I could see you were alright in the rearview mirror. I breathed a sigh of relief, and realized my chest was smashed as the very act of breathing hurt like a son of a bitch. All my bones were broken. I didn't have a chance in hell of living. I didn't want to leave you or your Mother, but baby, I had no choice in the matter."

I was beyond sad. The grief I had never felt grabbed me tightly. Tears ran down my face. I looked into my Father's eyes, and realized that Richard South was really my Dad. I knew it inside of me. Then, another voice came from behind me.

"I can fill it in from here," Landon said.

I turned, gulping in breaths of air between silent sobs. Neither of us had heard him enter. He looked at South, who motioned for him to continue. He walked toward us, speaking as he advanced.

"I was out for a stroll that night, looking for my next meal, and I smelled all the blood. The drunk driver, I finished killing for my meal, because he was already dead. Then, I turned to your car. I was going to take the blood from each of you. But, for whatever reason, when I saw your Mom broken beyond recognition as a human, and your father upside down, blood flowing from his body, I wasn't hungry any more. His blood was covering you, Noel. You were, quite literally, covered in so much blood, you weren't recognizable as a human baby. I took pity on your father, and I told him the police would be there soon along with the ambulance and fire trucks. I offered him life eternal as a vampire, but that he could never see you, again. I told him that he could still watch over you, and I promised that I would assist him. He agreed."

South picked up the story from there.

"Landon took me from the car, but only after taking you down and out of the car. He explained that it would be best for the authorities to think that you were never in the car with them, and it would be a blessing if no one really looked for you. So, he used his super vampire speed, and left you on the step of the nearest church. You were crying the last time I saw you, and all I wanted to do was hold you, but I couldn't. I was about gone."

Landon interjected.

"I took Richard, and turned him. He became my friend and mentor into a better life than I had been living. I realized that he would be a truly great leader. He accepted, but with one stipulation…that I watch after you for him. When I saw that you had stumbled into our world, and that you knew Ronnie, I had to tell your Father. The truth is that Damian and I have always been at odds with each other. He and your Dad have had a feud going for many years."

I was completely stunned silent. My Dad was a powerful vampire. He had a lackey named Landon, who was watching after me all my life. I was blood-bonded and mated to his enemy, and they had been fighting a very long time. Landon had saved my life for whatever reason. Suddenly, I was shaking, only I wasn't shaking. Landon had me in a death grip, but I could hear him yelling something.

"Breathe, Noel! Breathe!"

I stared at him, realizing I'd been holding my breath! I took a very, deep breath, and began shaking. I stared at South.

"What was my name?" I asked him.

"It was always Noel. Your Mom really wanted you to be named after Christmas, so you would always remember, and love it." Then, South said something I was not expecting, and since it was a complete secret known only to my parents and me, I knew that he told the truth.

"Noel…use it! It will tell you the truth of who I am!"

I stared at him in shock. What?

"Noel." South was standing in my space, and whispering into my ear so softly, I doubted that any vampire could hear him, because I almost didn't. "Your gift…use your gift!"

My mouth opened and closed like a fish. In the next instant, he was standing back at his desk. How did he know about my gift? How? I stared into his eyes, and suddenly, I was transported into a place and time in my past. The past of the wreck. My gift included one other very important fact…no one could lie to me. I could push past anything that I perceived as a lie. And, only my Father and Mother could have known this.

Landon's head whipped back and forth between us, with a deep frown marring his gorgeous, angelic face.

"Gift? What gift?" he demanded.

My Mom was gone, but my Father was real; was a vampire; and he was standing in front of me!

~ 17 ~

~ NOEL ~

"Oh. My. God!" My words were said on a shuddering sigh as I whispered, "Dad? It really is you!"

South smiled at me, and nodded. Landon was still looking from my Dad and back to me – several times, and frowning. He was obviously trying to figure out what we were talking about, and it almost made me want to stick out my tongue at him!

"Yes, squirmels," he said.

That was the final puzzle piece. Daddy had called me that special name, simply because I always squirmed when I saw squirrels, because I loved the little creatures. My bottom lip trembled, and tears ran down my cheeks once more.

"I don't think she would ever have wanted any of this to have happened – Daddy."

His smile lit up the room.

"No she wouldn't. I agree. But, one thing I do know. If I didn't protect you, even from afar, she would come and haunt my ass!"

I giggled, and nodded.

"She would! Look, Dad, we have to come to some kind of resolution here. You know that I am blood-bonded to Damian."

I debated telling South – my Dad – that I was his mate, but quickly discarded that idea. If they had been at odds all these years, I sure didn't want this to get in the way. Best for him not to know that right now. At least not until I spoke to Damian, but I knew it might come down to the fact that I would be forced to tell him about my gift, and that unnerved me. But, if I had to, I would. I suddenly needed blood…Damian's blood! I grabbed my stomach as a mild pain hit me.

"I really need to go back."

South nodded, seeing my discomfort.

"I understand. I was really hoping we could get to you so you could spend the night and we could talk. But, your bond is far too new. Before you go, though, I need to tell you something else. Damian and I have always had our differences, but that changes as of today. There is another of our kind who has been sowing havoc everywhere. I'm certain he knows this, but on the outside chance he doesn't, I need you to tell him. This was the second thing that prompted me to have this visit, because I know Damian would never have given me the time of day. Now, listen, Noel. If this evil finds out that you are not only my daughter, but the blood-bonded human to Damian, they will come after you."

"But, I thought that a blood-bond kept other vamps away."

"Typically, yes. But, there are some who do not like the new ways. They prefer the old ways of blood and turning those who they feel would be an ally to them. And, even worse? You are in even more danger, because of your gift."

Landon jumped in with his take.

"What gift? You keep saying that! What are you talking about, Richard?" Landon demanded.

My Dad said nothing. He would never betray me, so, I had to ask.

"How would he even know?"

"This particular evil has an inborn sense for those around him, and he can actually sense things when he is around them."

Landon added his own two cents.

"He's bad, Noel. Very bad. Worse than any even I have encountered. And, he hates…absolutely hates, Damian! Your true identity must remain a secret at all costs."

"Do you think you can talk Damian into a meeting with me?" her Father asked.

I wasn't sure whether that was a good idea or not, but….

"Who is this other vamp?" I asked.

"Curttis Drakow is his name."

"He's a volcano?" I squeaked in disbelief.

"No. That is Krakatoa. Curttis is even more volatile than any volcano!"

"Annnd?" she prompted.

"And, his territory is quite large," Landon finished.

"Is he here?"

"No. His territory is in South America, but he feels that America is his, and was stolen from him – by Damian."

My eyes widened.

"Damian *owns* America?"

South laughed along with Landon.

"No. He doesn't own it, but it is his territory, and he rules it."

"I had no idea! He never told me that! So, if that's true, then why are you here?"

"He granted me this territory, because of my human daughter.

My mouth dropped.

"But, I thought you and he were at odds with each other. How did he know about me?"

South shook his head.

"No. He never knew who you were or where you lived. But, he felt my true fear. We just argue over minor things these days, but they are enough to keep us against each other."

"You really do want to talk to him, don't you?" I asked. Seeing him nod, I told him, "I can't promise he will talk, but alright. I will ask him."

"That is enough for now. Tell him to contact me by the usual method."

"And, that would be?"

"He knows. May I give my daughter a hug?" South asked, and even though he didn't move at all, I felt him all around me. I sighed.

"Sure."

South was in front of me faster than I could see, and he gently pulled me into his arms. I was shocked. I knew those arms. I could feel them from somewhere in my past. He really was my Father, and I would know that even without my gift! I put my arms around him, and gave him a slight squeeze – as if he could feel it. Slowly he let me go, and I stepped back.

"Landon, please return her to Damian," South said. Then, turned to him. "Let nothing happen to her, or you will cease this life!"

Landon gave him one, sharp nod. I took one last look at my Dad, and wiping tears from my face, I followed Landon out the door. It didn't take Landon long to take me back to the gates of Damian's house. Vampire speed really comes in handy. Man, did I feel small compared to everything going on around me. Except, it seemed that I was going to be forever sick to my stomach anytime some vamp decided to grab me, and use their preternatural speed. Landon set me down on my feet, and turned to me.

"Remember, Noel. Do your best to get Damian to meet with South. It is to our benefit and his, and it provides more protection for you. With Curttis on the loose, no one is safe – not even the vamps. And, keep it on the DL, too."

"Well, kidnapping me right out from under Damian's nose isn't going to go well for you or my Dad, but I will do whatever I can."

"Are you OK? I mean...now that you know?"

"I'm not sure how I feel at the moment, Landon. I've lived my whole life, thinking my Dad and Mom were both dead, and to find out that he lived, but as a vampire? That's the things that sci-fi writers would give their eyeteeth to have on their plate."

"NOEL!"

I heard Damian scream my name, and I melted into a pile of goo. He truly had the ability to make my legs buckle under me like rubber! I turned to look at him, running across the yard toward the gate. I turned to Landon.

"I'll try, but I just can't make promises."

Landon nodded once more, and was gone instantly. Right at that moment, Damian and Ronnie burst through the gates, and I was thrown over his shoulder. With Ronnie on guard, we were inside the house, before I ever realized I wasn't at the gate any more. Damn vampire, cool powers! I wish I could do.... I stopped. Was I really contemplating becoming a vampire as Damian's mate? To become like him? Like my Dad? My head was swimming from all the things I knew and all the things I didn't want to think about right now.

The second we were inside his bedroom, Damian's luscious and delicious lips were on mine. I threw my arms around his neck, and pressed against him as I devoured his lips and tongue with my own.

"I won't lose you again, Noel. Ever! Do you understand me? No one will take you from me!"

I didn't even have time to answer him, because only seconds went by before I was naked and on my back on the bed with Damian pushing into my heat with his rod of steel! I cried out in the pleasure I felt as he buried himself inside me to the hilt! And, I didn't hold back my screams of ecstasy, and I also didn't give a fuck who heard me! I wanted him! I wanted his fangs deep into my neck, drinking from me, and I so wanted his blood inside me! I had no idea how much I needed it! His claw gouged a large hole in his own neck, and pulled my head to it. My mouth closed on it at the same time his fangs struck into my neck! The pull as he suckled on me, served to cause my walls to grasp his cock hard, and we both orgasmed immediately! But we were not done yet. He continued to move his velvety steel inside of me, while we sucked more blood. It was so delicious that I didn't ever want to be without him. I could have lived like this forever! The giving and taking from both of us was addictive! My hands went to his head, and I pushed him harder against my neck, begging him to take more without speaking. Damian gave me that and more. I began to feel strange, but incredible! As he filled me with his blood, I filled him with mine. We exchanged blood without a thought! And, then, my second climax hit me so hard, I had to lift my head from his neck to scream as he pumped his seed deep into my body.

"MORE, Damian! Oh, MORE! "I screamed. "HARDER!"

His own scream caused him pound into me harder and harder, and it just enhanced our orgasms as we continued to rock our bodies into each other. His balls slapped my ass so hard, I could hear the pounding of our flesh, as he thrust into me harder with each second. He filled me – not only with his rod of steel, but with his seed! I could feel it coating my womb and my channel. I could feel it filling my womb to overflowing, and I still wanted more! I never wanted to stop! Even as our climaxes waned, I didn't want to stop! I needed him more than air! And, he needed me. I realized that he had not closed the wounds in my neck, and blood was flowing down my breasts and my back onto the bed. His wound was healing quickly, but not before his blood flowed over his neck and chest, and dripped onto me. His eyes were red with lust and hunger as he noticed that we were red with blood, and I wouldn't deny him.

"Damian, please? Lick me!" I begged.

While his cock was still inside me, he began licking my breasts with his tongue, lapping up the blood that covered my nipples as he suckled them, sending waves of desire throughout my body. I arched my back so he could take me even easier again, but he stopped, and pulled his hard dick out of me. I opened my mouth to protest, but he silenced me with his kiss. Damian picked me up, and instantly, we were in his shower. I put my hand up on my neck, feeling the warmth of my life oozing slowly from the two tiny wounds that had yet to be sealed. But, I wasn't upset. I covered my hands with my own blood, and wiped them on my neck, my breasts, my abdomen, and between my legs. Damian licked my wounds, and they began to heal. He sank to his knees, and buried his head between my legs, licking the blood from where I had smeared it. I grabbed his head as he licked my clit, and pushed against it with his tongue. OH! He was a master at this! I didn't really want to know how he knew how to do this, so I pushed that away from my consciousness. I wanted something else from him.

"Damian?" I gasped between pants.

"Hmmmm???" he muttered, not taking his tongue from my pussy.

"Bite me," I demanded quietly.

His mouth stopped sucking me, and his head lifted to look at me.

"What?" he asked, as if he hadn't thought he'd heard correctly.

I sank to my own knees, and placed my bloody hands on his head. We had not yet gotten under the shower, so we were not rinsed off as yet.

"I want you to bite me. I want you to bite my pussy," I told him. If I had to beg, I would. "Please?"

"You want me to bite you? I mean, here?" he asked, placing his fingers on my pussy, and stroking.

"Yes!" I gasped in desire. No. I was in lust!

"Are you sure?"

In answer, I laid on the cool tile, and lifted my legs, placing them on either side of his head, opening my pussy to him. I was so much in the throes of lust, I couldn't see straight. In fact, everything I saw right now seemed to have a reddish haze to it! I had closed my eyes waiting for his tongue and his fangs, opened my eyes, and met his. He gasped in shock, even though I didn't understand why, I bucked against his head. Moments later, his head dipped, and his tongue began to stroke my pussy. I felt every, single amazing lick!

"Are you sure about this?" Damian asked once more.

"I have never been as sure in my life!"

His fangs descended and struck. I didn't really know what I expected, but I did not expect the high I got when he began to suck my blood and his seed from my body. I screamed so loud, I could feel my throat constrict, yet I didn't care who heard me! If we had been in a crowd, and Damian had laid me out for all to see as he fucked me, I wouldn't have cared one bit! He was mine; I was his! I heard him groan as he sucked me. I grabbed his head. I didn't ever want him to stop suckling my pussy! But, then, his fangs pulled from my flesh, and he licked me. Sliding upward, he thrust his cock deep into me once more, and we hit our orgasms within seconds. More of his seed warmed me inside, until finally, he collapsed onto me, but not enough to smash me. I held his head to my breasts in wonder and in awe at the most amazing sex I knew I would ever have in my life! For the first time, I knew I'd have to thank Ronnie for bringing me to Damian – to be his mate.

~ DAMIAN ~

We were both lying on the tile floor of my shower, and my head was buried in her gorgeous tits, after the most amazing sex in my long life! Never had I ever had such long, powerful, and incredible orgasms! When Noel asked me to bite her pussy, I thought my dick would never stop twitching. And, I wanted to do it! I don't know what had possessed me not to seal her wounds in her neck earlier, but I just couldn't do it, when I took her from the bed into the shower. Watching her own hands spread her life-giving blood all over her tits, stomach, and pussy, was the most beautiful site I had ever seen! But, I needed to seal the bites, before I could take from her later. I licked her body free of our blood, and licked the wounds.

When she asked me to bite her pussy, then lay down, placing her legs on my shoulders, but still opening her pussy to me, I had to do what she wanted. The biggest shock I had ever had, though, were her red eyes as she looked at me! I had no idea how her eyes could be red, but at that moment, I just couldn't care. When I buried my fangs into her on either side of her opening, the flavor of her blood and my semen flowing from her was unbelievable! I suckled, until I thought I needed to stop. I didn't want to stop suckling her pussy, but I managed to do so, licking her wounds, and sealing them. My dick was so ready to fuck her senseless! I climbed up her body, and thrust into her only to deposit my seed once more inside her heat; inside her womb. My head descended to her tits, and she held me to them, as we both tried to calm our excitement. I wanted more of her, but she was human, and I had to curb my lust. Her cries before I bit her, sure didn't curb my lust at all!

I needed to know if she was alright, when I saw her at the gates of my home. Noel was my home; she was my life; she was my blood-bonded human and my mate. I needed her like I needed blood to fill me with life. No. That wasn't quite true. I needed HER blood to fill me with life! Only hers would ever satisfy me forever. I knew this. This was far stronger than any blood-bond or even as a mate. This was at the molecular level!

I slowly worked my way up to my knees, pulling her with me. Gently, I held her up, because her legs were wobbly. I have to admit, I felt a little smug at knowing my body had done that to her! I gently held her to me as I scrubbed her body clean, making sure I was very careful of her nipples. They were much larger from my suckling, and I knew they might be a bit sore. If she were a vampire, it would not have been a big deal. I stoked my secret desire for her to become like me, and focused on her. Her eyes were brilliant green again. Now, it wasn't all that unusual for a blood-bonded human to have red eyes on occasion, but hers had turned a dark crimson red, which was very unusual. I'd have to do some research on that particular phenomenon.

Finally, we were both clean, and I dried her off with a thick, dark gray towel. Dark colors were a must for vampires. I picked Noel up, who was already asleep against my chest, and carried her to my bed…our bed. I climbed in beside her, and pulled her into my arms, her head laying on my chest. I closed my eyes, and wondered how South had gotten hold of her, but even more curious, I wondered why Landon brought her back. None of this made sense, but I wasn't going to yell at her. I was bound and determined to find out what happened.

For the moment, though, I just decided to meditate, since vamps didn't sleep. Tomorrow she would plunge into decorating, and for the first time since I was human, I was actually looking forward to having a Christmas with her and my family. Right now, though, I just relished in holding my mate and lover next to me.

~ 18 ~

~ NOEL ~

I. Felt. Amazing! I slowly opened my eyes, then shut them against the bright sunlight flooding Damian's bedroom. I looked to where he had slept next to me all night – uh, I mean day. This night and day thing was confusing at the moment! Damian was already gone. Did he even sleep? Making a mental note to ask him, I did notice that he'd changed the sheets from last night. Oh, CREATOR! Last night had been the best night of my entire life! He had flooded me with his seed in amounts that my body could never hold, but when he bit my pussy? I had just thought ecstasy existed! I reached down to touch myself. It felt normal, but I sure could still feel the moment his fangs bit me. I clinched as more desired fired through my body in waves as hard as if it were ocean waves crashing onto rocks!

"I gotta stop this!" I said to no one. Then, I remembered. "Wait! My Christmas decorations should be here!"

That was enough to distract me from my desire, which had me bounding out of the bed. I bounced to the bathroom, only to realize I didn't have anything to wear! How was I supposed to get back to my room? Maybe no one would see me if I ran fast enough? OK. That was just a ridiculous thought with a house full of vampires! No. I guess I could just borrow some of his clothes. I walked to the massive dresser, and started to pull drawers open, thinking to find a t-shirt or something, when I stopped in surprise. These were my clothes! I pulled out a bra that I knew I'd left at my apartment. I shuffled around in the drawer, and found more items I knew I didn't bring. Pulling open more drawers, I found all my loungewear, aka pajamas, and I had a little hunch. Damian had a massive walk-in closet, and I had yet to see it. Well, let's face it. I had no reason to do so, until now. Holding my underwear and bra in my left hand, I walked to the closet and opened the double door. Hesitating for a moment, I stepped inside it, turned on the light, and gasped.

"When did he have time to do all of this?" I muttered in shock.

Hanging on the right side of the closet, I saw every piece of clothing that I owned including shoes, sandals, and boots. But, what stunned me was that there were also new clothes hanging alongside my own clothing! In front of me, the closet had a large divider down the center, separating the closet into two separate, but connected, rooms. I ran my hand along the deep, rich mahogany. To the left, Damian's clothing hung in perfect rows. I turned right, and walked into the side where my clothes were, feeling a bit weird. I never in my life shared a closet with a man. But, seeing my clothing hanging across from his gave me a cozy and warm feeling. On the right side, I assumed it was mine, based on the fact it was all women's clothing. Blouses and skirts were separated into top and bottom, while dresses, evening gowns, and even robes were in their own longer spaces. To the left, and my mouth dropped, was the epitome of a woman's dream dressing area. A vanity sat in the middle of the divider, and had all the bells and whistles, including a large mirror with bulbs ringing it. Makeup of all types adorned the vanity in a neat, orderly fashion. Ronnie. Had to be. I knew she had been shopping – her very favorite pastime! To the right of the vanity, were rows on rows of drawers, their contents hiding, just waiting to be discovered. At the back of the closet, was a massive shoe rack, sporting the one pair of boots I had, the one pair of dress pumps, a pair of sandals, and my tennis shoes. They were in serious need of replacing. But, there were more new shoes for every occasion, lining halfway up the wall, while purses of all sizes and colors were stacked above, and colorized, for any occasion! I did know that I would never be able to wear or carry all of them! To the left of the vanity, was a built-in padded bench to sit while dressing. My insides were warming with love as I just realized he had moved me into his room. I didn't know what he had done with my little apartment that I had been about to lose, but, looking at all this, I was pretty sure I wouldn't be moving back there. Then, curiosity got the better of me, and I just had to open a couple of drawers. I almost passed out from what I saw! Jewelry! I had never had much in the way of jewelry. I had nothing but fake jewelry. A couple of hoops, two sets of studs, no rings whatsoever, bracelets, and a couple of necklaces were all I had. But, that's not what was in these drawers! I didn't really want to think about it, and my mind refused to believe that what I was looking at was real, even though my gut said the pieces were. Diamonds in suites lined the drawer of one, while emeralds and rubies, also in suites, lined the second drawer. I slammed them both, not even wanting to think about what was in the other drawers! I started to hyperventilate. I knew that Damian, Ronnie, and Caleb were wealthy, true. I mean…look at this house and their cars! But, all of this was just a bit too much for me! I hadn't been brought up in the lap of luxury, so it was so hard for me to accept these things. My mind compensated, thankfully, and sent it into another direction, which made much more sense to my overwhelmed mind. I realized what all of this really meant! I would be lying in his bed, in his arms, every night, now, and that gave me the most wonderful jitters! I felt my core getting wet. I shook my head, trying to dampen that desire down a bit, and left the closet, returning to the dresser. I found a dark green, long sleeve, crew neck t-shirt, which I had never seen before, and walked back into the closet, where I found brand new jeans, washed and hanging neatly with the other pants and skirts. I quickly dressed, and turned, viewing the closet once more. I sat down on the makeup chair, and looked at myself in the mirror. It was official. We were living together. Excitement and terror gripped me at the same time, and I honestly couldn't tell which was the stronger emotion. All I did know was that I was madly in love with him. And, the key word, here, was mad! Was I insane being in love with a vampire? The logical answer was yes. But, nothing about any of this was logical! If someone had told me, just three months ago, that I would not only be bonded – by blood, no less – to a supernatural being, but that I was also his mate, who moved me into his home to live with him, and I was now actually contemplating becoming one of them…well, I'd have called the white coats on myself to take me to the looney bin!

I still had to talk to Damian about South – and Curttis. I knew last night, he was making sure that I was alright, because we had both needed blood by the time I had returned. And, he wanted to make love to me to reassure himself that I was here with him. Truth was, that's the reason I needed him as well! But, I also knew that Damian had a business to run, even if I didn't exactly know what that was, so all of that would have to wait.

I slipped on a pair of house slippers. They were fuzzy, and I love fuzzy! I left his room, and skipped down the hallway, I was so excited! I pretended to tap dance down the stairs, and looked for my merchandise. Where was everything?

"I wonder where they put…," I asked to no one, but was answered.

"In here!" Caleb yelled.

I turned, and for the first time, I noticed a door in the foyer, in between the two staircases, and walked toward the door. Inside, there was a huge room – a ballroom, for it could be nothing less. It was massive, and at the far end was a curved wall of glass, looking out onto the most beautiful scene of mountains and a pool! The other walls were lined with alternating mirrors and mahogany. The floor was wood, but then, I wasn't really sure what kind. I wasn't all that versed in ballroom flooring. But, I did know how to decorate them! In the middle of the room. lay a large pile of boxes. And Caleb was standing in the middle of them, opening each box.

"OK. I think everything you ordered is here, but I have no idea what these are!" he complained, lifting a long garland of cedar, and scratching his head.

All I could do was laugh at him. Watching this big, burly vampire standing in the middle of all that greenery was just hilarious! I broke out in laughter, only to see his scowl turn on me. Tears of laughter ran down my cheeks.

"I-I'm s-sorry, C-Caleb! But, you have to admit that you look so f-funny among all that g-greenery!" I heard Ronnie laughing behind me, joined by a deeper male voice. It was Sam.

"Ha, ha. Very funny. Will you three quit standing there, and get to work!" Caleb grouched, his hands on his hips, and his face scowling at us.

After a few more minutes of laughter, Ronnie, Sam, and I walked to the center of the room, and we helped Caleb remove the rest of the lids from the boxes. I was giddy with excitement as I pulled out the garland for the staircases.

"OK, boss. Tell us what to do," Sam said.

Gathering up the garland, I pointed to the other boxes.

"Find all the garland that you can, and meet me in the foyer."

Minutes later, we all stood in the foyer, and I was giving each of them directions of exactly where I wanted everything to be. I was thrilled with the fact that I had the best doggone helpers on earth – vampires with speed. They placed the garland in the places I had indicated so fast, it made my head spin. Then, we traipsed back into the ballroom to gather more greenery. I explained where to put it all, while I picked up two boxes that had small silver bells and red bows. I wanted traditional with a touch of wow, and this would do it.

While the others were continuing to put up garlands and wreaths, I marched up the stairs, and started attaching the bows all the way down the garland. Then, I began attaching the silver bells that I had ordered as a last second idea. When I was almost finished, I heard a little sniffle, and saw Ronnie staring at the silver bells on the garland almost wistfully. I walked down the few remaining steps.

"Ronnie?" I said. "Are you OK?"

She looked at me, her eyes slightly red, and sat down on the bottom step. I followed her, putting my arm around her shoulders. I don't remember ever having seen her so upset, and it kind of threw me for a loop. Ronnie had never exhibited sadness before, and that was really worrying, especially because she was a vampire.

"My family loved Christmas," she hesitated a bit. She looked up at me, and saw surprise on her face. "No. I mean my human family, Noel. I was born in 386 AD, and back when I was small, it was the dark ages."

OK. Damian was really old, but by contrast, Ronnie was probably the equivalent of a teenager. I didn't say anything, and just let her talk at her leisure. After a few more sniffs, she continued.

"In those days, there were two classes – poor and rich. My family was of royal aristocracy, so we were, by no means, poor. Every year, my Mother would have professionals come into the house to decorate for Christmas. My last Christmas as a human, the black plague was running rampant. At some point, I was gasping for breath, and the powers that be ordered that anyone on the verge of death be piled into carts. I guess you'd call them wheelbarrows today. I was taken from my home, and thrown onto one of the carts. Both my parents had already died, as did my brother and my sister." She looked at me. "Damian found me, barely alive. He lost his sister when he was young, and I reminded him of her. That's why he said he turned me. I mean, Noel, how could I turn that offer of life down?" She paused a moment, looking up the banister. "Sorry. My Mother's favorite decoration was green garland tied with red ribbons, and glass bells. It was the one thing that she did herself. She dripped the bells everywhere, even on the chandeliers all over the house. They hung down like little prisms, and every time a breeze came through the house as people walked, they bounced and glittered." She turned back to me. "How did you know this was my favorite decoration?"

I stared at her, and I wondered if my gift had somehow picked up on her deep thoughts? Envisioning the finished project, I had added the silver bells as a last minute idea. It had to be. There could not be another explanation for my last minute and expensive order. Her mouth turned up in happiness, and she burst into a smile that would light up an entire city if it could be attached to a grid.

"I don't know how you did it, or why you did it Noel, but thank you! I haven't felt like this was my real home at Christmas – until now. Love ya, girlfriend!" She hugged me, then remembered something. "Oh, hell! I have to do some Christmas shopping, if you don't mind?" She asked, and I shook my head. "I'll see you later!"

Ronnie was gone. I looked up at the silver bells that had given her such happiness. I had never had anything like she had, but I was beginning to realized that these vampires were once human, like me, and had real lives before being turned. I wanted so much to find out what they thought of as Christmas for each of their time periods. After all, I viewed this place as my home, too. And, not like my apartment, where it was just a place to lay my head, but a real home. And, in truth, wasn't it? Damian had brought the little I owned, and moved it into this house…into his room…and me, into his bed. Could she dare to believe that she had a home, after never having one all of her life?

~ 19 ~

~ NOEL ~

"Whatcha thinking so hard about, Noel?"

Startled, I looked up at the face behind the voice. It was Caleb. Suddenly, I had an interesting idea.

"Hey, Caleb. Can I ask you something?"

"Shoot!" then, for whatever reason, Caleb had to explain what he meant. "Uh...I mean...you know. Tell me...not shoot as in shoot with a gun or bow. What I mean to say is that I don't mean a 'gun-gun', you know, like in silver bullets – or silver arrow tips – I mean...."

By this time, I was doubled over in laughter.

"Caleb, please! You're killing me! Don't hurt yourself!" He grinned sheepishly at me, and nodded. "So. Did you have Christmas in your home when you were human?"

Surprise made his eyebrows rise, before he answered.

"I haven't thought about that in a long time." I waited for him to speak, as I had done with Ronnie. I also wondered why everyone else's life had been much more exciting than mine. "I was born in 1871. Christmas everywhere was about the same. Of course, candles were used on trees, in windows, and around the house. I didn't have a house, but my parents, brother, and I lieved in a two bedroom flat. We had very, very little, but somehow, there was always food on our table. On Christmas Eve, we would go into the woods behind our apartment building to cut down a small tree. It was a true highlight of my life! My brother and always looked forward to it. We'd all take a part of the cut tree, and bring it back, setting it up in the common room - living room. We strung popcorn, cranberries, and on occasion, we would put candles on the tree. But, ordinarily, we just made our ornaments to hang, and Mom would put candles in the windows. We only were able to receive one small gift at Christmas time. Usually it was some food that we loved. Unfortunately, not everyone was careful. The last Christmas I had as a human was the end of me. One of the apartments was set ablaze with candles that were placed on a dry Christmas tree. It burned to the ground. My Dad and brother didn't make it out, and Mom died three days later from third degree burns."

I gasped, and he smiled.

"It's ok, Noel. It was best that she went. The pain was far too bad for her to live through. I, too, made it out, but I was burned over ninety percent of my body. The pain I cannot describe to you, but I remember how labored my breathing had become after four days in a healing house. In fact, I knew I was about to breathe my last, and I was looking forward to leaving this world to be with my family. That is when Damian found me. He trolled the healing houses in those days, looking for those who might need him. I was barely conscious, and to me, everything had become just too hard. I wanted to die. But, Damian would never have allowed it. Just as I took my last breath, he turned me. I was angry at first, but after about fifty years, I realized what a true gift had been given to me. But, I needed to warn people about candles and their dangers being on trees, and I needed to do it for my family who perished though not their fault. I began a campaign, with

Damian's help, to stop people from putting candles on Christmas trees. The problem was that people just didn't listen. It wasn't until Mr. Edison made his first string of lights and used them to light up his building at Christmas time, that people saw the need for candles as passé. But, there was nothing more warm and cozy than seeing candles on trees and in our windows. I'll never forget the way my Mom decorated our home with candle light and simple decorations. It brought back more memories than I ever believed." He smiled down at me. "Even though the tragedy happened to me at Christmas, I still get a warm feeling when I think about that time of year. I hadn't though of that in years! Thank you for that memory, Noel." He broke off, and looked at his watch. "Well, I gotta go do some errands for Damian. See you later – at dinner?"

My eyes darted to him in fear, only to see his smirky grin, letting me see his playful side, once more. I grinned back, and he took off at his vampire speed. I knew that Damian was born right at the time of Christ, or at least in that vicinity, so that era had no Christmas, but they did have Solstice. I ran into the ballroom, and rooted around in the boxes till I found what I wanted. While not real, I had bought several strings of cranberries and popcorn, but they sure as hell looked real! I grabbed a very tall ladder that Caleb had brought into the ballroom, and placed it where I could get to the chandelier in the foyer. I climbed up, and tied the silver bells all over it, letting them drape downward. Then, I took the cranberry and popcorn strings, and looped and draped them all over the chandelier. I climbed down, and looked up. It was simple, but beautiful. This way, both Caleb and Ronnie's memories would be included. Next, I took the other strings of cranberries and popcorn, and wove them in and out of the green garland. I had so many, the garland looked heavy with fruit and popcorn. It gave the whole place warmth I never realized. That's when Sam came into the foyer.

"Beautiful, Noel! That was so kind of you to incorporate Ronnie and Caleb's past Christmases."

"Thanks…but, how?"

"Vampire hearing," he said, pointing to his head. "Did Damian tell you about his Christmases past?

"What? He had Christmases?"

"Yes. He was married, once, you know."

I froze. Married? Damian was married? Seeing my stunned face, he apologized.

"Oh, I'm so sorry, Noel. I thought you knew!"

I just shook my head.

"Look…don't tell him I told you."

"It's ok, Sam," I told him, even though deep down, I wondered if I would have to compete against a ghost. Then, I realized just who Rebecca was. I asked him about her. "His 'wife' did Christmas?"

"I've known Damian a very long time. Her name was Rebecca Angelos, and she managed to make Christmas special for him in the two years she lived here. She was a lovely young woman, but as I said, they were not married long. When they married, Rebecca had pancreatic cancer, and she was dying. There was an almost otherworldly glow about her, and we all knew that she was too good for this world. Rebecca loved mistletoe and poinsettias, and would always have these scattered throughout the house in some of the strangest places – once she even had one hanging over the showers in the bathrooms! And, heaven help the person who tried to remove them! If someone stood under one of them, she would point it out, and there was a lot of kissing!"

I giggled. She sounded like someone I would have liked to have as a friend. I listened with awe as he told the tragic, but loving story of a young woman who never really deserved to suffer.

"Anyway, as I said, she covered the whole house in mistletoe and poinsettias, but she added her own touch to the little white balls on the mistletoe. There were a lot of unused prisms that had come from some old chandeliers, and she loved using those to tie little red ribbons on them, so when they swung, the prisms glistened, letting an unsuspecting guinea pig know that they were under it. It was really a little thing, but it was something that always made Damian smile."

"She sounds like she was a very special woman," I said softly.

"She was," Sam answered.

I nodded. I had actually ordered quite a few mistletoe balls myself, and wondered if the prisms were still around. But, I didn't have any poinsettias. Where the hell would I find those? I smiled as Sam waved goodbye, before he stopped. And, it was as if he read my mind.

"By the way…Rebecca had her own greenhouse out back beyond the tree line." He pointed toward the curved windows. "Damian had them built for her. You might take a look back there, but I don't think anyone's taken care of them in ages. She grew her own poinsettias," he added. Before he left the room, he turned back. "She also had some mistletoe growing. As long as it has been, it's possible the mistletoe may have taken over everything."

Rebecca grew her own potted plants? I was off to these greenhouses to see and give me some inspiration, then, I would explore the attic for the prisms. I had a plan to include everyone's ideas in my own, but I needed to find the poinsettias! I decided, later that evening, to see if Rebecca's greenhouses might still have anything in them. I asked Sam to go with me, after he returned.

As soon as he finished with his business, he met me in the backyard, and we began walking toward the greenhouses.

"Do you think anything remains out here?" I asked him.

"I honestly don't know if anyone has been out here in a long time, Noel. Damian never mentions it."

I had to admit. The idea that Damian had been married, even if Rebecca was sick, really hurt a little bit. But, I couldn't be afraid of a ghost.

"Why didn't he turn her?" That was the first, logical question that came to my mind.

"You have to remember when this was, Noel. It was back at the turn of the 20th Century. She was twenty in 1918, and had cancer. Damian did offer to turn her, because she was such a kind person. Yet, she still refused him. Rebecca just didn't want to live like him. She saw vampirism as an evil and completely against her Christian belief. It caused him great sadness, but he respected her decision."

I stopped, and he did as well.

"What?   Then,   why   did   she   marry Damian? Why did he marry her?"

Sam just shook his head, and didn't answer. This was just confusing, and made no sense.

"That's just so...so...strange!" I said, then started walking once again. 1918? That just seemed like eons ago, but it was only 100 years. All in all, a very short time to a vampire. I sighed, and decided to ask

Damian about her later. So, I dropped the subject for the time being. We had to go through a large, overgrown hedge, and then, we burst into a meadow. It was beautiful in the moonlight! And, there, in front of us, stood a massive greenhouse, gleaming as if new in the light from the moon. We looked at each other in surprise.

"Did you know about this?" I asked, not really expecting an answer, because I already knew it.

He just shook his head, and I followed him as we made our way to the greenhouse. Opening the door. We stood in shock and surprise, finding ourselves surrounded by beautiful poinsettias of all sizes and colors! Reds, white, pinks, peach, variegated colors of all kinds, creams, lavenders...the colors were literally endless! But, the most amazing color? A deep, almost blood red crimson color with pale pink and white centers!

I left Sam's side to wandered down each of the seven rows. The largest were on the right side of the greenhouse, and decreased in size from right to left. I had never seen anything like this! I reached out to touch a lavender one. It would be perfect for Easter in a cold climate! Well, Arkansas wasn't cold quite a bit of the time, but....

Turning, I found a deep crimson plant. I wondered why this color? The color of blood. There had to have been a reason that Rebecca had developed this crimson poinsettia, and it had to be because of Damian. I mean, why else would it be unique? In her own way, I think that she did love him, and I found a tear running down my cheek that at least someone had cared about him at one time in his life. But, who had been cultivating and taking care of these all this time?

"Hey, Sam?" I called to him, as I turned to make my way back to him. "Who do you think has been tending the green...."

Not paying attention, I ran into a solid rock wall, and arms came around me. My head tilted up. I knew those arms. The arms that had held me tightly, making love to me over and over again. The arms that held me to his chest, now.

"Damian?" I gasped. His head tilted down, and he kissed me. I threw my arms around his neck, and held him to me as I kissed him back. I loved him! I loved him! There was no doubt in my heart or my mind. The revelation was earth shaking!

"Noel," he sighed against my lips.

~ DAMIAN ~

The only reason that Noel stood here was that she found out about Rebecca. And, the man who told her was walking around the corner right now. But, still, Damian couldn't help but thank him. He doubted that he would ever have had the courage to tell her.

"Oh!" Sam said, startled. "Sorry, boss! I didn't see you there!"

Damian looked up at his friend, and raised an eyebrow. He gave a little nod toward Sam, who nodded in understanding, and walked out of the green house, leaving us alone.

"Noel," he sighed again, his mouth devouring mine. I needed her so badly right now, I could taste it!

"Strip me, Damian! Please?" she begged.

Grinning from ear to ear, I slowly took off Noel's clothing, taking time with each loss of clothing to suckle her nipples and breasts. I went to my knees to take off her pants and panties in one movement, then I spread her legs, and dipped my head and mouth onto her pussy. She stood, totally nude in front of me, in the green house of my dead wife, letting me nuzzle her pussy and clit. My hands kneaded her breasts, and flipped her taut, rosy nipples. She cried out in pleasure as I brought her to her first orgasm, then lapped her juices as if they were fine wine! In seconds, I stripped naked, pushing into her welcoming, wet heat with one, massive thrust of my cock. Noel screamed my name as I fucked her senseless. Her legs wrapped around my waist, while my hands and arms held her hips as I pounded her body into oblivion! When I cried out her name, I felt my seed shoot deep into her body and womb. I kept thrusting into her until she milked every single drop of it from me! I held her tightly as we both spiraled back down to Earth! I buried my face into her neck, quenched, but wanting more. I was always wanting more, and so was she.

~ NOEL ~

"That was...that was...," I tried hard to find the word.

"Incredible?" Damian answered, his smug grin plastered on his face, while his cock was throbbing inside of me. I slapped his shoulder.

"Arrogant much?" I asked with a giggle.

"Nope. Just honest with my mate."

He kissed me slowly, then allowed me to slide off of his cock. Reluctantly, we dressed. My pussy was flooding with the evidence of his desire, and my womb jumped several times as I thought of his seed inside of me. Too bad there would be no child, but I could never leave him. I had one, very important decision to make, and I knew I wasn't ready. Not yet. But, something told me that I would allow him to take my life, and replace it with his blood at some point. And, somehow, that was less upsetting, now. I mean...I wouldn't have to suck a human being dry of blood, because they actually had several manufacturing companies supplying them with blood, and a long list of donors who were happy to do it. If I didn't have to kill anyone, I'd consider it more seriously.

"Damian?" I began.

"Yes? Want more?" he grinned, and I grinned back.

"I will always want more of you!"

Damian kissed me deeply, then sighed as he let me go.

"What did you want to know?"

"Tell me about Rebecca?" I asked in a tentative voice, not too sure how he would answer.

He looked at me while we dressed.

"There has never been another woman for me, but you, Noel. I want you to know that."

"I understand that, Damian, but she was your wife for two years. She must have meant something to you for you to put a ring on her finger."

Damian dropped his head. He knew she deserved to know. He nodded his head, then looked at her. Leaning back on the rack behind him, he began.

"It was really simple. Rebecca was involved with the mob."

I gasped. Whatever I had expected, that hadn't been it!

"Yes. Her boyfriend was one of the top mob bosses in Chicago. That's where we lived for many years, before coming here. Anyway, his second raped her, and she became pregnant. Her boyfriend went off the deep end, and tried to murder both her and his second. I was there the night he truly lost it, and started using his Tommy gun in his own speakeasy. He was shooting everyone in it. Rebecca had been kind to me, and had allowed me to feed off of her, when she discovered I was a vampire."

I felt my stomach clench with jealousy when he said that, but tamped it down. It was 100 years ago, for goodness sakes, and she was dead! So, I remained quiet, and he continued.

"I took her out of there, and eventually, we moved here. Because she was pregnant, and in those days, a woman who was knocked up, but not married, was a tramp, I asked her to marry me just to give her child a name. In exchange, she would be my food, and we would raise the child together."

"And, then, she got cancer." I said in a flat voice to which he nodded.

"It was aggressive, and she was in her eighth month. She refused treatment, because she wanted to give her child the chance she never had. I agreed, but I did ask her to let me turn her, and she could raise her child with me. But, she didn't want to live like me – depending on humans for food. She preferred to let nature take its course. In February, after two years of marriage, and delivering her child barely a year before, she passed quietly at home. She made me promise to give her child to be adopted by a human family, and in my weakness, I agreed." He looked into my eyes, which were full of sadness and sympathy. "I kept that promise, and found the perfect family to raise her."

"A girl? Did you ever seen her again?" I asked.

"I kept tabs on her for most of her life, until she passed at the age of seventy-three. She left behind a daughter and a son, and five grandchildren."

I smiled. That seemed like a very happy ending to me. And, then I thought about something else.

"Do you still keep an eye out on her family?"

Quietly, I watched him nod, but it didn't seem very happy.

"I do. Two grandsons were killed in Iraq. A third lives in Australia with his husband. One of the girls died in childbirth, and the other girl? Just disappeared as if she had never been."

"Oh! Damian! How sad! Three out of five died. Did you ever find the other girl?"

"Yes. She lives with her husband and two children in Ontario."

"And, you still keep tabs on her," I said, already knowing the answer.

"Yes. I have some friends up there who keep an eye on her."

"That's such a sad story!" I laid my hand on his arm. "I'm so sorry. But, she was happy in her last two years?"

He smiled.

"She was. Watching her grow with her child was one of the favorite things I have ever witnessed and been a part of. I just wish...."

I could fill in the blanks. He wanted his own child, and because of being a vampire, he would never have it...and neither would I, if I stayed with him. Or, was that still true after what Ronnie theorized. I looked at his sad face hanging down, and knew that it didn't really matter if I never had a child. But, I would have him, and our life could be amazing together. I realized, at that point, that I was really and truly his mate. My hand went to his head, and I pulled it down to kiss him gently. His arms went around me, and he buried his face into my neck. I knew he needed me – my blood – so, I tilted my head back and to the side to give him access. His fangs pierced my flesh, and my lifeblood poured from me as he drank. I held him to me tightly. I made my decision right then.

"Damian?"

"Umm hmmm," he managed to get out as he drank.

"I'm ready."

His fangs retracted, and he licked the wounds, before he looked at me.

"For what?"

I pulled him to me, and put my mouth at his ear.

"To become yours forever." I whispered

~ 20 ~

~ NOEL ~

I expected him to be happy. I knew he wanted me to be a part of his world, but instead, he pushed me away from him, and I fell on my ass.

"NO! You are not ready!"

Then, he stormed out of the greenhouse, leaving me alone.

"What the fuck?" I asked myself, knowing that he wasn't exactly mad at her, as much as it seemed he was mad at himself.

Scratching my head, I stood, and brushed my butt off thoroughly. I proceeded to choose the plants that I would want for the interior of the house. After I did, I put the chosen plants by the door, then left. On my way back, I breathed in the clean, icy cold, crisp air! I started dancing toward the house. Nothing was like Christmas! It was my favorite time of year, and I almost wished that it were every day! OK. So, the truth about that was the old "too much of a good thing" argument might be true for most people. Not for me, though! Before I got to the back door, I stopped a moment. Looking to the left, then the right, making sure no one was around, I stretched out my arms.

"I LOVE CHRISTMAS!" I shouted to the universe.

~ DAMIAN ~

I was thrown completely off my guard when Noel and Sam walked through the hothouse doors! It had been only a matter of time, before someone would find out that I had kept Rebecca's dream alive in these poinsettias – and to tell Noel. For years, I'd used the greenhouse to get away so I could just think.

But, her admonition that she was ready a minute ago, was too much for me. I stomped through the house, out the door, and with my vampire speed, traveled a while, before I sat down in my favorite place to think. I ran my hands through my hair. Why had I done that? Noel had just told me everything I wanted that was buried deep in my soul! She had just told me that she wanted to be with me...forever! She wanted to be turned! Yet, all I could think of was Rebecca when she turned down my offer of immortality. It was nothing personal with her, though. She just didn't want it. Her reasoning was that people shouldn't be allowed to live forever, because it wasn't in God's plan. I remembered arguing with her, and asking if that were true, then why had vampires been allowed to thrive? What about werewolves, and some of the other creatures in the paranormal world? Her answer? None of us was normal. That we were abominations in her sight! Well, all except the ones that lived in this house and me. I stared out over the massive valley in front of me. For this moment, I felt like the gap between Noel and me was far too vast to bring together. So, here I sat...brooding about what could be, but questioning whether or not it was a good idea to turn her. For a while, I really hoped that Ronnie might be right, but what if she were not right? To ask Noel to give up living and breathing, as well as the other things that are so important to a human woman, such as the one thing I could not give her, was far too selfish!

~ NOEL ~

Well, puzzling out what was wrong with Damian was just way to difficult, and quite frankly, rather annoying. So, I turned to what I did best to push him from my mind for a while. First thing I did, when I entered the mansion, was to find one of the family members named Lydia. She was tall and lanky, the housekeeper, and one of the nicest women I'd ever met. She had blue-black hair that hung to her waist when it was down, although usually, she had it pulled up into a ponytail or a bun on top of her head. Her eyes were full on black, her lips were lusciously red, and her skin a slight olive. She stood no less than five-foot ten, and had a figure that I would kill to have! If and when I became one of them, I wondered if I would get that same gorgeousness of vamps?

"Hey, Noel! What can I do for you?"

"Can you get someone, to bring some of the poinsettias I left sitting by the front door of the greenhouse?

"Greenhouse? Wait. You've seen it?" She seemed strangely surprised. "Uh, well, uh, I guess. Uh, Sure!" she answered carefully.

"Damian and I discussed the plants, and said that everything was OK to use."

"No worries!" She turned to go get her husband, but stopped and turned her head to look at me. "We are just so excited that you are here, Noel! You've brought back joy and Christmas into our lives! Any of us will do anything for you! And, more than that? Damian is happier than we have ever seen him. You really love him?"

I smiled at her.

"Yes, Lydia, I love him."

She smiled as I thanked her. She turned, and hurried off to get Sam.

"Oh, Lydia!" I called.

She turned.

"Speaking of our Lord and Master," I grinned at her, receiving a grin right back. "Do you know where Damian went? He kind of took off in a funk, and I really need to talk to him."

I needed to know why he had acted the way he did, when I was only giving him what he wanted.

"Funk, huh?" She rolled her eyes. I knew what she was thinking, because I was thinking the same thing – Men! "But, I can tell you where he does go when he needs to think," she told me. Then added, "It's quite a way from here. I can take you there if you want. If you drove, it would take you thirteen hours to get there. I can have you there in just under ten minutes."

I was in need to get to him, so it didn't register that Lydia had said ten minutes. And, the last thing I did know was that I did not know that I could take myself. I didn't stop to consider how a human could travel at vampire speed, and I certainly had no idea, at the time, that I had the vampire speed due to being blood-bonded.

"If you don't mind?" I asked.

"Well, then! Hop on my back!"

I was a bit skeptical, but she just let her eyebrows raise as if to say, "Are you seriously going to pull that face?" Sighing, I'd barely grabbed hold of her, and we were off at a speed that was making me nauseous. I really needed to get some motion sickness pills if I were going to indulge in this kind of travel. Ten minutes later, we stopped. I had no idea where we were, but I didn't really care. It was already getting dark, and my stomach was still roiling with the speed we had traveled.

"I'll take you to the base of the rock, but you'll have to take it from there. All you have to do is to follow the short trail. He loves coming to Spouting Hole to think."

"Where are we?" I asked her.

"It's kind of a bit off the beaten path. I only know where it is, not *where* it is."

I did a double take.

"You know where it is, but not *where* it is? Is that some type of code or something?"

All Lydia did was just smirk.

"He's right up there, Noel."

"Thank you, Lydia."

"Always welcome, dear."

Suddenly, she was gone, before I had time to look behind me. Darkness was falling, but thankfully, it was light enough for me to follow the narrow trail that ran next to a sheer drop off, and had me shaking. I really didn't like heights. I made sure that I did not look down as I walked. Once I reached a slight clearing, I saw some steep rocks that were arranged as if they were stairs. I took a deep breath, and began to climb. I was at the top quickly. Being as short as I was, the steep stairs caused me to lift my legs almost abnormally high to climb, but I did it – panting from lack of breath, to be sure, but I made it. At the top, I rounded a corner, and stopped, gasping in awe! Before me was a large and very shallow lake with a multiple waterfalls! The lake was surrounded by large trees, overhanging the water making it almost hidden from the outside world. In the middle of it, there was a branch of some kind stretching across the lake from the right side, half in and half out of the water. So clear, that anyone could see the bottom as if there was no water at all! I had to explore this place, before the sun was gone. I walked all the way around it trying to find this Spouting Hole, but found nothing. I walked back to the entrance area, and looked to my right.   There, on the rocks, was a small sign saying Spouting Hole.   I looked upward, and noticed that there did seem to be a path that led upwards.

I slipped a couple of times on the loose gravel and dirt, but finally made it. To my right, the waterfall splashed onto protruding rocks below that looked as if they had tumbled at some point in history from a rockslide or maybe even an earthquake. In turn, I could see that the waterfall fed a short, shallow stream that meandered lazily along. I looked above me, and with the fading, twilight disappearing rapidly, I could barely see him, sitting at the top of the waterfall. In moments, darkness descended, but the starlight highlighted his face, which looked almost forlorn. I needed to get to him, but how? I sat down on one of the rocks, and stared at the water splashing onto the rocks, trying to figure out what to do. It was an almost black night except for the stars shining above me. I looked back at Damian. He had not moved. And...

"Wait! It's dark! How can I see so easily in the dark?" I asked myself.

That's when I realized that Lydia was also bonded, like me, but she had super vampire speed! Did that mean that I, too, might have some of these abilities? Of course! I could easily see in the pitch black. I looked up, and wondered if I could scale the height above me. I'd never climbed rocks before, but with my newfound abilities, did that mean I could? Well, there was no time like the present to try it. I stood, and placed my hands on the rock in front of me…and, I began to climb. I couldn't believe this! I was rock climbing! And, more than that…it was really very easy! I felt light as I jumped from one rock to another. This was incredible! I had no idea how much fun it was! OK. I'd never, ever try it if I was still fully human, but this was just too cool! I truly wanted to be with Damian in his world forever. Sacrifice was just a small part of it. And, I was willing. But, I needed to know why Damian had changed his mind. I reached the top, and quietly sat down beside him. He didn't acknowledge that I was there, but he knew it. After a while, he spoke.

"I love you, Noel. I do want you with me forever." He turned to me, and staring into my eyes. "But, not at a cost to your soul."

~ DAMIAN ~

When I had run out of the greenhouse, I knew I had taken the coward's way out, but I just couldn't do it! Yes! I wanted Noel to be like me; to be with me forever. But, when she had told me that she was ready, I panicked. I'd remembered how sure Rebecca had been about not turning her, despite the fact that she would never live to raise her little girl. But, remembering what she had told me at the time was only reinforced when Noel had told him she was ready to become a vampire. I remembered Rebecca as she lay dying in her hospital bed just after her daughter was born. I had even tried one more time to reason with her, even using her daughter as bribery.

"But, why not Rebecca? You will live to see your daughter grow, and thrive. You can raise her! We can!" I had insisted.

She stubbornly shook her head.

"That's not it, Damian. I would have to watch her die, too. And, then, her children's children, and on and on. I can't do that! I just can't! Even though my baby's Father is a rapist, and a mobster, I'd rather die from my cancer, than to outlive my children for virtually forever! At least, this way, I will have a chance of seeing them."

She had placed her hand on mine, and begged me to understand.

"I know what I am giving up. Truly, I do. But, Damian, my little baby will have you. I know you will watch over her, and her progeny."

I had looked into her tear-stained eyes with sadness. I did understand. If I had a choice to choose to be turned or not, I would have chosen life. But, I was never accorded that right, and I would never have taken away that choice from her.

"You know I will watch them forever, Rebecca. They will never want for anything. I promise you," I had vowed.

"I know. I will die in happiness knowing you will. Don't tell her of me, please. I don't want her to know that her Mother was a coward and chose badly, nor that her Father is a rapist. Find a wonderful family to adopt her."

She was quiet for a minute. Then, she continued. "Damian, do not mourn for me. I go to my God in the knowledge that I have been forgiven, and will live on another plane of existence. One I happily embrace. But, would you do me one other favor?"

"I will," I had vowed.

She had said something that had almost floored me, because I had no idea she had an ability that was almost like an oracle.

"Will you look after the greenhouses for me? Grow poinsettias, and care for them? Someday, you will find your true mate, and let her take over my heritage of decorating for Christmas. When that day comes, you will have everything you have ever wanted…a mate, a wife, and the Mother of your child. But, know this! You will be able to procreate with her, and her alone. I have seen this in one of my visions. She will embody everything about Christmas, and will happily join you in your life as a vampire. But, beware! Do not let her do so, until she becomes pregnant. As a bonded human, she will be able to conceive and carry a hybrid child, who will also live as long as both of you, when she reaches adulthood. Your daughter will be able to conceive in any form with any human or super being. Also, beware of the evil that is coming to your doorstep. Do not be quick to dismiss help that is close to you, for that help will come in a surprising manner. Do not let this evil take your mate, but if he does, you must defeat it, before your kind will be able to embark on an unbelievable transition!"

I had just sat holding her hand with my mouth gaping. I shook my head.

"No. Damian. I have been told this. With my sacrifice, not only will my own child live, but you will be able to procreate. Another will be the first, because she will understand that which your kind did not. It will be a girl, although, a surprise will also be on the horizon as well."

She had smiled at me while taking one, last breath, and with that smileon her face, she closed her eyes leaving this life. I had always thought that she was delusional at the end, but with the entrance of my true mate, Noel – a human – and lover of Christmas, I had to concede that Rebecca might have been right. That's why I couldn't turn Noel when she asked. I needed to live out the final end of all of this. If she were right, Noel would grow heavy with my child, and give birth to our daughter. Just the prospect of that was so far out of my dreams, it was almost impossible to believe in this prophecy. But, with Curttis, I had no idea how that was going to work. I wondered if I should even tell her that she would carry my child at some point, because I just still didn't really believe it. That was so hard for me to wrap my head around, but I couldn't deny that, so far, Rebecca had been absolutely correct. I honestly didn't know if it were even possible. To my knowledge, no human and vampire had ever had a child. Two vampires were absolutely a no! On that note, I spoke to her.

"I love you, Noel. I do want you with me forever." I turned to her, and stared into her eyes, taking her hands in mine, and told her, "but, not at a cost to your future."

"And, what the hell does that even mean?" she asked me, trying to pull her hands from mine. I wouldn't let her, of course.

"Rebecca."

I watched the puzzlement form on her beautiful face.

"Rebecca? What does she have to do with this?" Noel demanded.

"Something she said, just before she died."

"And, that would be???"

"She told me that I couldn't turn you until…."

"Until…what, exactly?"

I took a deep breath, and plunged right in, hoping she didn't think I was stark raving nuts!

"Until I placed my seed inside you, and it grows."

I saw all kinds of emotions run through her face: shock, awe, disbelief, anger, ecstasy, and finally….

"No fucking way! You are a vampire! Have any vampire/human produced a kid?" she asked me with a squeal.

"No, but…"

"There! You see? We can't get pregnant! Why would she say something like that on her death bed?"

"I don't know. I wondered if she had lost it, but honestly? Now that you are in my life, and she said that you would be, I'm not sure any more. Like you, Noel, she also had a gift – the gift of visions. And, she saw you."

Her mouth dropped over my statement. Slowly, she shook her head in disbelief.

"If what you are saying is true, then…"

I nodded my head. "So far, everything she has said has come true. I'm beginning to believe the rest of what she said is a possibility, now."

All of that sounded strange coming out of my mouth! Even I couldn't believe I'd just voiced what had been in my head. Apparently, Noel felt the same.

"Y-you think that w-we can have a-a-a…" she stuttered, not wanting to say it aloud.

"Baby?"

I didn't answer immediately, as I played what Rebecca had said in my head again. Finally, I said, "Yes. I think that Rebecca was more than just a young woman who had gotten caught up in the evil of her time."

"And, that would be?"

"I believe she was what was known, long in the past, an oracle."

Noel cocked her head at me in question.

"An Oracle was a prophet, of sorts. Someone who sees visions, and one who makes predictions of the future."

"Well, shit!" Noel exclaimed.

"Exactly…" I replied, adding to my own thoughts, "…just like me?"

~ 21 ~

~ NOEL ~

Had I just heard Damian right? His ex had made a prediction that I would come into his life, that we would be together, and that we would actually be able to produce a baby? Automatically, my hand went to my belly. The thought of carrying his baby was as unbelievable as my turning into an energizer bunny! OK. Using a bunny was probably a bad example, and maybe the wrong thing to say, but hell! What he had just told me? I just couldn't get my head around it! I loved him with every breath I drew. Everything evolved around the two of us! I was so willing to become fully his...to live his life with him. But, what if he did turn me? What if Rebecca was right, and doing so would prevent us from carrying out a future that neither of us could have imagined. I stared up into Damian's eyes, and the hope that lay within them only served to make my own hope grow within me. I couldn't do it. I couldn't ask him to turn me. At least not yet. If there were even the slightest bit of hope for this miracle, I would accept it, and become what I was meant to be. Afterward? Well, if I still wanted him to turn me, then I knew he would. I couldn't live a mortal life with him. Well, I could for a short time, but that wasn't the point. I didn't want to live a mortal life with him. I wanted an immortal life with him. And, if she was also right, and we had a child, and that child would live as long as did he, then I wasn't about give up the opportunity to live with them both. But, right now, I needed to talk to him about the other pressing matter at hand. My Father.

"I guess we need to put this all on the backburner for the moment," I said. "I need to talk to you."

"OK. What do you wish to speak to me about?" Damian asked, willing to put the subject aside for the moment.

"Can we go home? I'm almost positive that you will want Caleb and Ronnie with us when I try to explain this."

Damian drew me onto his shoulders, and his vampire speed had us back home in a matter of minutes. I'm quite sure I could have kept up with him, but until I knew for certain what my powers might be, I would accept the ride. I was tired, and still a bit stunned over everything, but we still had to talk – and I was really nauseous this time. I needed the bathroom first. I streaked for it as soon as we arrived, leaving Damian to call after me, wondering what was wrong. I darted into the bathroom, and threw everything up in the toilet, before flushing. Ick! I hated throwing up, and it always made my mouth taste awful. I tried to rinse it out as best as I could, but I still felt yucky. I quickly searched for my toothbrush, and used it. After I was done, I threw it into the trashcan, and opened the door. I followed the voices that were still in the foyer. It wasn't just Damian alone any more.

Ready for bed?" he asked me, waggling his eyebrows when I approached.

I laughed, and slapped his arm playfully. Sometimes, he was just so doggone playful! I bet most other vampires wouldn't have liked to be called that, and I was sure my vampire wouldn't either. But, he was just going to have to live with it! I wrapped my arms around his neck, and his mouth passionately descended on mine. He started to pick me up, and carry me to bed, when I pushed him away from me so suddenly, it threw him. He frowned at me.

"What the fuck, Noel?"

"Oh, buddy! You'll get me, but I need to talk to you first."

"About what?" he asked, sounding a bit frustrated, while Ronnie and Sam started laughing.

They had joined him, while I was in the bathroom throwing up my guts.

"We need Caleb, too. What I have to say needs to be heard by everyone, so let's go downstairs. I've put it off for way too long. And, you know how I hate to repeat myself."

His eyes narrowed at me, but the four of them walked back downstairs and into the living room. Caleb joined us, and he was not a happy camper.

"Why the hell did you two drag me out of my 'I just got to sleep' mode?" he muttered.

"Sleep mode? That's what you're calling it, now?" Damian laughed, then pointed at me.

"Gee…thanks!" I sarcastically said. Turning to Caleb, I grinned at his scowl, and said, "You're most welcome!" Then, I continued. "I'm sorry guys, but I really, really have to tell you all this."

"Well, we are not getting any younger, here! Spill already!" Sam quipped.

I did a double take. Was he kidding? Not getting any younger? I shook my head.

"Yeah. Well…" I started. Walking to the mantel of the living room, I leaned against the side of it. "It's about South."

"I really don't want to hear about that jackass, Noel." Damian hesitated. "What about him?"

He didn't want to hear about a jackass, but he asks about the jackass? Shaking my head, I knew Damian was still furious that he had allowed me to be captured right from under his nose, but the truth was, it really wasn't his fault. It was mine. I had gone with them of my own free will. They always say curiosity killed the cat? Well, in my case? It was curiosity was going to kill me if I didn't get the answers I had wanted all my life. I knew they had all wanted to know what had happened, but I just wasn't ready to speak at the time. Now, I was.

"First off, I need to tell you that South is not who you think he is."

"Huh?" Ronnie asked. "What do you mean?"

"What are you talking about? He's a rat!" Caleb sneered.

I shook my head, finishing in a very, very quiet voice that only a vampire would hear, "He is my Father."

Silence. Total and complete silence. The calm before the storm. One, two, thr….

"What!!!" Sam and Ronnie yelled at the same time. "You can't be serious?"

"No! That isn't possible! How could he be your Father? That makes no sense! You've been tricked!" Caleb said as he flew out of his chair, and the next thing I knew, I was being held by my throat on the wall.

Damian was infuriated as he darted to Caleb, yanked him away from his mate, and threw him back against one of the plate glass windows, which broke from the force. Caleb landed in the huge fountain outside. The speed at which Damian traveled to grab him by the throat again, happened so fast, he was able to spin back to Noel, and catch her with the other arm, before she fell to the floor.

"That is enough!" Damian yelled. "Do you have a death wish?"

"I-I'm sorry, Noel."

I smiled slightly.

"Damian, let him go. Please, let him go. I'm OK."

Damian dropped Caleb who landed with a thud on the floor, then started to go to Noel who held up a hand.

"No, please." I barely made it to the nearest wingback, and sat down. "If everyone will calm down, I can tell you all about it."

Damian yanked me up, turned, and sat down with me on his lap.

"Uh…do I really need to sit in your lap?" I almost snickered.

"Yes."

Well, that was succinct. I looked around at the still surprised faces surrounding me. I shrugged.

"South is my Father – my biological Father." I stopped anyone from saying anything by glaring at them. If they could glare at me, so could I.

"Why do you believe that?" Damian asked me.

"He knew something only my Mom and Dad would have known."

"What?"

Shit! I was hoping I could scamper by that without anyone asking me. I looked at Ronnie, who was frowning, then Sam, whose face was skeptical, and Caleb who sat with his massive arms crossed over his chest, staring at me with disgust.

I looked at Damian, who understood immediately, and he urged me to continue. It gave me the courage to let go of my deep secret.

"I have always had this ability to know what people were feeling. I don't know what drives it, but it's there just the same. I get these feelings, I guess. Anyway, for whatever reason, I know what others are feeling."

"I believe she is an empath," Damian told everyone, after the silence had continued for about five minutes.

Ronnie's hand flew to her mouth in shock, and both Caleb and Sam just shook their heads side to side in denial.

"The feelings, for whatever reason, let me see what is behind them. I have used them, been ridiculed, and many times, people are terrified of me. Sometimes, they don't want anyone to know their secrets. It took me a long time to realize that I was odd. When I did, I made sure that I did not use my gift again. Or, at least if I did, I would keep my mouth shut."

"Go on, love," Damian said.

"Anyway, South knew about it. It appears that both South and Landon have been watching over me all this time, and…."

Damian jumped up, and I fell on my ass on the floor. What the hell?

"Are you telling me that you are the one South was talking about? He said he had a human daughter, but I had no idea it was you!"

I picked my butt off the floor, and fisted my hands as they landed on my hips.

"I am going to forget that you just dumped my ass on the floor, and didn't even help me up, you jerk!

But, right this moment, rest assured, your 'vampireness', I will have retribution!"

Everyone else snickered, and then rolled out the huge laughs, earning each of us narrowed eyes, and set mouth from Damian. And, that only made me laugh harder. He rolled his eyes.

"You three done yet?" he asked.

The three of us all looked at each other, and back to Damian. All three of us shook our head no, and threw our head back in full-on laughter.

After a few minutes of the levity, she continued.

"Now, that your little temper tantrum is over, and Caleb has no further need to try and kill me, yes. My parents and I were involved in an accident when I was really little. I don't remember a whole lot, but I was not injured. My Mom was killed, and my Dad was dying. At some point, before the authorities got there, a young man came along and offered Daddy eternal life. He accepted because he wanted to protect me. So, Landon took me to a church, and left me on the steps. Then he turned my Dad. Cue Damian giving South permission to watch over me from afar." I paused for a few minutes. "South was offered the leadership of their clan, and he accepted. Unfortunately, I had a lousy upbringing, and that's where I came in to meet Ronnie."

"Wow! What a story," Sam exclaimed.

"It really is!" Caleb agreed.

"There was something else?" Damian was trying to keep me focused.

"Oh, yeah. He talked about some vamp named Curttis Drakow? Something about he is here, now, and I am not safe."

"Oy vey!" Ronnie threw her head back on the chair.

"You ain't just whistling Dixie!" Caleb muttered.

Oh, come on! You were thinking it!

"Drakow is here? In my territory? And, he hasn't said anything?"

"I guess that's what Daddy meant. I'm not really sure about anything at the moment."

"Noel, I hate to do this, but this is vampire business."

I rolled my eyes.

"Translation? Get lost!" I grouched. "I'm the one in danger. It's my Dad, but hey! It's vampire business, so you aren't welcome! Right."

I shuffled out of the room, and decided that this was a great time to take a damn walk outside to cool my heels. I stayed within the boundaries of the house as I walked. It was calm, and not windy. I decided to test out my theory of vampire speed. I bent in a "take-off" crouch,. My foot was down, ready to push off for the run, when a sudden wind crossed my path. I felt a horrible crack on the back of my head with blackness following right behind.

~ DAMIAN ~

I knew that Noel was angry with me, but she didn't need to be around us, while we discussed the death of another person. Maybe several. Strategy was necessary after what she had told us. I walked up the stairs, noticing all the decorations, and my heart melted. She was trying so hard to make our house a home. It was hers as much as ours. It was then I realized I wasn't feeling Noel. Anywhere. I quickly looked into our room. She wasn't there. I ran back downstairs where everyone was still sitting talking.

"Have you seen Noel?" I asked, hope dropping by the second.

"No. Why?"

"She's not in our room, and I can't feel her – at all!"

Ronnie, Sam, and Caleb took a few seconds with me. We scoured the inside of the house and the outside. She was nowhere! We all met back into the living room. Ronnie was beside herself with worry, and I was about to panic. So much so, I whipped out my phone, and called South.

"What do you want, Damian?" he growled.

"Is Noel with you?"

"No. Why? Wait. She's not with you?"

"No. She's nowhere on the grounds, either."

For the first time, I heard panic in my voice, and so did South, which sent him into panic mode. In the seconds between asking him, and him being their, my stomach plummeted.

"I'm outside the gate. Do I have permission to enter?" he asked.

"Yes."

Seconds later both South and Landon were standing in my living room.

"Where can she be?" Ronnie sniffled.

"It has to be Curttis," South said.

"Why?"

"Because he must know she is your mate and my daughter. Two dangerous combinations. I hadn't thought he would figure that out this soon!"

"Now what?" Ronnie asked.

No one answered, because they had no idea where to begin. For the first time in my life, I was actually terrified.

~ 22 ~

~ NOEL ~

I woke up on my back, and tried to turn on my side. The musky, moldy scent caused me to wrinkle my nose at the sickening smell, that was accompanied by another scent like a sewer.

"Ouch!" I squealed.

Geez, why was Damian's bed hard – and cold? Reaching out my hand, I patted the bed, trying to make it a bit more comfortable. Where was the sheet? I slapped my hand even harder, and the pain that shot through my hand caused me to sit up in an instant with a wave of dizziness and nausea. I slapped my hand to my forehead, and closed my eyes for a minute, waiting for the vertigo to leave.

"Frickin' A!" I muttered, as the pain began to subside. Slowly, I opened one eye at a time, hoping there wasn't any bright light.

As my eyes became accustomed to the darkness, I was able to make out shapes. I realized that there was a soft, golden glow around the room. I also noticed dark, vertical lines all around me. I squinted. Are those…?

"Bars?" Shock reverberated in my voice.

"Yes, they are," another voice replied.

I whipped my head to the direction of the voice. A figure was inching its way from the dark into the pale, gold light. It was a woman with long hair, and she looked emaciated. She was starving!

"If you really want to see me, you could come a bit closer to me, you know."

Cautiously, as I scooted across the floor, my hand came into contact with something thick and moderately wet. I yanked her hand up, afraid of what it might be. I sniffed.

"Just in case you're wondering, my dear, you're smelling blood on your hand," the voice snickered, it offered as an explanation.

Sure enough, I could actually smell the tangy iron scent.

"Oh, yuck!" I tried to wipe it off on the concrete. "You know you could have warned me."

"And, why would I do that? I've had such little entertainment in this hellhole, I needed a bit of a laugh."

"Oh, crap. More vamps?" I huffed.

There was no answer at first, and I noticed I could see the woman's face fairly clearly, now. Her incisors were glistening in the golden light. Why the hell couldn't I get my teeth that white? Why would I even think that was an issue right now?

"Vamps? I don't understand the word," the woman frowned.

"You're a vampire," I reasoned, heaving a deep sigh in resignation.

"Really? Wow! I never would have guessed!" she answered with sarcasm. "I have absolutely no idea what you mean."

"Riiiiight. Sure you don't." I sighed. "Look. I'm really, really not in the mood to bandy words with anyone, so how about we just level with each other, since we seem to be in the same situation?"

Nothing from the vamp.

"OK. Let's start with the basics, alright? Where are we?"

"What am I? Damn, bloody Waze? I don't exactly know where hell we are. This room, however, is a basement, obviously. And, those iron thingies around us? Just in case you don't recognize them are called bars."

"What is that? Sarcasm? Well, you certainly have the concept down!" I snarled. "No kidding! How did we get here?" I demanded.

"Me? I haven't a clue how I got here, and I can only guess at how long I've been here. You, however? They brought you into the prison, and threw you in the cell next to me almost twenty-four hours ago – give or take six."

"Six?" I frowned. Well, that probably explained why my side was hurting. If I'd been laying on the concrete floor that long, no wonder I'm hurting! I decided to change tactics.

"Ok. So, guess. How long have you been here?" I asked.

"Oh…I don't know, because you know how it is when you're just having way too much fun. You have a tendency to lose track of time. Maybe about ten years? Give or take three."

"Ten years!!" My voice had raised an octave. "Why? I mean…never mind. Don't answer that."

"Well, I wasn't going to answer you, anyway, but alright." The voice laughed.

"Who are you?" I asked.

"I am called, Salinda," she replied.

My eyebrows rose.

"That's a very unusual name."

"Yeah, well when I was turned, it was rather popular."

"Oh. I didn't mean…what I meant was I think it's beautiful!" Noel offered by way of an apology.

"Glad you like it."

Silence ensued for a few minutes. Then, Salinda reacted rather oddly by sniffing the air. She reached out and grabbed Noel by the throat, causing her to squeak. I knew it was a mistake to get closer.

"Who are you?" she demanded, teeth bared.

Noel clawed at her hands, but she didn't let go. What is it with vamps? They were always attacking me!

"L-leg-go."

"Your Eggo?" she joked. "Now. Let's try this again. Who the fuck are you?"

She let her hand open enough so Noel could gasp out a squeak.

"My name is Noel. Noel Snow."

"Why do you smell like Damian?"

Surprise showed on Noel's face. This woman knew Damian?

"H-how do you know D-Damian?"

"None of your business, and you are in no shape to ask me anything. Answer. My. Question!" she enunciated.

"B-because…I-I'm his…m-mate!" I gasped between breaths.

Salinda eyes widened in shock, and her hands dropped from my throat. She sat back in stunned silence. Damian was mated? No way!

"No! You can't be! But…but…you're human!" she exclaimed harshly. "You had better not be lying to me!"

"Why would I lie about that? I smell like him, don't I? I understand that when a vampire takes a mate, the mate begins to smell like them."

"Well, shit! I would never have believed that…. How long have you been mated?"

"First, so not your damn business, and two, not until you tell me who you are!"

"Very well. As I said, my name is Salinda. Salinda Blood. I was taken from my home almost eight hundred years ago, and turned by the very monster, who now imprisons us both. I managed to escape him for years, but about ten years ago, he tracked me down. I've been trying to escape ever since."

I sat there, rubbing my throat. It was easing up, but still I was having a bit of trouble talking. Blood? Wait.

"Geez! What is about you guys that you can't get an answer without trying to strangle me?" Wait. "Damian's name is also Blood. Who are you?" Noel demanded, curiosity telling her "don't ask…don't ask".

"Damian is my brother – my biological brother."
I was blindsided.
"Well, hell! I sure didn't see that one coming!" I murmured.

"Did you not know he had a sister?" she gasped in shock.

Well, he hadn't exactly told her, but I wasn't going to let her know it! It would be a sign of weakness on her part if she did.

"I did, but he told me that she had died."

"Typical male macho crap," she muttered. "To be fair, though, he probably did think I was dead."

"We've only been together for a short time. Really, not long enough for us to have had time to talk at length about our families." I wasn't going to tell her about my Father, because I just didn't want her to know right now. She shrugged. "I don't really have a family.

Salinda looked startled.

"What do you mean you have no family?"

In this case, though, I wasn't going to give up anything until I knew more.

"I was given up for adoption when I was a baby. It was at Christmas."

Salinda started laughing so hard, she curled up into a ball. Try as she might, laughter is catching, and moments later, I joined her. The whole situation wasn't at all funny, but laughing was better than crying. To all intents and purposes, Salinda was my sister-in-law, and the two of them sounded like a couple of horses as they snorted.

Suddenly, a door flew open, and the laughter dwindled.

"What the fucking hell do you two fucking bitches have to fucking laugh about?" a huge man demanded.

Both women broke off to look at him.

"I don't fucking know, you fucking son of a fucking bitch!" Salinda growled at him.

"Shut the fuck up, Salinda!"

"Make me, Ranken!" Salinda challenged.

He just glared at her, as he walked down a few steps. He was carrying something, and one of those somethings, he threw at Salinda.

"Just like you like it, bitch! Hot!" he sneered, throwing a bag of blood at her.

"I'll tell you what's going to be hot, bastard. It's going to be you, when I send you into the fires of Hell!"

Ignoring her, he stepped over to Noel's cage, and slid a plate of something through the bars.

"Eat, bitch! The boss says that he can't wait to get his hands on your tits and plunge his cock into your cunt! He wants to spread his seed all over your body, and put his fucking kid inside you! So, he needs you to eat well. Keep up your strength, so to speak!" he laughed heartily. "Then, after his kid comes out of you, he's going to throw you to the rest of us to fuck all we want, until we make you bleed from every hole in your body!" He moved to the bars, and his mouth opened, his tongue slipping out raking across his yellow canines. Then, he unzipped his pants, and grabbed his cock, stroking it as he continued. I felt a sick shudder race through my body at the sight of his flaccid dick. "I can't wait, either! I'm going to plunge my cock into your pussy over and over till my seed floods you, and sink my teeth into your tits. Then, I'm going to eat your cunt, and bite it till you bleed. Next, I'll fuck your asshole till you bleed, and make you suck my bloody cock while you are dying! Oh, girlie! I can't wait to get my fucking dick in your pussy!

He had been masturbating the entire time he was talking, and he roared as his seed shot out of his cock all over the food he'd placed on the floor of her cell. Then, laughing, he turned, walked up the stairs, and slammed the door.

I started to throw up, tears finally running down my cheeks. A soft voice interrupted me.

"Damian will be here, and he will kill these bastards! He'll get us out of here!" Salinda vowed.

"Oh, I know he'll get here, but will it be in time?" I asked her. And, for that, she didn't have an answer.

~ DAMIAN ~

"Damn! Damn! Damn! Damn!" Damian shouted at the top of his lungs.

"You are not 'enry 'iggins," Ronnie snorted.

He whirled on her.

"What?"

"Will you stop your caterwauling!" Caleb said to him.

"I agree. We will never find her if you keep this crap up! So, calm the hell down!" Ronnie said. Inside she was a mess. Her best friend was gone! And, yet, it was useless to be angry, because there is no way even she could be calm.

"Calm? Like you are? She's your best friend, but my mate, Ronnie!"

Damian plopped down in the chair, leaned over, and put his head in his hands.

"I'm sorry," he told them.

Ronnie put her hand on his shoulder, while Caleb put his on the other.

"OK. First, identify the culprit. Second, kill the bastard. The end."

Damian looked up at Caleb, and smirked a bit. South was not gone, and was sitting in the darkness around the fireplace.

"Caleb…get South back here!"

Caleb grinned, and whipped out his cell phone.

"No need, son." His voice was so angry, we could all hear it in his voice. "It's time to fucking kick this guy's ass!"

"I don't know where to look!" Damian said.

"Lucky, then, that Landon and I do."

They all let an evil grin spread across their faces.

~ NOEL ~

"And, that is what happened to me. The asshole turned me, and made me his slave for a very long time."

"Wow! What a story, Salinda! I can't even imagine!"

"Well, it's just the way it is. I fought him for a long time, until I finally realized I could not get away from him. I finally let him do whatever he wanted to me. It took years, of course, but I did it anyway. I had literally given up."

"How did you get away?" I was curious.

"Easy. I seduced two of my guards into helping me." Salinda tapped a finger on her cheek as if trying to remember something. "Then, after we were out, I killed them."

That admission bothered me a bit, but how could I fault her for killing them, when I would have done the same thing?

"Just who is this son-of-bitch?" I asked.

"His name? Curttis Drakow. Why?"

"Drakow!" I croaked.

"Yes. He turned both Damian and me."

Crap! Crap! Crap!

"I must get away from him! If he finds out what I may be, we're all going to be screwed!"

"What you are?" Salinda asked with a frown.

"Yeah. According to Damian, I'm an empath. And, my Father's name is South."

Salinda just stared at me in shock.

"You. Are. An. Empath."

"Yes. That's exactly what I said."

"So. You are Damian's mate; South's daughter; and an empath?" She slapped her head. "Out of all those, he isn't wanting you because of your gift. He's wanting you because of Damian and South."

"Why do you say that?" I asked her.

"He sired both Damian and me."

"And, he's had you here for almost ten years."

"Yes. And, the one thing he wanted to do most of all was to…"

"Hurt Damian in some way? But, for what?"

"Damian betrayed him – or at least that's what he thinks."

"How?"

"Drakow is every bit as evil as Dracula, if not more. His exploits are not even in the same universe as Dracula. Damian tried to hunt down Drakow afterward. He was going to kill him for all that he had done. There had been a huge altercation between them after he turned Damian. Damian almost killed him, but he let him live."

"I see. He thinks that it's all his fault that Drakow committed countless crimes."

"Yes. Damian is good man; he was a great brother; and a wonderful son. But, when he was turned, it killed him that he had to hurt someone to live."

"How do you know all of this? You haven't seen him in all this time, have you?"

"No. Drakow told me."

I didn't know what to think. It actually made a lot of sense, but still, it seemed a bit out there.

"Be that as it may, we have to get the hell out of here, Salinda. We just have to! I have no doubt that this Drakow guy is going to kill us. I cannot let him take us away from Damian."

"I agree. The consequences could be devastating."

"So, how do we do this? I'm not really into escaping impossible places."

"Me, either." She closed her eyes as if she was thinking. "Ok. When Ranken comes back, I'll try and get him to get closer to my cage. If I can get him close enough, I can take care of...."

Before Salinda could finish what she was telling me, the door opened to the basement.

"Speak of the devil," I thought.

Ranken came quickly down the stairs holding their food. He threw my food through the slot on the floor, then stepped to the bars where Salinda was. But, this time, he had no blood with him. The last bag had been Salinda's once a week feeding, and it was pitifully scant. Maybe a half a cup. If we were to get out of this nasty place, she needed more from a fresh source. I made up my mind before I could chicken out, and scooted toward her side of the bars. Ranken sneered at her.

"Boss said no more blood for you for a while, bitch. He's decided to extend your once a week ration to once a month," he told her, laughing as he ascended the stairs, again.

Holy shit! If we were here even another week without her feeding? I didn't really want to think about what might happen. Speaking of blood, I was feeling weaker myself.

"Salinda! How long have I been here?"

"Oh, guessing maybe just over a week." She frowned. "Blood. You haven't had blood."

"Yeah. Look, Salinda. To overtake Ranken, you need blood."

"So?"

I rolled up my sleeve, and presented my arm to her.

"Take what you need."

I splayed my arm through the bars, and she crawled closely to me.

"No. I do not take human blood through the source. I have never done it!"

"Look! You are our only hope of getting the hell out of this place! You are far too weak to do anything, dammit! Now, take what you need!" I ordered.

Salinda grabbed my wrist, and her fangs lowered. She met my eyes.

"It will weaken you even more. Are you sure about this?" she asked. "But, what about your baby?"

"Honestly? I'm scared to death, but I'm human, and I can't hold my own against this maniac! So, we will do what we have to do. I want you to take what you need from me to get us.............! Wait! What did you just say? Baby? What baby?"

"The one I hear inside your belly, of course. I don't know how you got pregnant with my brother, but hell! I'm not going to argue about it!"

I was stunned. Baby? I was pregnant? Oh, shit! Would it be safe to let her have my blood now? My hand flew to my belly as if protecting it. I didn't even have time to wonder how it happened.

"I will make sure I don't take too much, Salinda promised.

I knew there was no way that we would not get out of here without her strong enough. So, I nodded.

"Take what you need," I told her, and crossed my fingers that the baby – did I really just say that – would be alright.

She grinned at me. "Well, when you put it that way!"

Salinda struck fast and hard, suckling my blood from my wrist. I knew that I might have to stop her, but I needn't have worried. She said she wasn't like most vampires, and what choice did we have whether or not I did or did not trust her? None at all.

That was when several things happened at once. The door was thrown open, and Ranken flew down the stairs. His eyes were red, and darting everywhere as if looking for an exit somewhere. I could swear he wasn't paying attention at all. Then, an explosion resounded above us somewhere, and the entire building shook hard, dislodging bits of concrete and dust raining down on top of us. Ranken had made a crucial mistake. He had taken one wrong step too close to Salinda's side of the bars, turned his back, and looked upward when the explosion resounded. I stuck out my foot. He turned and tripped, landing him close to the bars of Salinda's cage. Without a miss, Salinda had him in a headlock, before he could even sit. She was so quick, it was all over, before I could even blink once. I had never seen someone tear off a head, but the crunch sound was sickening. Some of Ranken's blood spritzed on my arms, and although I tried to get it off, I just succeeded in smearing it. Yuck! Even the guy's blood stunk like rancid meat! I threw up all over the floor, again, then wiped my mouth. A glass of water that the bastard had brought earlier, along with what looked like more semen-covered food, looked as if it had not missed the inside of the glass. I crawled to it, drank, rinsed, and then downed the rest in one gulp. The, I turned and glared at Salinda, who was patting the headless body down.

"Where are the keys, you dumbass mother-fucker?" she muttered.

Huh. Well, Damian's sister certainly had no filters on her mouth. That was a plus in these situations.

"Damn it! Where are th…ah! Finally!" she said, putting the key ring on her finger, and twirling it around in the air. She looked at me. "You ready to blow this joint?"

I was more than ready, so I nodded once. She opened the door to her cage then mine. I had never moved so fast in my life, despite the weakness I felt. She put her finger to her mouth, then whispered to me.

"Now, listen to me. Do whatever I tell you, and we might…just might, get out of this still alive!"

I gave her a brief nod. No way was I going to jeopardize my only chance to get out of here. At least we didn't have to worry about Ranken any longer.

"This way," she whispered.

"How do you know?" I whispered back.

"Vampire hearing," she explained, tapping her right ear, while giving me a "what the hell look".

I rolled my eyes, and followed her. I heard a squeak, and stopped immediately. I looked down, and realized my shoes were making the sound. She scowled at me. I took them off quickly, and continued to follow Salinda. We walked forever…or it actually felt like that anyway. When she stopped this time, I heard voices and what sounded like a fight. She put a finger to her lips for me to keep quiet, and I nodded. She slowly opened the door, and we were able to hear the words without the muffling of the door between us. We both stilled.

"I'll not ask you, again," I heard a demanding voice.

DAMIAN! I wanted to feel his arms around me once more! To feel his lips and his cock moving inside of me!

Only a gurgle answered him, and I couldn't understand it at all.

"Broocemn," it said.

Salinda looked at me with raised eyebrows. I shook my head, and shrugged. I had no idea what that was all about that meant, either.

Suddenly, I felt something grab my neck, and a soft voice.

"Move, and you die," it said. Well, wasn't this a fine kettle of fish!

He pushed me from behind, which caused me to push on Salinda. She stumbled out of the door, but he continued to hold my neck backward toward his chest, the knife at my throat. This guy wasn't kidding. He would kill me. I kept absolutely quiet as he propelled me forward. Any fighting could get me killed. Sometimes, the strangest things cross your mind at the weirdest times. Right now, I had an epiphany about where I wanted to put one, gigantic wreath. Really?

~ 23 ~

~ DAMIAN ~

I heard a rough and deep voice resound throughout the room, and my feet froze.

"Let. My. Man. Go," it threatened, "or I will slit her throat."

"Curttis," I said.

Quiet erupted over the room as everyone else stopped fighting, and turned. I saw one hand at Noel's throat was crushing her windpipe, while the other was slicing a shallow streak across her neck. I hear her whimper in pain. Damn! Curttis was a dead asshole! I noticed that her mouth quirked up like she was laughing at the vampires in the room. All of us were like statues, frozen in time! No movement, no sound at all. But, it was clear from the horror in Noel's eyes that she was on her way to freaking. When I didn't release the guy immediately, I saw him rake the knife against her white throat, and he cut another shallow, three-inch line in the front. Blood slowly trickled down her neck. I had never thought about how terrified I could get, because I had never been terrified. It's terrifying enough to know you might live forever. But, in that instant, seeing Noel's neck forced back, and that damn knife at it, terrified me more than anything I had ever seen in my life! No! I couldn't let her die, and I knew that I could never live without her in my life. So, I slowly lowered his man, then I threw him across the room, and he hit hard, neck first, then just slipped to the floor, but everyone had heard the crack. He was still alive, but with a broken neck. It would heal in a very long while, but it would be damn painful as it did. Knitting and repairing bones was the hardest, and most painful thing that a vampire could experience.

After what seemed like forever, Damian stood to his full height.

~ NOEL ~

Was something wrong with her? Damian was here, and even though my neck was in pain from the cut Curttis had just inflicted, I was so damned turned on at that very moment for him! Of course it wasn't because he was hot as hell. I felt the incision with the knife, again. I wanted to cry out, but pride kept me from doing so. My warm blood ran down my throat, and I felt a finger rake through it. I couldn't see him, but I heard a slurping sound, as he sucked my blood off of his finger. Oh, shit! That was so damned disgusting! Then, if that bastard holding the knife, cut into my neck just a bit deeper. Damn! That hurt, and I couldn't keep the tears from flooding down my face.

"Good, Damian Now, we will talk," Curttis sneered.

~ DAMIAN ~

Damn the fucking bastard! I knew I had to do something, but at the moment, I had no idea how to get Noel away from him – not without Curttis killing her! My eyes darted around me, looking for something…anything…to give me an answer as to how to rescue Noel. And, that is when I saw someone standing to the side of Curttis and Noel, who seemed rather familiar, but my I didn't stop, until I did a double take, and met eyes that I hadn't seen, since before I as turned. Eyes of one who I loved to distraction, and tried to protect at all costs. Only here she was! But, that wasn't possible! The illusion was hidden slightly behind a bend in the wall – just enough where Curttis couldn't see her. She wiggled her fingers at me, and grinned at me with a smirk.

"Lindy?" I barely mouthed, without speaking aloud. How could I truly believe my eyes. I'd gone crazy! Worse? The illusion nodded back at me – and wiggled her fingers, again!

"It's me, Cus-cus!" she mouthed back with the nickname she had for me.

I had no idea what to do. My mouth dropped in surprise and shock, but I managed to stop it before it got lower. I glared.

"You're dead!" I mouthed back at her.

She shook her head fiercely.

"I'll explain later. But, we have to get Noel away from him! He's one, sick mother fucker!"

Well, my sister was really alive! She was standing right there. That's when she grinned at me.

"Chant," she mouthed.

Well, I'll be damned! She was right! If she were real, then she would sing one, long, high-pitched note that was hers alone – one that had shattered even some rocks in our day. We had discovered she had one mean voice, when I was teaching her to defend herself! She had practiced that same note for a while, and perfected it to break blood vessels in one's eyes! She kept the person focused on the pain in their heads, while I pretended to take them out, rushing toward them head-on.

I nodded.

"Do it!" I mouthed.

Moments later, a low keening began, and it began to rise quickly. I was immune to the sound, but I knew it was working when even my own vampires slapped their hands over their ears. Curttis, though, was fighting it. He knew if he let Noel go, his leverage would change, so he fought it. I saw Lindy frown, and she went for the juggler as the note rose higher, until even Curttis could not take it any more. He dropped his hand from Noel's throat, and the knife fell to the floor, as he slapped his own hands over his ears, and Noel threw herself away from him. I could see her ears were beginning to bleed, and I knew I had only seconds, before Lindy burst everyone's eardrums. I watched Lindy walking toward me, and completely missed Curttis's final desperate move. He raised his hand with a gun, and I was willing to bet the bullets were silver. He fired.

"Noooo!!!!!!!!!!!!!" came a scream.

In a split second, Noel used her vampire speed, and threw herself in front of Lindy, her eyes widening in shock as she hit the concrete floor with a wumpf. Noel's movements were slow as she started to stand. Kneeling on one knee, and the other foot on the floor to stand, her eyes grew wide, and she looked down at her chest. A bright red stain of blood began to spread onto her dirty white shirt. As if in slow motion, she slowly looked into my eyes, and I saw hers glaze. Noel started to fall back down. I was at her side in seconds, and reached out to catch her. Lindy darted toward Curttis, and Caleb rushed to Curttis's other side. I dropped to my knees, cradling my mate in my arms. My dying mate.

"I-I…" she coughed hard, gushes of blood flowing from her mouth. "…l-love y-you."

Her whispered love sent me over the edge, and I looked to see that Caleb had seized Curttis in a death grip so tight, that he couldn't escape. He fought like a wildcat to get away. I motioned to Lindy and Ronnie, who was just rising to her feet after the ear-splitting sound of Lindy's voice. She saw her friend's chest covered in blood, and was horror stricken as she ran to my side in the blink of an eye. Ronnie reached us at about the same time.

"Take care of her," I whispered to Lindy and Ronnie.

"We will," Ronnie said, trying whatever she could to staunch the rapidly spreading blood across my mate's chest.

I didn't want to leave her, but as her mate, it was my right to destroy the one who had tried to take her life! I was in Curttis's face immediately. All he did was sneer at me. Caleb held him tightly.

"Oops! I guess I kind of missed, didn't I? I meant to hit you!" he laughed maniacally. "Nah! It's my great happiness to get to watch you fall apart, Damian! Taking the life of your mate, and my biggest enemy, is sweet revenge!"

That was when real terror gripped me. The bullet was silver. And, because Noel and I, now, exchanged blood, she was just as vulnerable to silver bullets as any of us! I looked back at Ronnie and Lindy who were both looking terror-struck as they realized what he had said. I turned back to Curttis, and motioned with my head for Caleb to leave. He did so without a moment's thought, and rushed over to where the other girls were. My eyes narrowed at Curttis to the point that I could feel the blood flood into the whites of my eyes, and my pupils, which were turning black as coal.

I heard Lindy tell me in her quiet voice to kill the bastard. I had Curttis in my grip, and I quickly twisted his arms behind his back, and leaned in to whisper in his ear.

"Run!"

That single word spurred Curttis into action, and he turned to run. His screams didn't faze me at all.

"I should have killed you when you turned me."

"You can't kill me! And, you know exactly why!"

"I do."

And, I did. Curttis was the one who changed me. He was the one who had threatened to kill my parents and my baby sister if I did not let him change me. I had no choice. Had he turned his sister?

"But, you know what? I don't care. Run!" I said to him again.

"I see your little sister made the transition well," he choked out the words, rubbing his throat. "Isn't that right, Salinda? Or, was it Lindy?"

Lindy turned to him, and was in his face in a second.

"You are no longer relevant, Curttis. My brother is going to tear your head off your shoulders, and then we are burning your stinking carcass!"

She was back by Noel's side just as fast as she had appeared next to Curttis.

"Well, you are right about that, dear sister. Only, I think I'm going to play with my food for a bit."

I kicked in his kneecap so that it bent backward. His scream was music to my ears. I couldn't wait to make him suffer!

"Now, I said, *RUN!*"

Curttis took off, and I followed. I heard someone scream, "NOOOOOO!" as I ran by South. I wanted to tell him I was sorry, but I had more important things on my mind.

~ NOEL ~

I saw Damian hesitate a moment as he looked to the side. He'd seen his sister! Then, a sound unlike anything I'd ever heard before, began low, like singing, but continued to rise higher and higher. My ears were hurting, and I could feel warm liquid run from them. Blood! It had to be. I'd heard of sounds that could burst an eardrum, but never had I ever experienced it. That's when I realized that I could no longer hear anything. I was fairly certain I had just been rendered permanently deaf.

I felt Curttis's hands drop from me, and I started toward a smiling Damian. At the same time, I saw Salinda walking toward Damian, and hear a shot. Without thinking, I ran to put myself between her and Drakow. I felt something hit me in the back, and it knocked me to the floor. I immediately stood, and made it to one knee, when I stopped and stared at Damian feeling my eyes widen. I slowly turned my head down to see what the warmth was coming from my chest. Blood. A lot of blood spreading throughout my shirt, and fast. I should have been scared, but surprisingly I wasn't. I almost felt...relieved. Then, I remembered, that I carried a precious life inside of me. If Salinda had not heard the tiny heartbeat, I would never have known. My baby would die with me. Strangely enough, though. I was at peace with it. But, my mate would never meet or know his child he wanted so much just as I would not know him or her. And, it made me sad. I hadn't even had time to tell him! I looked back up at him, and I felt my sight going as my eyes glazed. I stared into his beautiful face, and fell forward. Damian caught me, of course, but with the blood I was losing, I knew it was a lost cause. That was funny considering I was in a room of vampires, and I was shot by one of them! How cliché was it? I was tired. I closed my eyes as darkness took me from this life.

~ DAMIAN ~

I finally had broken every bone inside his pathetic body. And, now, it was time to remove his head. But, I was still feeling vengeful, so I reached out to grab the knife with which Curttis would have killed Noel, and slowly began to saw away at his neck. He screamed and gurgled, but I felt nothing, but pure, unadulterated hatred for him. Blood gushed from him onto me, and I wanted to bathe in it! I continued to saw very, very slowly, until I reached his spine, then I threw the knife down on the floor, and twisted his head off the rest of the way. I tossed it into the corner. We'd gather up what was left of him, and burn his body outside. I hadn't had time to look at Noel, since I had been lost in revenge, but now I looked over at her, and what I saw made my heart stop still. I ran to her quickly, and dropped to my knees. I reached out, and took Noel in my arms.

"She is dying, Damian." Ronnie shook her head with sadness.

I knew that none of them would ever attempt to turn her into what I was, unless there was no other choice. I knew they were right, but my heart was cautious that now she would want to share in my world wholly and completely. But, would she hate it?

218

Would she finally change her mind, and join me as a vampire?

And, then, Noel reached out her hand to me to say goodbye.

~ 24 ~

~ NOEL ~

What woke me was the warm, thick liquid flooding down my throat. It was a heavenly flavor! Wait just a doggone minute!   While I drank, I frantically searched my mind, which was rather fuzzy at the moment, but had a hard time pulling whatever was alluding me. I was obviously in and out of conscious, but I just couldn't quite stay awake. I remembered a pain in my chest that was unlike anything I had ever suffered in my life. I tried once again to open my eyes. This time, I succeeded, and it would seem I was in a room that was completely snow white and stainless steel. I blinked once, and saw a dim figure to my left. I had such a deep feeling for him, but I couldn't make a connection with who it was. Another figure was to my right. Female, I think. Someone I knew, but didn't know very well. I also smelled something coppery and iron. I liked it! It made my body feel…alive! More alive than I had ever been in my life! All my senses, except for my sight, seemed heightened, and it was as if I could actually feel light. I also felt as if I had no weight at all, which was really, really weird, but it felt great! I took a breath, and more scents assailed me from every direction. Now, all of it was combining and confusing the hell out of me! I couldn't take this! I craved the darkness, and I allowed myself to fall back into the blackness, that was my familiar friend.

~ DAMIAN ~

"How much longer?" I asked Salinda. I still couldn't believe that my sister was here.

"I estimate…oh…maybe about another two hours. That's the earliest timeline that I can give you. You know that most stay under for almost thirty-six hours, before they awaken. Noel is most unusual. In fact, I've never heard of anyone awaking and falling back to oblivion during the transition."

"Whose idea was it to give her your blood?" I asked.

"Mine," Ronnie said. South didn't break concentration.

My mouth dropped.

"Why?" I demanded, taking Noel's hand into mine. I was never going to let go.

Instead of Ronnie answering, South did.

"Because," he said, not looking at me. Again, I started to protest, but he shut me up in a second with his reason. He turned his head, his eyes meeting mine. "I am her biological Father. Who has a better right to bring her into our immortal lives, but the one who brought her into this world the first time? She may be your mate, Damian, but she is still my daughter in flesh and blood." He turned back to Noel, brushing a lock of hair from her sweating skin, a tear running down his face. "She should be my daughter in this life as well."

I studied South carefully. He had come with us to this fight, because he would not be left behind with his daughter in danger of being killed or worse. I had agreed, and he brought Landon with him. To tell the truth, if they had not come, I wouldn't have had the opportunity to kill Curttis. He and Landon, along with

Caleb, Sam, and Ronnie, had kept the minions busy while I killed him. Damn! I hated like hell to thank the man, but from this point forward, we would be allies and friends.

Silence fell around us, except for the light noise of Noel's sucking on South's wrist. I honestly couldn't find the words to protest his right. He was the man who brought her into this world and to me. He would bring her into our world, now, and again, bring her to me. Instead of being mad, I suddenly felt gratitude.

"Thank you, South. From this point forward, I welcome you to my house, and my Clan, if you will so have us."

South looked at me for a minute, as if judging if I meant it. He nodded, and crossed his hand to shake mine.

"I am most honored, Blood. As of this moment, all that I have is yours, and I offer my entire Clan to become part of yours. It will be an honor to be a part of my daughter's life and her family in this life."

With those words, the Clan of South was dissolved, and they became part of my Clan. He would be given a place of honor in my Clan, and become my advisor. I had never had one, before, even though most every clan had one. As for Landon…well, I guess I could make him my third. Despite the dislike I had for him taking Noel from me, I grudgingly admitted that having his skill as a warrior in my clan would be a huge boost. As it was, South's addition combined with mine would give us the largest clan in the world. Ronnie broke into my reverie.

"Does that mean that she'll remember it all, Salinda? The transition, I mean?" Ronnie asked in horror.

Excellent question, and one I would have asked if I hadn't been sidetracked.

"Since I've never heard of it before, your guess will be as good as mine."

"But, what is your best guess?" I asked.

She shrugged. "Knowing this one? I'd say she will."

That bothered me greatly. I hoped she was wrong. Noel had stopped feeding from her Father's wrist, and he pulled it away from her. She looked peaceful. I looked at him.

"I want her to awake in my arms, in our room."

South nodded.

I picked her up, and with vampire speed, we all sped back to my mansion.

"I shall be down here, if she should need me," South said, and went into the Living Room, followed by Landon.

Ronnie, Salinda, and Caleb followed me up the stairs into our bedroom. I laid Noel on the bed, then sat on the edge and looked at the others – specifically, Salinda.

"How?" I demanded of her. She knew exactly what I meant.

She flinched, then shrugged.

"I might as well tell you, because you never have been one to just let things go."

After brushing Noel's hair out of her face, I looked at her serene face, knowing she was suffering the fires inside of her. Her blonde, almost white hair was much longer, now. She was going to be a beauty – as if she already wasn't! I would hold her until her time to wake, but first, I turned back to my sister, and tilted my head, waiting for the explanation.

"There's not really all that much to tell. About two years after you disappeared, Curttis came to our house. Mom and Dad had passed this life six months before in a cart accident. You knew?" She saw me nod once, sadness taking over my face, remembering when I had found out that our parents were gone. "Anyway, I was by myself. Well, it might have been that I was truly afraid to be alone, if I even admit it. Curttis offered me the opportunity to have a long life, and I eagerly took it, ignorant of the consequences. I didn't relish spending the rest of my life alone." She had tears in her eyes. "After he turned me, I realized what monstrous act I had allowed to happen. He had a young boy, no more than fifteen, ready for me to feed upon when I awoke. When I sucked my first victim dry, and after the hunger within me was curbed, I dropped his body at my feet. I looked at myself. Every part of me was covered in an innocent's blood! I was dripping with it! I was horrified at what I had done, and vowed to never, again, feed on a human being." She looked at me, and a sense of pride made her stand taller. "To Curttis's disappointment, I never have! I was able to get away from him for a very long time. About ten years ago, though, he tracked me down. He tried starving me and punishing me in every way, including stabbing, burning, and raping me, but still, I refused to take blood from a human being...until I met Noel."

I knew, at that point, that my face showed a fanatical kind of anger, but before I even thought about lunging for her, she continued.

"Damian, when Noel was placed in the cage next to me, she saw how weak I had become. I hadn't fed in a very, very long time. In fact, I did not know how long it had been. You know how long it takes a vampire to die from starvation, and I was right at the end of my life, when she was thrown into the cage next to me. But, after speaking to Noel, discovering that I had a sister-in-law by being your mate, I found that her mind was very sharp, and she was very wise. When Ranken was going to rape and kill her, I was her only chance. But to help her, I needed to feed, and she understood. So, she offered her blood to me, Damian. I didn't want to feed on her. I hadn't bitten a human in so long, and I was absolutely determined not to do it again. However, I realized that she did have a point. I was terrified to do it, but she told me that if I was Damian's sister, that if he had been in a similar situation, he would feed from an offer of nourishment to help us escape our cages. So, I took it – this one time, and one time only – until now, of course. Damian, without Noel, I would not be here, and neither would she. I owe her my life; I owe her my loyalty; I owe her my protection. Even though South is, technically, her sire, I drained her, so she is part my child as well. As I said...I owe her. I will never let her be alone, but both of us are happy that you have found one another, and, of course, I also approve."

I turned up the left side of my lip, and gave her a mocking glare. She laughed, and suddenly, I joined her as well.

"Well, she will awaken soon. I can hear her heart beat slowing. Soon, it will not beat again, and she will wake. I'm kind of dreading her anger about all of this."

"Well, I wouldn't," Ronnie said. "She loves you. Besides, look at it this way. If she is angry, you'll have great make-up sex!"

"Yeah. What Ronnie said," Caleb repeated.

Salinda turned to him in disgust.

"You are a jackass, Caleb! Where did you find this coward, brother?"

"I beg your pardon!" Caleb snarled. "I am almost as strong as Damian, bitch! How dare you!"

"D-did you just call me a '*bitch*'?" Salinda said in shock.

I had to hide a smile, and saw Ronnie doing the same. Lindy was not a pushover, either as a human or apparently, as a vampire. But then, neither was Caleb. Might be a bit of fun to watch them butt heads! Only God knew how much they all needed a laugh, right now!

"I did, and my manners are not such that I would be prevented from saying it again!" Caleb smirked at her, watching anger rise in her face. God, she was beautiful! Her breasts heaving heavily from the air she sucked into her lungs. She was magnificent – and sexy as hell, Caleb was thinking, but he'd never let her know it! Fighting might just be way too much fun with her.

"Why you mother fucking, son-of-a...."

"Watch that gorgeous mouth of yours, Princess! Or I'll watch it for you!" Caleb warned, his true vampire self-beginning to show.

Salinda dropped her mouth, and for the first time in forever, she was speechless, and I almost hooted aloud, watching her! Instead, I looked at Noel, before I turned to the other three.

"That's enough out of all you. Take it downstairs or somewhere else. My mate won't need you hyenas around her when she wakes. I'm going to have enough problems trying to explain things to her. Now...get out!" I ordered.

All three waltzed toward the door. Caleb and Lindy tried to get through the door at the same time. Ronnie shuffled along behind them, giggling hard at Caleb and Salinda's antics. They were definitely mates, but just how long would it be before either of them realized it? Ronnie couldn't wait for the drama to unfold, and followed the angry, stomping Salinda, who had lost the door struggle in favor of Caleb! She shut the door behind her, leaving Damian with his vampire mate, waiting for her reaction when she awoke.

I chuckled at poor Caleb, because my sister would claim him for everything he had – and he would be powerless and hopelessly in love, before Lindy finished with him! Lucky bastard that he was, Lindy would have him tamed in no time, and he'd fall in line with her every wish! I sighed, then I gently stripped Noel to her skin to see the change. Oh! What a beauty she was in life, but as an immortal? She would be unparalleled! I stripped, and climbed into the bed with her to hold her tightly in my arms. Would she be able to adapt to this life – my life? After what happened with my wife, I had no idea, and all I could do was wait until she woke. I loved Noel. She was everything that I wasn't – good, kind, loving, caring, and above all, honest. I closed my eyes to wait on her awakening.

~ 25 ~

~ NOEL ~

I could hear things – really, really well! My senses were on overdrive. I could hear… conversations and footsteps and…Sam and Ronnie making love? OK. I really didn't need to hear that in any way! Caleb was arguing with…whose voice is that? Salinda! Salinda is Damian's sister! I listened to them for a few moments, and grinned. There was no doubt about it in my mind at all. The two of them were mates! They loved arguing, apparently, and that's how they showed their desire for each other. That would be good for both of them. Caleb was such a stickler for all the rules, and I knew, for a fact, that Salinda would break all the rules! She almost giggled, then stopped. What was going on? My skin felt like tiny ants crawling all over me, and yet, it was a pleasant feeling! I could smell something cooking in the kitchen – pot roast? Yes, that's what it was, and it smelled absolutely…revolting! So horrible, I almost gagged. That was one of my favorite meals! My mouth was watering; my throat scratchy and burning; my stomach was growling. I needed – something in it, but what? Soup? No. Lobster bisque? Ick! No freakin' way! Tomato soup? No, not that either. Dammit! I needed something red and thick and tangy with iron and…! And, then, I knew exactly what I wanted – needed! Blood! I need blood! Just the thought of it had me flipping my tongue out, and raking it across my lips with hunger. A shuffle. Someone was in the same room with me. I could smell him. Damian. My mate, my soul, my love.

My eyes flew open, and I saw that I was in our bedroom. Hmmm, I was comfortable. I needed to stretch, and in doing so, I was enjoying the coolness of the night. Yes. It was night, cold, and I was totally nude! A gentle breeze blew overhead – a fan spun gently overhead, raking its gentle air over my legs and arms. My breasts and nipples peaked into hard nubs. I slid my hands over them, and pinched them between my fingers, then spread my legs wide, allowing the decadent air to cool my pussy. Remembering Damian was in the room with me, my pussy flooded with juices. My womb clinched tightly, wanting his dick inside of me. The cool air was stroking my molten hot core, making me ripe with desire – lust. I wanted blood and sex, but not necessarily in that order! I turned my head to see Damian standing in the open window, the moon spotlighting his nude body and extremely erect cock, its outline showing it attached to his body, and extending up and out from his abdomen. My core clenched in desire. His eyes were closed, as he sniffed.

"I smell your arousal, mate," he said without opening them.

I answered him.

"I see your hard dick. Is it wanting something?" I commented, with the sound of need in my voice.

Without looking at me, he gripped his cock, pumping his hand up and down it, causing me to groan aloud in desire. Watching him masturbate was the biggest turn on ever! I began to stroke my nipples with one hand, while lowering my other one to my extremely wet pussy, where I spread my legs wide, and stroked my fingers between my lips, slipping one inside of me. I needed him in me, but the truth was, I also wanted to watch him pump himself, and above all, wanted to watch his seed shoot from his tip onto my breasts! I'd never been much of a voyeur, but at the moment, I wanted to be one! My pussy clenched tighter, and juices flooded from me onto the bed. I stopped stroking, stretched, and then bounded upon my knees, turning so that he could see my ass ready for him. I wiggled and grinned at him. Suddenly, I felt a hard, and much larger than I knew him to have, dick thrusting into my pussy with a force I had never felt. I wanted harder!

"More! Harder!" I cried out, yelling, "Please, Damian! Fuck me harder!"

"As you wish," he said, repeating my favorite romantic line from The Princess Bride. It always turned me on!

Damian slammed into my body harder than ever. I wanted harder, more, harder, and even harder. I had no idea how I could take him this hard, but I was desperate for his body inside of me!

"I'm coming!" I screamed at him, not caring that I was so loud, others in the house could easily hear me. I just didn't care. If he wanted to fuck me in front of everyone, I'd get naked and turn my ass up so everyone could see that he was mine, as he thrust in and out of me! Let them see him shoot his seed inside my body!

"Oh!" I screamed as I came, squeezing his cock so tight, I thought I might pinch it! But, all I could think of was feeling his cum fill my pussy and my womb!

~ DAMIAN ~

I knew the moment she was awake, and sniffed. Her pussy was ripe for me!

"I smell your arousal, mate," he said without opening them.

"And, I see your hard dick. Is it wanting something?"

I grasped my hard cock, pumping it. I turned slowly to see her hands stroking her nipple and pussy – two fingers were pushed inside her, and she was pumping them in and out of it! In seconds, she had bounded to her knees, whipped around, and stuck her ass in the air. She wiggled it, and I was on her in seconds, slamming into her as deep as I could! It didn't take long at all, when moments later, I felt my cum fill Noel's immortal body for the first time! But, I couldn't stop! I continued to thrust into her, until my dick was good and dry! Then, I pulled out of her, hearing her groan in protest. I pulled her to my chest, and lay down next to her.

"Easy, love," I told her. "You've been dead for just over thirty hours. You need to rest."

She looked up at me with a raised eyebrow. I just smirked at her.

"Oh, Damian…that was…that was…." She tried, desperately, to explain what she was feeling, but she just couldn't. "I want more, Damian! I want you to shoot it on my tits! I want to spread your semen all over me!"

Damn! My cock jumped, and I felt my balls fill once more with my seed at her words! Trying to keep the boy at bay, I needed to get her fed, before we continued – which we would. And, I would not leave her pussy, until we were finished – which would probably be never!

"I know. And, I will fill you all you want. But, first, you must feed. This night will be new for us both, and you must have nourishment to keep you ready for what I am going to do to you!" I told her, waggling my eyebrows.

I could see that only one word got through to her. And, that word was "feed".

~ NOEL ~

I was confused. Why would he use that particular word? Only vampires fed, and…. My eyes flew wide open, now, and I sat up so fast, it was as if I hadn't even moved at all. It startled Damian, who sat up next to her.

"F-feed?" I asked him. Then, I remembered. I realized that my night vision was so good, I could easily see without any type of light whatsoever. My hands went to my chest, as I tried to feel where the hole should have been. I'd been shot!

"Stop, Noel! Please!"

He didn't want me to be upset about this, but he knew better.

"I-I was s-shot! I know I was!" I turned to Damian, my eyes wide with terror. "Why am I not shot? Why is my skin as if it were never hurt?"

I suspected that I already knew the reason, but I was having a hard time realizing it. I shook my head, and looked at Damian with horror.

"I-I am one of you, now?" My hand went to my abdomen! My child! Their child! The secret that I had been hiding from everyone, waiting for the perfect time to tell Damian!

"Yes, my love. Lindy and Ronnie knew that the only way to keep you alive was to change you. You were dying. I was killing Curttis, and didn't know what they had done, until I returned for you. I'm sorry. I really didn't want this to happen. It's going to be a bit different for a while, but you will get use to it, my love. Trust me, I...."

"Don't lie to me, Damian! You did want me to become a vampire! You did!"

He looked at her sheepishly.

"OK. True, but I didn't want it to be like this. I wanted it to be your choice," he told me, and pulled me to him.

For minutes on end, I felt terrified, and worried, until I finally was able to tell him.

"Oh, my God! No! Damian! Y-you don't understand," I sounded panicky.

"What?"

"Our baby, Damian! I am pregnant!" I shouted at him.

If I had told him that he had become human again, I obviously couldn't have surprised him more! Then, his eyes went wide with the same terror. His hand reached mine, and placed it over my hand that was on my stomach.

"Are...are you sure?"

I nodded, tears starting to fall.

"Lindy heard the heartbeat!" I looked up at him. "I-I was going to tell you that evening. Damian...what about our baby? Am I really...a...a...vampire, now?"

Anger filled him with dread. "Lindy knew!!!!!!??"

"Yes. She's the one who told me!"

"She drained you, Noel! Drained you dry!"

"W-what? D-did she not tell you?"

"No, she did not!" I raged. "Noel, you and the baby would have died anyway, though."

I knew that. I did. But, still I felt horribly sad. I turned to look at him, and the sadness on his face was echoed in mine.

"It was obviously either you were turned or you both would die."

I nodded. Acceptance wasn't in my nature, but I knew that it would come at some point. Right now, though, I needed something else.

"I need blood!"

I started to shake all over, and my eyes shot next to the bed as he pointed. At least six bags of blood lay there waiting for me. My hunger overcame everything else at the moment, even the fact that I was no longer pregnant. I turned to him, and he nodded. I reached for the first bag of blood, feeling my fangs lower, and pierced the first bag. I sucked fast and furiously, taking only seconds to drain it. I gave it to Damian, who threw it into a trashcan, grabbing the next one. By the time I had reached my fifth bag of blood, I was feeling sort of sloshy. I was a fool, but still I wanted more.

"Why do I want more when I'm so full?"

"Because you are new and young. You will need the equivalent of a human being a week for the next year. It will then begin to drop off."

"But, Damian. I'm not saying how much. I'm saying I need more! Much, much more! But, I don't know why?"

An idea, albeit a "making me nervous sort of idea, popped into his head. He pushed me back on the bed, then leaned his ear to my belly.

"Damian?" she asked. "What is it?"

~ DAMIAN ~

In total and complete shock, I heard the blood sloshing a little bit inside of my mate. I also heard a tiny heartbeat! Did I really hear it? I listened carefully. There it was again! A tiny heart beating very slowly – like the end of a human's life. But, it was steady, not dwindling, or getting fainter. No. Instead, it was very, very slow, but getting stronger. Noel's change had not hurt their child! I became aware of Noel pushing me.

"Damian! What are you doing?"

Tears ran down her cheeks at the thought of the loss of the tiny little life. She tried to push me off her stomach, but I refused to budge.

"Damian!" she tried again.

I looked up at her, and shock hit her, as she saw tears in my eyes.

"Damian?"

I pushed her back, and crawled between her legs, nudging my hard cock at her opening.

"He's alive, Noel!"

"What?" she asked, puzzled.

"Our baby!" I placed my lips on her belly, and kissed it. "He's alive. I can hear his heartbeat!"

Noel's mouth dropped in surprise. Her tears dried up as she saw wonderment invade my eyes.

"W-what? H-how? A-are you sure?" she stuttered, not ready to believe. "How did he survive my change?"

"I don't know." I shook my head in a state of shock. "I don't know. But, he did."

"Or...it could be a she, you know," Noel reminded me with a smile like the sun.

I jerked! A girl? A *girl*? Who looked just like her Mother?

"Oh, fuck!" I said, frowning.

"What, Damian? What is it?"

"I'm going to have to kill an awful lot of boys and men in the future, aren't I?"

Noel threw her head back, and laughed uproariously. I just glared at her with a look of annoyance, which just made her laugh harder.

"Poor Daddy! And, no, you won't! She will have a mind of her own, and we will treat her as such. But, if some poor idiot does decide to...."

"Do *NOT* finish that sentence, Noel!" I demanded, only getting another snicker from my snarky mate.

Noel placed her hands over mine, and stared at her flat stomach. Her eyes beamed up at me. Then, she realized that she was hungry. She reached for the last bag of blood, and I let her sit to eat. After she finished, she wiped her mouth.

"Is that why I'm so hungry?"

I smiled, and nodded.

"It must be. Perhaps it's no different than a human mother who has a life growing inside of her. She needs to eat a lot, too!"

Noel slapped my arm in jest, and I just smirked.

"Are you saying I'm going to get fat?"

"No. I'm saying that I will have to keep you well supplied with plenty of blood for the next – hummmm. I wonder if there is precedence for a pregnant human turned vampire with a bun in the oven?" I grinned.

Her eyes widened, then narrowed as she looked at me.

"But no humans, right? If Salinda can do it, so can I!"

I laughed outright.

"No. No humans. Just donors. A lot of them. Good thing we have many."

"Funny. Now, mate...come fuck me again!" she demanded. "It's apparent that I'm going to need lots and lots of sex during my pregnancy!"

I had no problem with that at all, and plunged back into her warm, welcoming heat!

~ Epilogue ~

~ 10 Years Later ~

~ DAMIAN ~

I sat down heavily, and leaned back in my distressed, brown leather, wingback chair – something I refused to let my mate and wife get rid of when she went on a decorating spree a couple of years ago. I need it, because it's a comfort to me. Noel always said that she understood after I explained, and had patted my back with sympathy. It wasn't the chair as it is, now, but what it was long ago in a time when I had just been changed by my sire. It wasn't so much a need as a want and was the one place I retreated when he was on the warpath. For some reason, it gave me comfort even today. It had been recovered numerous times over the years, and Noel had surprised me with a new recover for my last birthday.

God! I loved that woman! Staring into the fire that Noel insisted be blazing every night in the winter, even though we no longer needed it, the evening was quiet. Everyone had gone into the city for the New Year's Eve fireworks display that Caleb and Lindy had sponsored over the last five years. I just let my mind wander around on its own.

It was a comfort that my sister was in my clan, now. The two of them were explosive! They fought at every turn, and yet, neither saw another person of the opposite sex, since meeting the night Curttis was destroyed, when I had almost lost Noel to his damn bullet! Thanks to South, though, she was now my mate in both life and in un-life. It was actually fitting that South, being Noel's biological Father would also become her Father in this life as well. But, right now, I wanted to kill the bastard! If Landon hadn't been in his clan when I added them, none of this would have ever happened! Dammit!

After Noel's amazing success with the magazine that covered her Christmas Decorations, she had more clients than even she could ever have imagined. She had received the highest awards possible, and our house was always the number one destination for tourists during Christmas. I chuckled. Noel wouldn't let anyone call us the "undead" any longer, and demanded I change the laws as such. That was something I refused to do, and all she did was giggle at me.

"Hmmpf! So much for being on the DL," I muttered quietly.

This day had been full of surprises, but the biggest?

"Landon. Did it just have to be *Landon*?" I angrily muttered.

Arms snaked around my neck from behind, followed by long, blood red nails. I had known Noel came into the room, of course, and my dick responded accordingly. It always did when I was around her.

"Now, come on, Damian. Holly and Landon were mates from the moment they met, and you know it. Thank you for giving them a mating party! He'll protect her with his life." Noel said to me. She started laughing. You heard what she said?"

I nodded, and wrinkled my nose. But, did Noel just have to repeat it? It was so corny!

"I think she was hilarious when she asked everyone, 'My Christmas Present...has WHAT'?"

Noel bent over in laughter, and then squealed when I pulled her onto my lap. I put my hand on her arm, and lazily stroked it, while I chuckled. It was funny. It was truly a strange world, now. Since our daughter, Holly Marie Blood, was born, she had progressed at a rapid growth, and was already the equivalent of a twenty-two year-old woman. Only time would tell her true longevity. But, there had been another oddity as well. She was brilliant. A lot more than anyone we knew. We pretended to send her to a private boarding school in the Alps, but secretly, we kept her at the mansion, and we all taught her. Because she was obviously fully matured by that time, we had placed her in a local high school for her last year. But, she had been so smart, the faculty had decided that she needed to proceed on to college, and as a fourth year student, although most said that she was beyond that stage.

Landon made me really, really angry when he had first laid eyes on her at the age of two months, she had smiled back at him, and I had groaned. I didn't want to believe it. The last man I wanted around my daughter was Landon. He was a player! And, now, they were mated, and off on a mating honeymoon! I wanted to gag.

"Now, what's on the DL, Damian?" Noel purred, her voice soft and seductive.

"Oh, Holly. I was just thinking back to when she was born."

My hand automatically began to caress her breast. So, sue me! Her breasts were luscious, and it took everything I had most of the time not to reach for them, even in public! Right now, she was rolling her eyes at me.

"Ah yes! Remember when I had just sat down on your lap, and my water broke?" Noel laughed aloud.

"How can I forget that?" I asked with a guffaw. "I had just wondered why your pussy had given up so much wetness, before you said, 'My water just broke!'"

Noel smirked.

~ NOEL ~

I decided to finish the story, since both of us knew it so well. Damn vampire faultless memory!

"I remember you saying, 'OK'. Then, you asked, 'Your what just broke?' And, I told you the baby was coming!"

"Oh, I remember, Noel. What puzzled me at the time was why you had any pain at all. You were a vampire at that point."

"I'm just so glad you panicked, because I didn't think it was fair that I was the only one." I said, and my mind drifted off to that day. "And, you called Dr. Marnart, who didn't arrive until after all the hard work was done."

"Yep. Typical," Damian laughed, and I joined him.

I was pregnant only three months, and I was big. I knew, somehow, that our child was coming soon. I had sat on his lap one night, when we had a rare moment alone, wrapping my arms around him, and thinking about how much my life, or lack thereof, had changed over the previous five months. I had met Damian through my best friend, Ronnie, discovered that they were vampires, Ronnie mated Sam, her long-time boyfriend and bonded human, became Damian's bonded human to save my life, had massive amounts of the most amazing sex ever, found that my Dad was his nemesis, who had been turned into a vampire after a car crash when I was two, who kidnapped me, sent me back to Damian, they became friends, found out I was pregnant, but before I could say anything, I was kidnapped by the nefarious Curttis, placed in a cage in a dirty basement, met Damian's sister, Salinda, let her feed from me to make her strong so we could escape, escaped only to be shot in the chest, turned into a vampire, Curttis was killed, (I had been sexually active almost constantly for those three months of pregnncy), our baby was not hurt by my turn, had her with some pain no one could ever explain, and finally, I won numerous awards for my Christmas decorations. Now, though, I had one more Christmas surprise for Damian.

Whew! That's a lot to think all at once! Anyway, back to the story. I had just leaned over to give Damian a mind-blowing kiss, because I was going to suggest I give him a blowjob, when I felt something pop inside of me. My hands gripped my abdomen as I experienced some pain. I felt warmth – a lot of it – flow from me, and I knew that there was no way that was anything but my water. And, of all the stupid times for it to happen? On my mate's lap! His wingback was totally ruined in that moment, which is why it was moved into the garage until we could recover it. It took quite a while to get around to doing it, since I had it recovered on his last birthday as a present.   But, the truth was, time wasn't at all important to a vampire. It was more of a human idea, after all, but even I realized how insignificant it was.

If only humans would just eliminate time, so much would be better!

"I can't reach Marnart, damn it!" Damian roared, throwing his phone against the wall.

"Damian! That's another phone you busted! What are we going to do?" I gasped with each pant.

"We do what we must," he had said as he scooped me up, and dashed to our bed.

"But the blood?" I whined.

Damian had looked at me like I had a monkey coming out of my butt, instead of beautiful little girl.

"Uh...blood? Noel, I don't think blood is going to bother either of us."

"Oh! Right! Forgot...vampire!" I yelled in pain at that point.

"But, you may need additional blood. I'll be right back."

Before I realized he was gone, Damian was back with loads of blood. I smirked through a particularly hard contraction.

"What took you so long?" I gasped.

Damian looked at me, and couldn't help laughing through my pain. It was really funny, now. Then? Not so much.

"I love you, Noel. I'm going to have to deliver our baby."

"I love you, too, Damian! The final pain struck, and I had to push. As I did, I screamed at him. "But, Dammit! If you ever touch me with that dick of yours again, I'll cut it off! AHHHHHHHHHHH!!!!!!!!!!!"

Of course, I was being overly dramatic at the time. I'd had his cock every which way since then, but at the time, I really meant it.

"Ah! Remembering when you threatened to cut off my dick?" he guessed what the look on my face meant, and snickered.

"Yep." I laughed as he pulled my lips to his.

But, what really was making me smile was remembering the sight of my mate holding his tiny little daughter after she was born that had melted my cold, dead heart. It made it even cuter when he said, "Hey, Noel! Look! She has tiny little fangs!"

He had handed her to me, and I looked at the beautiful face staring back at me. Sure enough, she grinned at me, and there they were! Teeny, tiny little fangs! They had been so cute!

"I have a little surprise for you, Damian," I whispered into his ear, as I came back to the present.

Everything else was forgotten in the wake of the desire I constantly felt from him, when he nibbled down my neck and between my breasts.

"Ummmmhmmmm?" he muttered. "I'm busy."

"I don't know how it happened, but I'm pregnant," I said, pulling away from him to look into his eye.

As realization hit him, I smirked, nodded, and shrugged.

"How?" he stammered.

"Well, let me explain those little birdies and bees. You see, when a girl and a boy love each other, and they are vampires, they go at each other like the energizer bunny." I giggled at his facial expression. "I don't really know how. But, it happened. Oh. And, one more thing?"

"I'm afraid to ask," Damian groaned.

"So are Ronnie and Lindy."

"What? All three of you?" Damian choked out the words. "At the same time??"

"Of course! Rebecca was right, Damian. She told you what would happen. She really was an oracle!"

We heard the other girls squealing and laughing in the entryway. Holly and Landon would be back on Christmas Eve for the huge party the Blood's always threw for their employees every year for the last ten years. And, they had Noel to thank for it.

Damian was stunned, and moments later, two male, shocked vampires, strolled into the living room, leaving the girls to their own devises. Sam and Caleb looked as if a hummer had rolled over them. I would almost laugh, if all three of them weren't in the same boat.

"You, too?" Caleb stuttered, asking Damian.

Damian nodded.

"I need a drink – a double!" said Sam.

"Yep," Damian declared.

Then, Damian looked at me as I entered the doorway, heading out with the girls. Next year, we'd have lots of children around us, just as Rebecca had predicted. Right then, if we had another girl, I wanted to call her Rebecca in honor of a very brave young woman. It warmed my heart, and gave me a very happy feeling. But, with that smile of complete happiness and love directed my way, I truly counted myself as the luckiest woman – dead or alive – in the world!

LK Kelley
the
ANAERRIS CODE

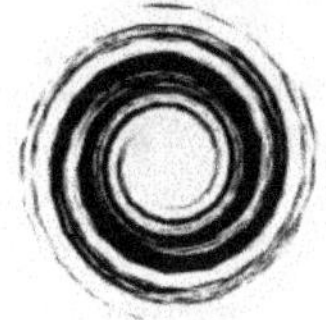

a Gemma Sinclaris Series

Jaxx
Part 2

By LK Kelley

~ Monologue ~

(Scene opens: Gem stands in front of a packed audience sitting in the cosmos)

Gem: "Thank you, everyone! Thank you for being here! I want to welcome you all here, and I'm so happy you will be front and center for my strange life!

So, are you ready?"

(Cue: Lots of applause and cheering)

"Alright, then! So, to bring you all up to date so far, you will remember that my life was boring, basically. I was a writer, and my publisher wanted me to write a supernatural book that had to do with vampires.

Next, these really strange storms happened, and I was drawn into a situation with Professor Jaxxon Hawkins, who, strangely enough, turns out to be one of the Fallen angels, who comes from a place called Onaerris. It's a moon somewhere in the cosmos out there."

(Cue Gem: Points to the heavens)

"Yep. That's right! Outer space, no less! From there, I discover that I am some sort of universal super being with massive powers (still waiting for all those), who is supposed to save my Mom's home moon, Anaerris, my Dad's home moon, Onaerris, another moon called Domaerra, Earth…and, oh! By the way! I'm supposed to save the whole damn universe, too! No pressure! Anyway, I also find out my bestie,

Taylor, is also one of the fallen, and Stan, the local car restorer. Both are married to Richard and Stacy, and together the six of us are trying to figure out what we are supposed to do.

To date, I have been chased by storms caused by the bad guy and girl, Eloran and Delinear, been put in a volcanic prison, somewhere in the cosmos, broken out of it, and jumped off an 8000 foot cliff only to find out my first power was the ability to create a Vorc'ara – or, I guess the best way to describe it is a stable wormhole of sorts. I also discovered a book in the library where I work that has the secrets that I will need, along with my mate, to save everyone, as well as my little pug, Lola, who turns out to be a Fae in disguise who has whisked Taylor and Rick's kids to safety in another realm, while Jaxx and I used the book, and the last thing I remember is a brilliant white light after it took me over, then blew up the cabin we were staying in. At least my friends are all OK! Well, I hope they are, anyway. And, why is it the cosmos keeps wanting to dump me in worlds with volcanoes? My mate is missing, and I am missing him terribly!"

(Cue: Commercial)

"What? Oh! Right! Well, gang, I'm being told that it's time for a commercial…have you ever wanted to eat when you are not hungry? Well, you have to try the most delicious nut bar I have ever tasted. And, you all know the name of my favorite life bar, right? So, what's it called?"

(Cue: Audience yelling followed by cheering)

"Nuttier than a Fruitcake by the Great Cosmos Nut Company!"

(Cue: Gem. She stands, grabs a bar from above her in the midst of the nighttime stars, and chomps down!)

Gem: That's right!

(Cue: The crowd of Lolas barked in a standing ovation!)

Gem rolls eyes: Could this get any more ridiculous? No. I really don't think so!

~ 1 ~

Waking up is Hard to Do! ~ Jaxx

Jaxxon Hawkins felt lethargic and extremely tired as he woke. But, he was sure that was only temporary. Well, until a terrible cold invaded his body. Somewhere, he wondered why being cold could happen to him? He never felt the elements like this! His mind began to wonder as he fell in and out of consciousness. Why? And, were those voices he was hearing? He slowly drifted as if his soul drifted on the wind.

"What do you think, Doctor?" a man asked. His voice was strangely familiar, and Jaxx struggled to figure out where he had heard it.

"I.Caaanot.Sssay.Myyy.Looord." a strange voice answered. It was guttural, raspy, and the sentences short and clipped with a voice hissed much like a snake.

"But, he will get better, right?" asked a soft voice, and while not as familiar, Jaxx thought he recognized it somewhere in the back of his mind.

"Yooour.Booodies.Arrre.Nooot.Suuuited.Tooo.T hisss.Cliiima..."

A strangled yelp ensued. It reminded him of a stuck pig!

"I am not interested in your opinions, Doctor! Only facts! Now...I ask you one more time. Will Jaxx make it?"

"Heee.Isss.Onaeeeris. Heee.Wiiil.Myyy.Looord!" the voice squeaked.

"Good!" the familiar voice said. Jaxx heard a thud, and then, the voice ordered, "Now, get out!"

Jaxx heard a door slam shut, and that soft voice spoke once again. Obviously female, he thought.

"Please, my love! It's not his fault that Jaxx is this way! Weren't you just a bit too aggressive?"

"Too aggressive? Hell! I wasn't aggressive enough with that sleazy son of a bitch! He would just as soon as killed Jaxx as look at him! I'm Onaerris, but I am not some fucking moron!"

"Well, perhaps you were right, when you put it that way. His kind has always made me shudder with disgust! I mean…a serpent? Really?"

"It's too bad we had to bring that son-of-a-sleaze bag to a place of such gentle creatures!"

"I agree. But the sweeties don't know the first thing about humanoid bodies, and unfortunately, that left Doctor Hsss! He's been imprisoned here for eons, and this is part of his sentence for trying to kill them. You and I both know that the gentle creatures are not always all that gentle!"

"Yeah. I know it; you know it," he snickered. "And, luckily Hsss does, too! He's absolutely terrified of them!"

Where the fuck had he heard that voice before, Jaxx wondered? He struggled to think about it. Ah, hell! He needed to open his eyes – now! They flew open, and immediately beheld his – brother? And, next to him was … Analyse! He tried to speak.

"J-Jolinaer?" he could barely get the name out of his mouth. His mouth was dry, and miserable.

"Jaxxon!" Jolinaer exclaimed. The bed shifted under the weight of Jolin as he sat.

He clasped Jaxx's arm, while Jaxx did as well, but his arm was weak.

"Jaxxon. It is good to see you, again, my brother!"

All Jaxx could do at the moment was to nod in acceptance. Then, Analyse stepped forward.

"How did you get here? We saw a bright light, and chased it down. We found you completely knocked unconscious!"

That brought Jaxx out of his momentary stupor of surprise, and he sprang up from the bed onto his feet in one, fluid movement. He grabbed Jolin's tight, black t-shirt to keep from falling, while Jaxx grabbed his brother's shoulder to keep him from falling.

"Where is she?" he demanded.

Jolin looked at Analyse with a very puzzled expression. She looked back at him, just as puzzled. Jolin looked at Jaxx, again.

"Who, Jaxx? There was no one with you," he said quietly, tolerantly. Maybe Jaxx had hit his head? He was certain that he didn't know what he was saying.

Jaxx huffed, and pushed Jolin so hard, he stumbled, but didn't fall. He stared at Jaxx in shock. It was as if he was fixated on something – or someone.

Analyse stepped forward, and placed her hand on his shoulder. He jerked around, and caught himself just before he grabbed her by the neck. He was angry. He had to find Gem! He wouldn't stop until he did.

"What do you mean, who? Gem! Who do you think I'm talking about?" As their faces continued to frown in puzzlement, he continued. "GEMMA! You know? Your DAUGHTER?"

Jaxx was yelling, and he knew he sounded like a maniac, but Gem was his life! His mate! He wouldn't rest until he found her. Analyse's eyes opened wide with horror, and she started to collapse. Jolinaer stopped her from falling. She looked up at him, pink tears in her eyes.

"Oh, Jolinaer!"

Jolinaer turned to look at the stricken face of his brother. The shock of finding him on Domaerra was almost too much for him, but Jaxx hadn't even questioned where they had been all these years! But, even that seemed pale by comparison. If his daughter was missing, then why was she missing. But, Jaxx was losing it, and he didn't know why. And, he needed answers.

"Jaxxon! Stop it! Calm down, brother!" Jolin ordered, raising his voice.

Jaxx frowned, and looked at Jolin. Was he kidding? His mate was nowhere to be found, and Jolin had the audacity to tell him to calm down? Over his immortal dead body, he'd calm down! But, before he could speak, Jolin had him in a headlock. He couldn't move. Damn! Jolin had always managed to immobilize him with this trick! He could never break out of it! A loud growl escaped from his throat.

"That is enough, Jaxxon!" Jolin looked at Analyse who had slipped to the floor anyway. She was sobbing silently. Watching her broken almost killed his heart! They had left to keep her safe, and now, it would seem, she was missing. He stopped a moment. "Hold it, Jaxx. Exactly how did you meet Gem, Jaxx?"

Jaxx looked up in surprise. The question shook him out of his fixation.

"Jolin? What the fucking hell, Jolin! Why are you on Domaerra? Why is she on Domaerra? Where the fuck have you two been all this time?" Without breaking his stream of questions, he continued in one breath. "I can't believe that you are showing up, now, of all times! How did you get here? Why did you leave Gem in the Fae realm until she was taken to Earth as a baby? Why did you let them give her human DNA? Eloran and Delinear are after all of us. Imaerra kidnapped her, too her to some volcanic realm in an alternate dimension, and luckily, she was able to open a Vorc'ara, and she didn't even know she did! Why are you here? What is the matter with both of you? Why won't you answer me! Did you hear what I said? *She is MISSING!*"

Jolin and Analyse dropped their mouths at his flood of questions. A thought came to Analyse.

"Jaxx. Answer us! How did you meet Gemma?"

Jaxx was breathing hard. Oh, sure, he didn't need to, but right now, it almost felt good. At least it kept him from making the mistake of his life – that being killing someone! He looked back and forth between them, breathed deeply, and finally calmed down a little bit.

"Holy shit! It really is you!" he gasped in surprise. "Where am I?"

Jolin finally was able to approach Jaxx.

"Yes. It really is me, Brother!" he said, and the two brothers embraced each other.

"You are on Domaerra. How did you get here?" Analyse asked him.

Jaxx backed up from Jolin to stare at Analyse. She looked just the same as she did when he saw her thousands of years ago! And she was still beautiful, but not quite as beautiful as her daughter. Gem was the most beautiful woman he had ever seen in all of his existence!

"Is it true? You really know our daughter?" Analyse asked, grabbing Jolin's hand.

Sighing, he replied.

"Oh, I know her, alright. She has a lot of protection – at least she had it until that damn book of yours got in our way! Not only do I know her, but…," he paused for effect. He wasn't really sure how they would act when he told them the truth. OK. So. He was actually feeling like a coward!

"Yes?" she asked him. "Please, Jaxx! Tell us how you met her?"

'…she is mated!"

Both Jolin and Analyse gasped aloud.

"M-mated? To Jaxx? I can't believe it!" she asked.

"Yes. Jaxx. We never expected to find out she was already mated at such a young age!"

Jaxx looked at them as if they were from another universe!

"Young age? Gem is twenty-two years old!" he answered.

"Well, technically, she would be about ten thousand and twenty-two years old," Jolin said calmly, looking off into space as if he was thinking about it.

Analyse turned around, and stared at him as if she had never seen him before. He turned, and saw her stare. Grinning, he laughed.

"What? OK, my love," he said, drawing her to him. "You know it's true!"

"I don't care if it's true! She's our little girl, and I want to know who the hell she is mated to, and when it happened!"

Analyse whirled on Jaxx, and grabbed him by the throat, lifting him into the air.

"I'm not going to ask you, again, Jaxx! Tell me who is she mated to?"

Looking down at her, she wasn't really hurting him. He looked at Jolin, then Analyse, then Jolin, and last, Analyse, again. His mouth turned up in an extremely evil, and slow grin.

"I thought you two understood?"

"What? What should we understand?" Jolin asked.

"OK. So, who, Jaxx! I'll snap your neck like a twig if you don't answer me right now!" Analyse demanded.

Grinning even wider, as Jaxx suddenly heard what he needed to hear so desperately, and answered with one word.

"Me!"

◎

Meanwhile, Gemma was in real trouble…

◎

Gemma screamed when she saw the dark figures approaching her. One of them grabbed her, and slapped his hand over her mouth, dragging her behind a large rock. She growled behind the hand, until he growled back at her.

"Shhh! Are you trying to get us all killed?" the man said to her.

That answer silenced her faster than anything else could have. Killed? How could she get them killed? She had no idea where the hell she was! All she knew was she groaned, because, once again, she was standing in the middle of a volcanic world! Why the hell was she constantly getting put into this kind of situation?

She saw him motion to some others to get down behind some other rocks close by them, and they scattered fast. When she got out of this – for the alternative was not acceptable – she was going to kill something … or someone!

"Are you going to be quiet?" the man asked her without moving his hand from her mouth.

She looked up, but the steam and clouds were so heavy, he was just a figure in the mist. She could see him in a general outline, but that was about it. She took a deep breath, and decided she could trust him – at least for the moment, and she nodded. Gem knew she couldn't see him, but she could see his head nod up and down, and his dirty hand released her. She took a deep breath, but kept it silent. Then, Gem heard voices.

"O-over there! That's w-where I s-saw that l-light, m-my Lord!" a voice stuttered.

"You're sure about that, Navoer? You had better not be lying to me!"

She heard a sound as if someone was being slapped. For a moment, she almost felt sorry for the guy, then she realized that they had to be looking for her! Gem threw her own hands over her mouth to keep her from screaming.

"I-I p-promise I am n-not, m-my L-lord!" he answered with a sniff.

Was he bleeding? Shaking her head, why should she even care in the first place? She needed to keep quiet, and pressed her hands tighter to her mouth.

"I also saw the light, my Lord," another stronger voice told him.

"What was it?" the leader asked.

"I have no idea, but I do know that the light was brighter than a supernova! I have never seen anything like it before! Whatever it was, I also saw someone being thrown out of it! Because of the mist, I couldn't tell you who or what it was, but I do know that fact for sure!"

"Look around, and miss nothing! I am returning to the Citadel to report to the Mistress," he said. "But, be warned! Do NOT come back empty handed, because if you do, you will be thrown into the Lake of Fire! Do you understand me?"

Gem didn't hear an answer, but she was quite sure that they were nodding in fear. Who was the Mistress, she wondered. And, where the fuck was she? Maybe she needed to find that out, first!

"We cannot let anyone know that Onaerra is still occupied! It would ruin our plans to take Earth! And, the Mistress would kill me – and anyone else! So, remember that, because it means you!"

Gem's head popped up! Mistress? Onaerra? Take over Earth? She was on Onaerra! Why did the book send her here, and where the hell was Jaxx? Silent tears began to slowly stream down her face. Shit! Jaxx … where are you? The sound of many footsteps started moving. The sound of them lessened, and she realized that some of them were moving away from them. She almost sighed aloud, when she heard more voice.

"OK! Look everywhere, and don't leave one stone unturned! Our lives depend on us finding the being that was thrown out of that light! Do you hear me! Find it!"

Gem's stomach became tighter in terror when he heard many footsteps moving quickly. She knew that they were looking for her! But, being terrified would get her nowhere! She had to calm down! It would do her no good, and she knew it!

She heard a slight noise, and turned to see the person who had dragged her behind this stupid rock, saving her life, move his hand in a military style. A couple of figures a few feet away, moved quickly away from the rest of them. They took off at a run, and most of the other figures took off running after them. The figure behind her moved, and she heard an almost sickening sound of bones crunching. Knowing it would only incapacitate for only a few minutes, she started to stand, and the figure grabbed her arm, leading her in the opposite direction of where the others had run. She followed him without hesitating.

The air was stifling! Breathing hard, she could feel the heat bearing down on her with the extra exertion, when the figure admonished her.

"Stop breathing! You don't need to, and it will help you in the heat!"

Stunned, she realized that he was quite correct. She had forgotten that she did not need to breathe! The moment she did, she realized that it did help with the heat! Seconds of running turned into minutes, minutes turned into hours as they ran. Yet, surprisingly, she never felt tired! Whatever was happening to her, she knew she was evolving into something. But, what? And, all that paled, because she wanted Jaxx!

Finally, the silent runners stopped at a mountain – that wasn't running with lava! He placed his hand on the rock, and it turned to living lava, followed by his entire body! The area began to shimmer. In seconds, it was gone, and an opening appeared. She was pushed toward it. The moment she stepped into the opening, she was hit with a massive blast of icy cold air! She stopped suddenly, enjoying it, but it didn't last! She was pushed from behind.

"Go!" he ordered. "Don't stop!"

She ran, until she came to a huge room, and came to a halt, surprise on her face. It was massive! It kind of reminded her of the entrance to the Ministry in Harry Potter, but even a bit darker with torches scattered here and there.

"Over here," the man told her.

She followed.

"Is this really Onaerra, or did I just imagine I heard that?" she finally had the voice to demand.

"Please sit down, before you fall down, Gem," the man told her.

Surprise gripped her as tightly as his hand gripped her wrist, when the man said her name!

"How do you know who I … ?" she began, when the man turned around, and she gasped as he turned, and smiled at her. Then, "Mr. Simmons? I-is that you? B-but, h-how … ?"

How could Simmons be here? He was Onaerris? How in the hell was everyone around her fallen angels, and she never knew it?

"Shhh!" he shushed her. "The men here are the only ones I can trust! And, I do not need you giving us away!"

He looked nervously around. Satisfied, he took a deep breath, and using gestures that she guessed came from something like black ops, they scattered into the shadows of the room. He turned back to her.

"We don't have much time, Gem. The one who was looking for you has gone back to the Citadel, but he could still send his minions back here.

"Now, what?" she asked. "And, how in the hell did you get here, anyway?"

"That's not important right now. What is important is that we need to hide you. Where is Jaxxon?" he asked her.

"Jaxx?" she repeated, as if she was stupid.

"Yes. You know? Your mate?" His voice sounded contemptuous.

"Uh…" she started.

"Is he here, Gem? You have to tell me! These bastards don't fool around. This is a totally different world than he left! And, ruled by something that is just … indescribable. He needs to get you out of here! I don't know how you arrived on Onaerra, but you have to leave!"

"I can't leave," she gritted through clenched teeth.

He looked at her as if she had horns growing from her head.

"Vorc'ara?" he reminded her.

"Ooooh! Right! I wonder why I didn't think of it?" she said in a small voice. Of course, she didn't think of it. She just wasn't used to being able to open a vortex to the Creator knows where!

"Get the fuck out of he…," Simmons began, but hearing a squish coming down the hallway. "Oh, hell! How am I going to hide you?"

Simmons turned, and his head darted everywhere. Where was she? Gem was nowhere to be seen. Maybe she had already left by the Vorc'ara? She had to have done so. Good. Less problems with her there! He turned to see the ruler of Onaerra come slithering down the hallway. He grimaced. Every time he saw the "thing" that had taken over Onaerra, he cringed. He was glad that Gem would not be seeing it!

Gem opened her mouth to tell Simmons that she was right next to him, when she watched him look everywhere around him. He even looked straight at her, so why did he not see her? If she was confused before, she was even more so, now. The squishy sound coming from the hallway became louder and louder as it got closer to them. She stood by Simmons' side, and watched him grimace and cringe. As she wondered why, the squishy sound started into the torch light. It was beautiful! The face of the ethereal creature coming toward her made her feel almost lethargic. But, in an instant, she shook that feeling off as she stared at it. Everyone always imagines the big bad guy as a worm or reptile or some other creepy crawly thing! They are wrong. Evil could also come in the form of beauty, too. Especially at the moment. And, that was what slithered into the great room. She had no idea what it was, but one thing she did see, and it almost made her toss her cookies! It's front was a beautiful woman. She was stately, tall, glided instead of walked with the blackest hair she had ever seen on anyone that flowed down her back almost as long as she was tall – twenty feet tall, that is. Her eyes were the darkest black, but almost blue. Her complexion was a dark olive, her lips plump and red, and her boobs were at least a triple, what? X? They were massive! Her gown of pastel pink, gathered at the waist, which pushed her breasts upward, but just barely being held up, let alone her nipples covered! They bounced with each slither. Her gown drug the ground as she glided along. She watched Simmons bend over in a very deep bow as she passed by him. And, then, she saw the back of the "thing". Behind her, giant streams of fluorescent, blue slime was expelled behind her with each step, and left a trail on the floor. And, then, the second it touched the stone floor, it turned a dark, brownish green! OK. That was so disgusting! She caught herself, before she lost everything in her stomach as the rancid scent of decay and death hit her nose! From behind, it moved more like a serpent, and nothing even remotely resembling a humanoid being. She held her breath, because if she didn't, she would give away the fact that she was there. Gem still didn't get why no one could see her, but at the moment, she *really* didn't care. It was a good thing. She wasn't too sure why Simmons was here, but honestly … had she really been surrounded all these years by other fallen angels? The answer came to her in her mind, and almost made her gasp aloud.

"Yes, my love."

She closed her eyes in relief.

"Jaxx!" she exclaimed through their bond, catching herself just before she gave herself away with a gasp.

"I am with you, Gem. Where are you?"

"I don't believe this, but that damn book spit me out on Onaerra! How did that happen? Where the hell are you?"

"On Domaerra … with your Mother and Father!"

"What!" Gem yelled.

She was suddenly very afraid that she had given them all away, and quickly looked around her. She sighed when she realized the pink thing, which put out shit, was no longer in her vision.

Mr. Simmons looked in her direction.

"I thought you were gone!" Shaking her head, he continued. "Talking to your mate, my dear?" he asked with a sneer.

"Oh, hell, Jaxx! Simmons is here, and he is not smiling very nicely!"

"Simmons? What is he doing there?" Jaxx asked her.

"Don't you know?"

"*No.*"

As if she had paid no attention to him, she continued.

"*And, by the way, Jaxx. What is that filthy, twenty foot high stinky pink thing that looks just like a woman on the front, but from the back, looks and smells like a garbage dump?*"

"*Huh?*" Jaxx asked. "*What twenty foot high pink thing?*"

"*Wait! You don't know? But …*" her voice cut off in mid-sentence as Simmons raised his hand, and hit her in the face. She fell to the floor unconscious.

"*Gem!*" Jaxx cried, as he felt his mate leave his consciousness.

"*Gem?*" Nothing. Louder, "*GEM!*"

His face must have shown how distressed he was, because Analyse addressed him.

"Jaxx? Jaxx, what's wrong?" she demanded, her voice shaking.

"Jaxx," Jolin said. He knew that demanding wasn't going to get Analyse anywhere with him. Only a calm reasonable voice would do it.

Jaxx looked over at Jolin, and he saw Analyse's face. His face must have shown how distressed she was, because a tear streaked down her face.

"I don't know. I was talking to her, and she had just told me that Simmons was with her, and then … nothing."

"Who the hell is Simmons?" Jolin asked him.

"The local grocery store owner. I don't get it. Who…?" he started, when he heard a gasp from Analyse.

"Simmons? *Simmons?* That just isn't possible! It can't be him!" she cried.

Both Jolin and Jaxx looked at her in puzzlement. They looked at each other. How could she know Simmons?

"Analyse? You know him?" Jaxx asked her. "How?"

Silence met his question. He waited patiently for her to answer. It was obviously difficult.

Several minutes passed, and she answered him.

"I can't believe it! How is he still alive?" she spoke to herself.

"Who is he?" Jolin wrapped his arms around his mate. "Please, my love. Explain."

"Huh?" she asked turning her head, looking at him with blank eyes, before she realized that Jolin was waiting for her to answer him. "Oh. Simmons is not Simmons, but Simoche!"

Jolin stepped back in shock. Jaxx looked at him, and suddenly understood!

"No! He's dead! I killed him myself!" Jolin yelled.

"I know! He killed me! How, Jolin? How could he still be alive? You beheaded him!"

"I have no idea!" Jolin admitted.

"Hold it!" Jaxx said. "IF he is dead, then how is he alive?" he turned to Jolin. "How did I not recognize him?"

Jaxx shook his head in shock. Then, a horrible thought came to him. Simoche. How had he not recognized him? And, now, he had his mate! What would he do to her?

"I have to get to Onaerra! Now!" he demanded of Analyse.

She nodded silently.

"Wait," Jolin said. "We can't just appear on Onaerra! We are both wanted!"

"I can't worry about that right now! I have to go .... NOW!" Jaxx said, and Analyse nodded in agreement.

"Calm down. You both know what can happen if we try to go there without some type of plan!"

Jaxx just glared at him. His mate was in danger, and Jolin was telling him to wait?

"You both know it's not feasible for us to go running into danger without some type of plan!" Jolin's voice was the sound of reason.

"But..." Analyse started, then shut up when she saw her mate shake his head.

"No. I want to get him as much as you do, Jaxx, but if we get ourselves killed, then he will still have her in his clutches! We don't go into this with our eyes closed. We have to make sure that if we get there, we can rescue our daughter! We need some surveillance. My contact will tell me where we can enter Onaerra through your Vorc'ara safely!"

"Contact? You have a contact?" Analyse expressed surprise combined with suspicion at this revelation. "Why have you never told me that?"

"Because, my love, we have had no reason to contact my contact. Now, we do."

"But is he trustworthy?" Jaxx asked.

"Absolutely," he told them without a doubt. "But, it's not a him."

"What did you say?" she asked with suspicion in her voice.

He turned to Analyse, and grinned sheepishly.
"It's a her!"

~ 2 ~

If another immortal conquers the Fallen, then what
possible hope can there be for humans? ~ Gem

Gem watched the men all bow as the "thing"
passed them, and wondered how they had gotten
under her thumb? Aren't they all angels, she asked
herself? One thing she did know, that sure wasn't an
angel! What did she have over them? Honestly, she
was a bit unnerved by this fact. Immortal beings
being taken over by some creature from somewhere
else was a real scary thought. Especially since they
were *fallen angels*! That was even more terrifying, if
they were terrified! What could be worse than them?

After the thing left the room, Simmons breathed
a sigh of relief.

"Get after the plan," was all he said, and the
other scattered to openings all around the room.

Then, "Gem?" he asked, obviously still not being
able to see her.

She wasn't sure if she should answer for a few
minutes. What if he had something planned for her
that would result in being placed in some volcanic
prison? She'd already been there, done that, and
wasn't about to let it happen, again!

"Please, Gem! You have to get the fuck out of
here! The bitch will be back, and she will not hesitate
to try and kill you if you become visible!"

Gem huffed, and walked up behind him,
touching him on the shoulder, which only served to
make him jump. Simmons whirled around, and saw
Gem standing there. He huffed and puffed.

"You had me worried that you had actually left,
before I could tell you what I need Jaxx to know!"

He looked around the room, then satisfied, grabbed her hand, and led her to a small room off the large one, and shut the door. He waved his hand, and she heard a lock turn. Her heart sped up when she heard it. Was it necessary to lock the door?

"Sit down," he ordered. Then, thinking better of it, said, "Please?"

She glanced around the room, seeing only a small bench on one side of the room. She glared at him for a minute, then slowly walked to the bench, and sat down. She waited until he was able to actually speak, but for a few minutes, he paced back and forth across the small room, until finally, he came to a halt in front of her.

"Simmons?" she asked.

"OK. You have to get out of here! You need to use your Vorc'ara to get the hell out of here. How did you even get here in the first place?" he asked. Then, before she could answer, he waved his hand at her as she opened her mouth. "Never mind. I don't want to know, and quite frankly, it's not important at the moment. The more I know, the harder it will be for me to answer questions from that bitch!"

"Bitch? What is she? What happened here, Simmons? Why are you here, and how are you here?" she finally asked.

"It doesn't matter. None of that matters. Suffice it to say that I have been keeping an eye on you for many years for some members of the council. And, again, it doesn't matter why I am here," he stated, again waving his hand so she didn't talk. "Let me tell you what you need to know so you can tell Jaxx!"

"OK, OK! Tell me, Simmons."

"Look, you have to tell Jaxx that he can't come back here! We are slaves, now. Slaves to the Qyx.

They have been after our powers for eons, and there is a traitor among us, but we do not know who it is," Simmons almost whispered, but made sure that Gem could hear it.

Gem darted her head at him in surprise. A traitor? Against the Onaerris? That sounded like it might be a first.

"Eloran?" she whispered back to him.

"Hell, no! He's more like a mosquito that makes you itch. This traitor is the kind that is bent on destruction for power!"

Well, to Gem, that sure sounded like Eloran!

"She would sell out her soul, and others, for the ultimate power," he added.

"Wait…she? Ultimate power? What's that?" Gem asked.

"Trust me! You do not want to know!"

"Does it mean against the Creator?" she asked him. "Come on, Simmons. Ya gotta give me something more than that!"

"The ultimate power is not just the Creator's, Gem. It's the power of the chosen!"

Gem's eyes drew together. The chosen?

"Who are the chosen?" she asked, puzzled.

Simmons' eyebrows raised in astonishment. He couldn't believe she didn't understand!

"Not, who, Gem. You are the chosen!" he clarified.

"What!" she squeaked.

"Shhhhhh! Are you trying to get us killed?"

"What do you mean, me?"

"You still don't get it, do you? You are the one whose power she seeks to to absorb, Gem. You are Jaxx's mate, right?"

She nodded.

"Have you joined with the book, yet?"

Gem was silent. That was what they were trying to do, when the damn book sent them away! She slowly shook her head.

"Fuck!" said Simmons.

"*Gem! I've been listening! Ask Simmons who the traitor is,*" Jaxx asked.

"*Oh, thank God, you are still here, Jaxx!*"

"*Gem...focus!*"

"*Oh...right,*" she turned back to Simmons who was pacing back and forth, and she could swear she saw tracks on the rock where he had been pacing!

"Uh, Simmons. Who is the traitor?"

"I dare not even say her name, here, Gem! She has eyes and ears everywhere – just like our Creator!"

"But...," Gem began.

"No, Gem. Forget it! I won't say anything more!" Simmons looked around him. Then, he grabbed her shoulders. "Get the fuck out of here!"

Gem didn't have to be told again. She stepped back from him, concentrated on Domaerra's capital city, and the Vorc opened before her. She looked back at Simmons.

"Simmons? Come with?" she begged.

Sadly, he shook his head.

Gem nodded, then stepped through the Vorc, and to Jaxx and her parents.

◎

"Dammit! I have to get to her, Jolin! I must!" He looked at Analyse. "Please, Analyse? Please? I have to get to her! She's in danger!"

His anger was getting the best of him as both his brother and his mate shook their heads. He put his head in his hands, and literally felt tears begin to form. He was still amazed that he could even make them! He felt a gentle hand on his shoulder.

"Believe me, Jaxx," Analyse began. "I don't like her being on Onaerra any more than you, but you can't go there! Please believe me!"

Jaxx looked up, and glared at her, and asked her point blank, "Why?"

But, it was Jolin who answered.

"Lilith," was all he said.

"*What*?" Jaxx all but screeched. Not wanting to believe a word, he continued. "*Who did you say*?"

"Lilith is the traitor. She has joined with the Qyx, and together, they have taken over Onaerris," Jolinaer said quietly.

Jaxx stood, and grabbed the nearest thing laying around, which happened to be a lamp, and threw it as hard as he could. It pierced through the ice wall, and kept right on going. Where it landed, no one ever found it. It was assumed that it sailed until it hit the ice-covered ocean, pierced it as it pierced the wall, and was lost forever. Not that anyone was overly upset about it. But, it wasn't enough for him. He also threw other things around the room.

"Jaxxon! Stop it!" Jolinaer ordered. "You have to get yourself under control!"

Jaxx stopped, his chest heaving with his exertion. The book was keeping him from being reasonable. He fell into the closest chair.

"I'm sorry, but with the book still inside of me, I just can't seem to control myself!"

Jolin and Analyse were shocked.

"Wait! What do you mean the book is inside of you?" Jolin asked.

"It's what I've been telling you! We did exactly what the book told us to do, and the next thing we were thrown into different worlds – with the book inside of ME! I had no time to transfer it to my mate who is supposed to be the recipient of it!"

Analyse looked at Jolin in stunned surprise!

"Analyse, I don't remember you telling me that the book would go into Jaxx, first."

"That's because it wasn't supposed to do that, Jolin! It was very simple. She was just supposed to open the book with what I provided, and it was to transfer the knowledge to her. Her mate was to help her, but not take the book inside of him!" She turned to Jaxx. "I don't understand."

Jaxx took a very deep breath. It was apparent that whatever had happened was not supposed to happen, but whatever was going on, it must have taken on a life of its own! Jaxx turned to Analyse.

"OK. The book spoke to Gem, first, telling her that she had to – uh – 'join' *physically* with her. And, then, it spoke to me through Gem, and told me what had to be done. We followed the book's explicit directions, and the next thing I knew, I woke up on Domaerra – without my mate!"

Analyse nodded. "That actually makes sense," she said. The two men looked at her in puzzlement.

"I mean…it's not like I expected it to evolve in this manner, but it does make sense. Sex always transfers our consciousness to each other."

"But, it's a book, not a bloody physical body that can have sex!" Jaxx gritted his teeth. If he didn't mate with Gem soon, he wasn't going to make it! The book was causing him extreme anxiety, and it was actually making him crazy enough to lose it!

"That's true.   But, somehow, and honestly, I have no idea, it actually evolved into a physical being of some kind. It amassed so much knowledge – more than either you or I originally gave it, Jolin – that the only person able to hold it is Gem. And, for whatever reason, it wanted to transfer that information by having sex with her!"

"Analyse, are you even hearing yourself talk? That's the craziest thing I've ever heard!" Jolin said.

"I know. I don't get it either, but that has to be what happened."

"No shit!" Jaxx said, sarcasm dripping from his lips.

"*Jaxx*!" Jolin warned. "Go ahead, my love."

Jaxx just stared at him with anger in his heart. If he didn't get rid of this fucking thing within him soon, and spill it into his mate, he was going to do some very serious harm! And, that was intolerable!

"Well, it was written partially on Anaerra, partially in the Fae Realm, and sealed with our magic, Jolin. And, it is over ten thousand years old! I am going to speculate because of that, and then it was stored within my library on Earth all this time! So, then, yes. I believe something amazing could have happened!" She and Jolin looked over at Jaxx, whose hands were fisted tightly enough to draw blood, and which was dripping onto the lavender ice below him. "We have to get Gem from Onaerra…and soon."

Analyse nodded.

〇

Gem stepped out onto a world of lavender ice. And, it was flat! After getting her breath, because a

Vorc always took it away, she looked at her surroundings. In the distance was … flat and nothing; to her left … flat and nothing; to her right … flat and nothing. She turned around, and it was … fla …. Eyes widening, her mouth dropped.

"*No way!*" Gem gasped.

A mountain stretched from left to right, stretching as far as the eye could see in either direction! It was far away, but holy shit! It's height defied description. It reached into the sky until she could see no more sky, and still it continued into the clouds! She felt as if her neck were going to break as she leaned backward until she felt as if she might fall! Finally, she looked down, and noticed that there was a cave carved into the ice about ten feet above the ice floor.

"Hmmmm. Now why would it be higher?" she wondered.

After looking around a couple of minutes, she set out, walking toward the monster mountain. It seemed as if hours had passed by the time she almost made it to the mountain face. Man, she hoped that she would be able to see her mate soon! Gem sent out her mental connection, and received a mind back that almost knocked her on her ass! His mind was clouded and afraid. The book was doing something really bad to him! She tried to reach out over and over, but nothing came back except tremendous misery.

Gem was only minutes from the cave opening, so she set off at a run, and in seconds, was running faster than she had ever run in her entire life. Almost supernatural. Well, of course! Technically she was part of the supernatural, right? It was not minutes, but seconds, and she was going so fast, she almost ran into the mountain! Luckily, she was able to slam on the brakes before she smashed into it! Gem backed up slowly in order to gauge the height she would have to climb. She was right. It was only about ten feet off the ground. Easy, right? Wrong. Stretching her neck upward, she shook her head in wonder and frustration.

"This is really, really weird!" she said to no one in particular.

The opening to the cave was a perfect, symmetrical arch, indicating that it was definitely man-made … or something made, anyway! She huffed. Well, there was nothing for it, because either she climbed up ten feet on the ice mountain, or she didn't. At least she was in pants, and a long sleeve top, but that wasn't going to work forever, and already, she could feel the cold seeping into her body.

Whatever ridiculous notion she had, she tried to climb the slippery slope – and slid right back down! Of course, it was slippery.

"Now, what the hell am I going to do? I don't have climbing equipment for ice!" she grumbled.

Turning in frustration, she plopped her butt onto the ice, only to quickly jump back to her feet! The ice was so c-c-cold … with a capital COLD! Brushing her butt off, she walked back and forth in front of the cave. She stopped, and began to rub her temples. She was getting a headache! Gem let her hands fall, and she looked at the mountain again. She spied something unusual imbedded into the ice. Moving closer, her hand reached out to feel the indentation, also imbedded into the ice. As she looked carefully, she noticed there were more – all leading to the cave opening. They were the same color as the mountain, and so it made sense that they couldn't be seen. And, they were the right size for a foot and hand to grasp! She brushed her hands of the ice, then put her hand in the second grip, only to discover there was something like rubber in the floor of the indentation that allowed the climber to grip tightly!

"Well, that's very helpful," she muttered as she began to climb.

The ice was too cold, but the rubber grip kept the cold from completely getting to her hands. While she climbed, she still wondered why the cave was placed so far up the face of the mountain above the flat of the land. Shrugging, she kept climbing until her hand reached the floor to the opening of the cave. A large strip of the same, rubbery stuff allowed her to pull herself into the mouth fairly easily. She turned to sit, getting her breath. It wasn't that far of a climb, but the ice made it much harder despite the footholds. While she waited for her breath to calm, she noted a slight movement below her. She took another deep breath, then leaned over to see what it was. Nothing was there, but strangely, there was a disturbance in the air, and it appeared to be undulating in a rolling motion. It reminded her a bit of water that was in a rolling boil, but a gently roll.

While she watched, her eyes grew wide as she watched a mass begin to take shape. Her eyes widened with each change. The mass took shape, and below her was the most hideous "face" she had ever seen! Scooting quickly into the cave, she stood to run, and heard a sound behind her. She slowly turned, afraid of what she might see. The thing was huge! Far too big to enter the cave, thank goodness! It was the color of the lavender ice, giving it the best camouflage ever! It's face had no eyes, nose, or mouth that she could see, but it was riddled with openings, each orifice dripping with some type of "goo" that flooded the opening of the ice cave. Its "body" was covered in spikes, and she was quite sure that those things were sharp! Hearing cracks, she realized that the "goo" was melting the floor of the cave. That's when the smell hit her nose!

"Oh! My! God!" she exclaimed, slapping her hands over her mouth and nose, while trying to keep from throwing up everything she had ever eaten in her life! Far worse that the creature on Onaerris, it was melting the archway in order to get to her! The stench was so bad, she had a silly, yet random thought, that she needed a jumbo size bottle of "Poo-Pouri", used for spraying, before one – uh – went to keep the smell from permeating a bathroom! But, she doubted that would help in this case!

Gem couldn't stand up to run. Her eyes stung from the smell, but using every ounce of strength she had left, she managed to stand. The ooey-gooey thing tried to get into the mouth of the cave, but luckily, it was still too large to do so. Gem screamed, turned, and ran as fast as she could run into the depths of the cave. Anything was preferable to that thing!

After running forever, or so it seemed, she finally slowed down, and sat on the floor. So, that was why they had the archway ten feet up! That thing out there had intended Gem to be its dinner! She leaned her head against the ice wall of the cave. Cold always helped her headaches, and that is exactly what she had right now. Her blood pressure must have been well over three hundred, and her heart was beating fifty miles per hour, she was sure! Gem sat and waited until her breath calmed down. Once it was steady, she stood, and continued further into the cave. She looked around as she walked, and even though she had noticed when she was running, it had not penetrated her mind until now, that the cave was very, very bright! She slowed to a walk noticing that the cave glittered like diamonds, and where many would have felt claustrophobic, that was not the case. Instead, it appeared to have a great deal of open space. As she continued, colors of every hue began to take shape. And, like the Spired City of colors, there were colors everywhere. Colors she was familiar with, and others that just had no name to them, it glittered and sparkled as if they were beautiful jewels lodged into the ice!

Gem couldn't help oohing at each new color that appeared, until she was wrapped in a cocoon of color. She unexpectedly popped out into a cavern, and she found herself on a large landing just outside of the cave.

"Holy giant caves, Batman!" she exclaimed, using her own version of Robin to Batman from the old series.

It was massive. There were no words that could possible describe this enormous underworld. The cave she had entered had twisted and turned, led up and down, so she had no idea where she was, or if she was deep into the center of the planet. It was made of one, single domed ceiling of ice. The colors undulated above just like clouds in the sky above. It was absolutely beautiful! The closest description that she could come to in order to explain the enormity of the cavern was that it must have once contained a mighty ocean before the planet froze solid. Perhaps that might explain the flatness of the world above. Maybe at some time, the ocean had spilled out of this cavern into the open, and froze. She was no geologist, but that was logical enough in her mind to accept this massive structure.

She looked below her, and gasped. A great city lay at her feet! As far as the eye could see, there were rolling hills of lavender ice, and buildings built from the ice! And, not just any buildings! Many of the were massive skyscrapers rising to far above her, but never touching the ceiling of the cavern. Buildings of different hues glittered and gleamed in the artificial light generated from above. Connecting the entire complex were clear tubes winding their way in and out of the city in different configurations. Each tube had a slightly transparent and different color to it. Probably indicating what part of the city it serviced. Gem could see some type of transportation zipping around the city through these tubes. Above her flew strange, arrow shaped vehicles that were very, very fast. Much faster than the tubes. Even from this height, she could see different creatures bustling to and from wherever they were going, and a great many tiny creatures with lavender fur, their faces resembling the funny platypus on Earth. She didn't stop to wonder how in the world she could see them that clearly from the height she was standing.

Wait! Platypus? Wasn't that the description that Jaxx had told her the beings of Domaerra looked like?

"Woohoo!" Gem squealed aloud. She'd made it! That meant that somewhere, down there, was her mate! She looked for a way down.

"Of course, it wouldn't be that easy to get down there!" she remarked with sarcasm.

It was all such a strange combination. Tiny little furballs, coupled with other beings, and high technology to boot! It seemed so primitive, yet far more advanced than anything on Earth! While she was pondering this, a flying vehicle came to a stop just off the landing. Surprised, she watched the door open, and a ramp appear. She walked slowly toward it, stepped onto the ramp, and entered the vehicle.

Several passengers looked at her in surprise. She gave them a hesitant smile, and sat in the first seat that she came to that was empty. When the door closed, and the vehicle took flight, the passengers started to speak over each other, not paying her any more attention. It was obvious that they were used to seeing humans – or at least humanoids. Others humans were also on the transport as well.

Gem sat back, and let the vehicle fly her to wherever the hell it was taking her!

~ Books By LK Kelley ~

The White Wolf Prophecy Trilogy Series

The White Wolf Prophecy ~ Mating
The White Wolf Prophecy ~ Hall of Records
The White Wolf Prophecy ~ Scroll of Time

The Anaerris Code Series

The Anaerris Code ~ Gem
The Anaerris Code ~ Jaxx (Coming Soon)

Wolf Canyon Memory

My CHrIStMaS PreSeNt... HaS WHAT?

Please Leave a Review

Hi! I want to thank you for reading My Christmas Present…has WHAT? I hope you'll take a moment and leave a review! They have all received 5* ratings. Authors are always so happy and excited to read reviews of their hard work, and even though I know it might take a couple of minutes, if you will leave one — even a simple "I liked it", would truly be appreciated! And, please take a moment to look at my other books as well at the links below!

Again…thank you so much for reading my books!

The White Wolf Prophecy Trilogy Series

The White Wolf Prophecy ~ Mating
https://www.amazon.com/gp/product/B0718XCJHS/ref=dbs_a_def_rwt_bibl_vppi_i4

The White Wolf Prophecy ~ Hall of Records
https://www.amazon.com/gp/product/B071YMT1L7/ref=dbs_a_def_rwt_bibl_vppi_i1

The White Wolf Prophecy ~ Scroll of Time
https://www.amazon.com/gp/product/B07116DZJX/ref=dbs_a_def_rwt_bibl_vppi_i0

The Anaerris Code ~ Gem
https://www.amazon.com/gp/product/B071NL8M7H/ref=dbs_a_def_rwt_bibl_vppi_i3

Wolf Canyon Memory

https://www.amazon.com/gp/product/1615002014/ref=dbs_a_def_rwt_bibl_vppi_i2

About 5* Author, LK Kelley

LK Kelley's series, The White Wolf Prophecy Trilogy is not only a full, 5* series, but both The White Wolf Prophecy ~ Mating, as well as The White Wolf Prophecy ~ Scroll of Time have received 1 & 2 BESTSELLING awards for ebook (respectively)! Her 1st book has also been a number one seller @ Amazon.

Please checkout her website for her books, where to buy, information, reviews, photoshoots, and even more!

https://firebird4554.wixsite.com/lkkelley1

And, join her 34.9K followers on Twitter for a great time!

https://twitter.com/LKKelley1

"After I began writing paranormal romance books, it was specifically for the adult female ages 18 - 60. I just felt like there seemed to be a missing link for this age group. I also believe that even the supernatural world can begin at any age in life. I have no idea where my desire for writing came from, but Inhave always loved to write and things just seem to flow easily. I write using the same ideas that writers use for TV and movies. I use storyboarding, and scene development. Each scene my readers will read is done by taking the idea, running it through as s full scene as if it were for TV or movies, then I literally Act it out. Once done, then it is written."

LK was born in Little Rock, Arkansas, and adopted by Curtis and Jerry Smith. Her hometown from the age of seven months was Fort Smith, Arkansas. At 17, she toured Europe, and learned that not everything about World History was written! She also celebrated with the French on Bastille Day, July 14, on the Champs-Élysées.

She graduated from Westark Community College (now known as University of Arkansas Fort Smith, or UAFS) with an Associate of Arts Degree in Music, and a minor English. As of 2012, she is also a Freelance Book , Article, and website Editor.

She loves to read anything, and everything, but most specifically that which has to do with the Supernatural World and Romance. To date, she has written 5 books including Wolf Canyon Memory and My Christmas Present...has WHAT? – both stand-alone books! LK also has extensive interests in ancient alternative history as well as time travel.

LK Kelley lives in Barling, Arkansas. She has been married for 45 years to Wes, her true soul mate, and it feels as if it's only been a month. They have one daughter, Laura, who lives in Colorado, and a secret? Laura is the face of The White Wolf Prophecy Trilogy!

www.ingramcontent.com/pod-product-compliance
Lightning Source LLC
Chambersburg PA
CBHW070426120726

47910CB00003B/670